RED FLAME FI

by

Alexander Macpherson

PublishNation
www.publishnation.co.uk

DEDICATION

To my beautiful wife Jackie for all her patience and inspiration.

ACKNOWLEDGEMENTS

Gary Peussa again for his innovative cover design.
Simon David Smith.
To all the authors that have written about the trials of the Native Indian.

Alexander Macpherson was born in Scotland and educated in England before joining The Armed Forces and The Ministry of Defense, after which he became a Design Consultant. He presently spends his time between Florida and the U.K but has resided in Canada and France. He continues to travel.

Other books by Alexander Macpherson:

Tiptoe through the Alligators.

RED FLAME FIRES BACK

CHAPTER 1

He pulled up and listened, one second, two seconds, three seconds, yes, it sounded like a man sobbing. The constant whispering of the trees was making it difficult to decipher if it was a voice, the wind or his imagination. As he strained to listen each gust seemed to intensify and so he then doubted himself. Then suddenly a lull.

"No, no please. Oh God." A man called out but only just audible. He moved slightly forward, unlike the white man his mount did not have metal horseshoes and so was much quieter when moving in woodlands. He was about seven feet from the tree line, where the cart trail began, emphasized by the sun lighting up the short grass and dirt on the trail, he was surrounded by large Sweetgum trees. On the other side of the ten-foot-wide track were thousands of 100-foot-tall Sycamore trees that went on for miles, it was as though the trail had just been cut straight through the dense forest like a knife through butter. As he edged nearer to where the voice was coming from he saw a covered wagon and what appeared to be a man wearing a black suit and white shirt sitting upright in front of one of the wagon wheels. He strained to see, but It looked as though the man, a young man maybe in his late twenties, was tied to the wagon's front wheel, he thought he could see ropes securing him, but he was not sure. Suddenly the rustling leaves and wind stifled any other sounds.

Then a piercing scream that made him jump, a lady's scream. He turned slightly so that he could see towards the rear of the wagon and that was when he saw a man lying on top of a lady, the man's white red spotted arse was bobbing up and down and another man was holding her down by the arms. They were raping her. Both men were laughing to each other. By the look of their clothing they were ranch hands.

"My turn now," the man holding her down yelled, "come on. Get off her it's my turn."
The other man wasn't listening, he kept on going enthusiastically. She screamed again.

"David help me," she called out hysterically, "make them stop."

"Please don't hurt her. Please stop. God make them stop. "The young man yelled but he had obviously given up any hope of benevolence from the two men and any other sort of help from his own God.

Red Flame slowly and silently took the long bow off his back and carefully withdrew an arrow from his quiver, moving forward again slowly he positioned the arrow on the bow, he dug his heels into the sides of Laggon and as they charged out from the trees, riding without reins he sped towards where the man was still bobbing up and down, he withdrew the bow string and fired the arrow straight into the man's back. He threw down the bow and pulled his tomahawk from his belt and with one sweeping movement planted it straight into the skull of the man holding the girl down.

'Splat!' Just like a coconut being split.
He jumped down from Laggon and pulled the white spotty arsed man off the girl.

She lay frozen with fear, her knickers were lying on the grass about six feet from where she lay, her pretty pink blouse had been ripped off and thrown into the trees and her skirt was hoisted up around her neck, she suddenly saw him, a Redskin armed to the teeth and wearing only a loincloth. She looked even more terrified, her eyes wide in terror, she must have thought he was going to take over from where the white men had left off.

The man tied to the wheel saw all this and yelled out again.

"No. Please God help us." The man was sobbing, obviously grief stricken.

"It's ok, your safe." Red Flame said to the young woman. He pulled her dress down to conserve her dignity and reassure her he had no intentions of hurting her. He walked over to the tree's and pulled her blouse from the branches, picked up her knickers and handed them to her.

Suddenly off to his left, a man also wearing chaps on a large chestnut horse broke cover and rode off into the forest, he fumbled for his long bow in the grass but it was too late, the man had disappeared.

He ran to the man tied to the wheel and pulled his knife from its sheath, the man cowered thinking he was about to be scalped, instead Red Flame cut the ropes that bound him and threw them into the woods. The man sat frozen to the ground, unable or unwilling to move. Probably fear.

It took the man a while to absorb all that had gone on in the last few minutes. He looked to the sky.

"Thank you, God, thank you so much."

"Are you alright?" Asked Red Flame.

"Yes, I think so, is my wife ok? Anne are you ok?" The man called out.

"Anne will be fine when you go to her and reassure her."

"Yes. Yes. Of course." He replied.

The young man stood up, he was about 5'9" tall, fairly thin, with thinning hair for such a young man, he definitely was not a ranch hand, more like a banker or doctor. He had on what had been a smart tailored black pin stripe suit with a white shirt, black leather shoes and a black bow tie, but today due to all the dust and obvious weeks of travelling it looked as though he was a tramp, he would need to invest in a new wardrobe very soon.

The man moved quickly to his wife, he bent down and cuddled her, she was younger, maybe nineteen or twenty with long blonde hair, fairly thin but very attractive with freckles, he wasn't surprised that she had caught the eye of the ranch hands. Attractive ladies were not seen too often in these parts. She was having a similar fashion problem to her husband, her skirt and shoes were also from he guessed an expensive department store in one of the north eastern big cities, Boston or New York. She had been wearing a huge white hat until the ranchers decided they wanted action of a different kind, it was laying on the grass a few yards from her.

"Anne, Anne I'm so sorry," the man said throwing his arms around her again, "I wish I could have done more. I should have brought a new gun.......or something"

"It's not your fault, it's those evil men, it's their fault," said Anne through her tears, her voice breaking, "we must remain strong, it's what God wants." Who would have thought she had just been raped he thought to himself? A very strong-willed young Lady.

"Yes of course, it's what God wants. I prayed Anne, I prayed and God delivered, didn't he?"

"Yes, David he did, thank you for praying, I love you." She was obviously the stronger one in the relationship.

"I love you too Anne."

Red Flame stood, listening, without saying a word, if this is what they really believed then who was he to dispute it, but he pitied them quietly to himself.

"OK," he said after giving them a moment to gather their thoughts, "where are you folks heading, because you should get going now, one of those men got away and if they were from a local ranch they will return, they don't take kindly to their friends being killed especially by someone like me. A Redskin! There will be a bounty out on me within hours for anyone who will deliver my scalp."

"Your scalp? But white men don't do that, we were told it was only the Redskins that took scalps."

"No, history maintains the white men started it. Early Europeans they say. We just copied them."

"Oh my God. I didn't know that," the man looked terrified again but quickly gathered his thoughts, "we are heading south to Madison, we had paid those men to escort us there, they took that money and then stole the rest of the money we had. All of it."

"I'll check these men out and see if they have your money on them." He walked over to where the men lay and started to rummage through their pockets.

"Are you going to steal it then?" Asked Anne disapprovingly.

"No Mam, I don't steal money. I have no need to. What would I spend it on?"

"I'm sorry, I didn't mean to offend you, you saved our lives. That was very rude of me." She was obviously still coming to terms with what had just happened.

"No offense taken Mam," he continued to search the pockets of the two dead men, "No money here, the other man must have had the cash. These men's horses must be around here though, you could sell them and their guns, you could maybe recoup some of your loses."

"Hallelujah, thank you, thank you." Cried out David.

"We owe you so much, how can we ever repay you?" Anne asked.

"You don't have to do that but as I said you ought to get going, that other man will travel fast and be back with more ranch hands, and you have a long way to go. You should get going now, I will round up their horses and whatever rifles and revolvers I can find and will catch you up. But you better get going now. As fast as you can."

The couple immediately got up onto the wagons front seat, they kissed quickly on the lips, Anne replaced her white hat, picked up the reins and they lurched off at a fairly brisk pace.

He wandered into the trees and quickly found the two mounts contentedly chewing the moist grass, their dead rider's rifles were still in there sheaths. He led them to where Laggon was standing, picking up the men's gun belts as he passed their bodies. He mounted up and set off in pursuit of the clumsy slower moving wagon that had already disappeared from view.

He caught up with them after about a half mile, and as he passed the wagon he tied one horse to the wagons right rear cleat and the other to the left cleat and then rode alongside of the couple. They both looked a little more relaxed. David was tightly clutching an old single shot rifle which must have been at least thirty years old. It probably was a comfort thing.

"There are two horses tied to the back of the wagon, both have their past owner's rifles and handguns tied to their saddlebags. At the next town which is Jacksonville you can sell them to the general store, that's about sixty miles ahead. You have food and water?"

"Yes. Plenty." Replied Anne.

"You are heading straight to Madison?" He enquired.

"Yes." They answered together.

"Good, well just keep up this pace or faster if you can, those ranch hands will not be far behind."

"You're not leaving us? Please don't leave us," pleaded David, "we will pay you, I promise, but please don't leave us alone out here, they will come back, I know they will." David was beginning to panic again.

He thought momentarily, David was right, they probably wouldn't make it to Madison in one piece, it was a long way off and he knew he really should stay with them, even if it was just for moral support. They were in no fit state to travel at the moment, really no fit state for anything.

"Alright, I will stay with you until we reach Madison but I am going to go ahead, you won't see me but I will be watching you. Just keep going as fast as you can. We will speak later."

"Thank you. You won't leave us though?" Asked Anne suspiciously.

"No, you have my word." He smiled to them both. He turned Laggon and rode off to the southwest through some Fringe trees in full bloom and disappeared.

He knew the couple were scared and very anxious but if he'd stayed with them on the trail he would not be in a good position to defend them if any of the ranch hands did catch up. He climbed the undulating hills to the left of the wagon so he had a view of both the trail ahead and behind so he would know when and how many ranch hands he would have to deal with when they caught up and he knew they would, it was just a matter of time. He kept up an easy pace staying almost level with the wagon and the God-fearing couple but out of their sight.

They had been travelling for almost three hours, nobody in sight in either direction, until he saw the dust cloud rising about a mile behind them, he squinted as he looked back, he thought there were four riders making really good speed towards them, the ranch must have been closer than he originally thought. If nothing else, they would want the horses and the rifles that had been taken from their work mates, they might even want to sample again what one of their friends had already.

He sped up and went ahead of the wagon by about thirty yards, there he would stay until the ranchers had passed the wagon and stopped it. They wouldn't see him.

One of the men was the one who had fled the scene earlier, the man with the money the 'Hands' had stolen from the settlers, he recognized the large chestnut horse.

Within minutes all four had passed the wagon, stopping abruptly and turning to face the couple, blocking the wagons progress. The wagon stopped immediately with Anne yanking on the reins.

The one on the chestnut raised his hat sarcastically and smiled, he was obviously in charge.

"Well, we meet again," the man said, "we've come for some more of what we had earlier, until we were interrupted that is. Still got your old rifle as protection I see?" The other three laughed mockingly.

"Please don't hurt us, please don't, take what you want but don't hurt my wife." David yelled, fear had taken over again. He could not see Red Flame.

"We intend to, you should get some protection out here," the lead man said with a broad smile and then smirking at Anne, "this whiner isn't going to protect a fine Lady like you out here in these parts, you need a real man." There was a long pause as they stared steadily at each other. Almost like a standoff.

"How about him?" Anne said nodding in the direction of Red Flame who was sitting astride Laggon adjacent to the four about fifteen yards away, with his Winchester rifle pointing straight at the lead hands head.

The four turned quickly to see him and then tried clumsily to turn their mounts to face him, one went straight for his handgun. 'Crack', his chest exploded as the bullet from the Winchester hit him, he dropped sideways to the ground.

The second ranch hand had now got his pistol in his hand. 'Crack', Red Flames bullet struck him between his eyes, and he dropped to the ground. The third hesitated, his hand still hovering over his revolver, 'Crack', blood spurted from his chest. He hit the ground. That left the lead hand, who must have thought his men would easily take on a Redskin because he hadn't even moved. He stared at Red Flame, trying to make up his mind to grab his revolver or make a run for it again. Red Flame stared back, waiting.

"Make up your mind, your choice." He yelled. The man turned his horse away and whipped it with the reins to make a quick bid for safety. 'Crack'. the bullet hit him in the side of his neck and immediately he rolled backwards off his mount and hit the ground hard.

Red Flame rode forward to the wagon and dismounted. The couple just sat silently looking at the carnage in front of them. Without saying anything to Anne or David he collected all the rancher's hardware that was strewn across the track and threw them into the back of the covered wagon. He rounded up the four ranchers' horses and tied them alongside the other two that were already secured. After a search of the lead hands pockets he found the money that had been taken earlier from the couple and handed it to David.

Anne and David sat motionless, not saying a word. She had her hand up to her mouth in disbelief. They both appeared to be in some sort of shock. He doubted they had ever seen so much violence before, the blood lust that had become such a common thing in America in the last few decades.

"Ok, let's go." Red Flame said breaking the silence, mounting Laggon and setting off at a good pace. He heard the wagon rattling along behind him. The track was flat and they should make good progress he thought. After about thirty miles, he turned to the couple who had not said a word to each other since the incident.

"Are you both alright, do you need to stop for a while?"

"Would you mind? We'd like some water. All this dust, it's making us very dry." Asked David.

"Only if that's alright with you," Anne added quickly, "I'm sorry we haven't even asked your name, after all you have done for us. I'm sorry we have been so rude."

"Don't worry Mam, it's been a bit hectic. My name is Red Flame. Let's stop now and have a quick drink then we can get going."

It took just a few minutes to pass the water bottle around and then they were on their way again.

"Now, do you know the way?" He asked the couple.

"Yes, south and then towards the west coast, we follow this trail most of the way. We have a rough map we were given too." Replied David.

"Good. Well let's go."

He turned Laggon and headed off at a good pace in a south westerly direction with the wagon about twenty feet behind him. They rode for another two hours, he could hear the couple talking behind him about God and how he had saved them. If only life was that simple he thought to himself.

"Red Flame, shall we stop for the night soon?" David called out, "Anne wants to make you her beef stew as a thank you for all that you have done for us today."

It was getting late and he was hungry so he readily agreed they should stop soon.

"Let's keep going a little further until we find a suitable clearing, it shouldn't be too long. It's going to be sunset soon, so we need to get off the trail before it gets dark."

"Ok that's good." Agreed David.

It was less than an hour before he told them to pull into an opening that was protected by high Maple trees on three sides from the cart track so they would not be easily seen by any passing travelers.

While David unhitched his horses, Anne rummaged in the back of the wagon searching out cooking utensils and food. Red Flame scoured the woods looking for branches and kindling to make a fire, he then found a suitable area for it behind the wagon and within minutes it was raging. Anne set up her metal tripod and hung a pot of water off it. The three of them sat around in a semi-circle while Anne diced vegetables, cut up some beef and scraped it all into a large metal pot and hung it from the tripod.

David stood up as though he had forgotten something and went to the back of the wagon and returned with a bag of feed for the horses, all eight of them including Laggon. He spread some on the ground in front of each and then went from one to another with a bucket of water, he seemed a kind man but he did need to keep them healthy if he was to get a good price for those that had belonged to the ranch hands in Jacksonville.

David grabbed a log that was lying on the ground near the tree line and pulled it nearer to where Anne was preparing the meal. David beckoned to Red Flame to join him on the log.

"Thank you so much for what you did today."

"You don't need to thank me David."

"I hope you don't mind me saying so," said David apologetically, "but you don't seem to be the average native Indian, you are not what we had been told to expect," Red Flame smiled but didn't answer, "there's something about you that doesn't add up."

"In what way?"

"Well, your English sounds impeccable, as though you went to a school in England, your coloring and features are European. Not like any Indian I have seen before. Not that I have seen many."

"It's a very long story David."

"We have the time," David smiled, "how old are you? were you adopted or kidnapped? I have so many questions, give me a clue."

"Neither, my father was from Scotland and my mother was from the Apalachee tribe not far from here, and I'm twenty-one."

"Wow, how did they meet?"

"Their mutual love of fishing, my father from catching salmon in the Spey river and Loch Laggon, hence my ponies name, in the Highlands and my mother from catching trout in the local Black Warrior river. They met one day sharing the same river bank and that was it, they fell in love and I came along as they say."

"Really? What did your father do as a profession?"

"He was the local Doctor."

"No? They must have had a hard time, and so must have you."

"No, not really, I went to the village school with all the white kids, learnt all the normal things and my father taught me other stuff like how to read English from his own books and to understand William Shakespeare, how to fly fish of course, how to Box, about European history and then I would visit my cousins in the tribal village, and they taught me the Indian ways, like hunting with a bow and arrow, tracking, the spiritual side of their beliefs. I had a great childhood. Well, most of the time."

"Are your parents still alive?"

"No, my father died eight years ago. He was murdered." He was finding it very easy to talk to David.

10

"How terrible." Interrupted Anne, still cutting vegetables.

"Oh, I'm so sorry." Said David and sounding as though he meant it.

"No need to be sorry, not your fault, but thanks."

"Your Mother? Is she alive?"

"Yes. She lives in the tribal village with the rest of her family. West of here past Tallahassee."

"Do you see her often?"

"Yes, when I can. We are very close but it can be difficult at times."

"Why is that?"

"The Chief and I don't quite see eye to eye." Replied Red Flame.

"Can I ask why?"

"He wants to rid these lands of the white man. I can see his point of view after all the lies we have been told by the various Presidents, or great white chiefs as the Indian tribes call them. He remembers when the Carolina government partitioned the President to move the whole Cherokee nation west in 1848 and many lost their lives, in fact most of them did. He thinks the same is about to happen again but with all the tribes. He wants to fight. Who knows, he could be right."

"And you don't?"

"No, there are too many whites now and I believe if you can educate people properly they should be able to live together. Even if you have to segregate them, peace should always be possible if people really want it. It's just at the moment the whites don't really seem to want peace. Fighting won't achieve anything but more hatred. It's getting worse all the time, more killings, more scalping's, and I do think eventually it will come to an all-out war."

"You do? That's very profound."

"Well, my parents proved that we can all live together and learn from each other if we want to. It all depends on the people."

"That's very true. Would you mind if I took a photograph of you?" Asked David politely.

"A photograph? You have a camera with you?"

"Yes, I do, I use it in my work."

Red Flame paused a moment.

"Aren't you with the church?"

"No, I believe in God and the church but I'm a newspaper editor. I'm on my way to start a new job at the Madison news. I have been working in Boston for the past six years and decided I could do more if I moved south where newspapers are scarcer."

"Well good for you David. I wondered why all the questions, now I know. That's great. I wish you all the success." How did he get that so wrong he wondered?

"Thank you, Red Flame. That means a lot to me, and Anne."

"Yes, thank you Red Flame," she echoed, "that's very kind of you," Anne had been sitting just a few feet away listening but still stirring and checking the food, "not long to wait now, it will soon be ready. But can I ask you something Red Flame?"

"Of course, Anne."

"Are you married?"

"No," he shook his head, "I live a fairly nomadic life. I don't think a wife would like that or deserve it."

"No, I suppose not." She smiled and nodded in agreement.
David had already stood up and walked to the rear of the wagon, after rummaging in the back for several minutes he returned with a tripod which he set up six feet in front of the log where they had all been sitting. David returned to the wagon and appeared again carrying a large walnut box camera and flash holder, he fiddled with the contraption for several minutes.

"Right! We are just about ready to go. You sit where you are Red Flame."

He watched David set the camera up for action, he had been told by his father that cameras were common in Europe and he had seen pictures of them in books, but he had never seen one being used before. He was intrigued and asked several technical questions which David answered proudly and assuredly showing off his knowledge and expertise.
David fussed a little more with the mechanisms and then stood motionless looking through the lens with a black cloth over his head.

"Keep still Red Flame." David counted from one to ten. Then there was a large puff of white smoke and it was done.

"Good. Thank you, Red Flame. That will make a great story." David said as he removed the photo plate. He slowly and methodically dissembled the camera and returned it to the back of their wagon.

"Now let's eat." Anne said enthusiastically.
They had a superb meal and a very interesting discussion pursued about the Native American Indians place in an ever-changing America, the many Indian wars and the new peace agreements all hastily being signed as the masses of immigrants flooded across the country. They spoke about the Buffalo hunting grounds rapidly being eroded by the White man's roads and their Iron horses. He really enjoyed listening to both David and Anne's points of view, he was somewhat surprised by their knowledge of Indian affairs and from what they said he was pleased that their opinions were reciprocated by many other white folks in general.

That night he slept well on the ground behind some foliage about ten feet from the wagon where David and Anne had bedded down, just in case they should be attacked by any passing fur hunters or renegade Indians, he would have that extra few seconds to respond. He didn't need to have done so.

The next morning, they set off early after a delicious breakfast of bacon and eggs all cooked and supplied by Anne, he wondered how they could pack so much food into their wagon. Within an hour of waking they were on the road to Madison again on a beautiful crisp morning, bright blue skies and the trees absolutely were at their best, a montage of greens and the Fringe trees creamy white blossoms. It was a wonderful day, as long as he didn't encounter too many ranch hands on route.

They travelled for about two hours to Jacksonville where David and Anne went into the town and sold all the ranch hands horses and weapons they had acquired to the General Store, making a handsome profit. He waited on the outskirts of the town for them, out of sight for just over an hour and then when they returned they all got back on the trail south westerly towards Madison. He rode three hundred yards to the north of the wagon on higher ground, out of sight from any other travelers that might be using the trail but still maintaining sight of their wagon. These were dangerous times and so caution had to be maintained.

After another seven hours of constant riding and the sun about to go down, he said goodbye to David and Anne on the outskirts of Madison, a bustling town that he felt they would soon make their mark on. They hugged each other and said their goodbye's and soon the couple were back on their wagon rolling towards the main street, he watched them disappear into the mass of wooden shacks that would-be Madison.

CHAPTER 2

He turned Laggon and slowly headed back northwest, he had liked David and Anne and thought about their naivety when it came to the big bad world out there, it would be a great day when people like them didn't need to worry about who they were likely to meet on their travels, the people that would hurt and steal from them without even blinking. They had a long way to go yet, but he felt with others around them for protection they would one day make a name for themselves in the newspaper industry.

As always, he stayed off the main trails in case he should very quickly come face to face with an unwanted stranger and then he would have nowhere to turn, and that usually led to trouble. There were still many white men that believed in President Jefferson's saying 'The only good Indian is a dead Indian' and always looking for that easy $20 scalp bounty that Jefferson had promised.

Two days later after travelling almost nonstop he arrived at his mother's camp circle, over two hundred and fifty tepees all with wisps of smoke invading the evening sky and crossing the bright orange sunset. Children playing and shouting together, hundreds of ponies munching on grass, dogs barking and running in all directions. He missed the village life sometimes. Life was fairly simple, if you had enough food.

Red Flames mother was delighted to see him, it had been over a month since they last spent time together and of course she was going to spoil him like most mothers do. His mother was fairly small but fit, like most Indian squaws. She had the deepest blue eyes he had ever seen and her black hair shone like the sky at night. It was no wonder his father was infatuated by her as he used to tell Red Flame regularly.

"When did you last have a proper meal?" She asked immediately.

"Yesterday."

"What did you have?"

"Rabbit."

"Oh, ok," she sounded disappointed, "tonight, I will cook you Buffalo, that is still your favorite isn't it?"

"Yes ma, it still is." He knew it was best to agree.

"Good, sit down and tell me what you have been doing."

They spent the whole evening chatting about his travelling, about meeting Anne and David, remembering his father and of his intelligence, the things he had said and done over the years and how they both missed him, and of course the subject that all native Indians spoke about nonstop these days, which was the white folks killing their tribes off and stealing their lands and what they thought might eventually happen to the Indian nations.

Several of his old friends, Yellow Cloud, The Chief's son Little Bear, Man Walking Backward and Green Eyes dropped by to his mother's tepee later to catch up on all his news and again to talk about what they thought would be an imminent war with the whites over the constant stealing of lands and settlement of white families on their hunting grounds. He was surprised to hear that several tribes amounting to around 8000 warriors were gathering to the north west under the famous Sioux Chief Sitting Bull, and all of the young warriors thought they would be invincible if they joined them and were looking forward to a fight with the bluecoats. They would become legends among their own people or so they thought.

When he said he did not think that this was a good idea as there were ten times this number of bluecoat soldiers stationed at the Forts in the area, he was shouted down and even called a coward by Little bear.

"I am not a coward Little Bear. But there is a time and place to do these things and now is not yet the time. We cannot compete with the white man in an all-out battle, they have Howitzers that can kill at two hundred yards, they have rifles that can shoot bullets without reloading, a good soldier can bring down twenty of our braves with these repeating rifles. How many of these rifles do we have, I have one, do you?" he pointed to one of the braves, "do you, do you, do you," he pointed to the others in turn. None answered, "there is no point in fighting a war until we know we have a chance of winning. Many of our people are weak because they don't have enough food, our ponies are hungry, the bluecoat's horses are all fit and well fed and at the moment could easily outrun ours, we need to get properly

16

prepared before we even consider going to war, and that would be the last resort. I want to grow old with my family as we all do, without waiting for the next bluecoat attack."
The others listened intently and finally agreed with him that what he said was sensible.
Little Bear apologized to him. Later they talked about old times and Red Flames mother fed and watered them all and they left happy.

An hour later Little Bear reappeared at the tepee, his father Chief Yellow Bird had asked that Red Flame meet with him and some of the elders when the moon was high to discuss the conversation he'd had with Little bear earlier.
Although Red Flame and the Chief hadn't always agreed on things, Red Flame did respect him and readily agreed to meet. The Chief had always protected the tribe and particularly Red Flames mother since his father was killed and he had always respected him for that.

When the moon was at its highest Red Flame entered the tepee of Chief Yellow Bird to find eight of the tribe's elders and Little bear already sitting cross legged around the fire in deep conversation, the tepee was dark except for the glow of the fire highlighting all their rugged faces, he knew them all as they knew him, the smell of their calumet pipes made him catch his breath, it had been a while since he had been invited to such an important tribal meeting.
"Welcome Red Flame, and thank you for coming, you do us an honor." The Chief said.
"No Chief Yellow Bird, it is my honor."
"Your father taught you well with your language Red Flame."
"Thank you Chief."
"Little Bear has told me what you and he were discussing earlier about the tribes making war on the white man and how it is his wish and many of the young warriors to join Chief Sitting Bull to drive the white man off our lands. He says you disagree. I have asked you here to explain why, I believe he even called you a coward, is that right?"
"Yes Chief, he did."
"Are you a coward Red Flame?"
"I don't think so Chief."
"You don't think so? Do you not know?"

17

"Not really. I have fought many battles as you know against many men, both white and red and I have never had to run away, but I like to think that I make the right decisions before I enter battle, I always have a plan beforehand, I cannot honestly say that if I was forced into a situation that was going to get me or my fellow warriors killed, I wouldn't run away. I would, but only to rethink my attack to return to make sure I won. I would not want to die to lose a battle, but I would to win it."

The Chief sat studying his face, expressionless.

"As I said Red Flame, your father taught you well." The Chief smiled warmly at him.

"Thank you Chief. We the great tribes of this country have lost too many battles because we haven't studied our enemy's methods of making war, we have to get more intelligence on how they do things, the weapons we need to match theirs. Then we can beat them. Is this not how we are more successful at killing the Buffalo, we know their speed and direction, when they will turn, when they will run, this is from experience, we need this same information about the white man's bluecoat army, then we will defeat them. I still say we should not go to war, the white man will always outnumber us, but as a last resort when we have nothing else left we will have to fight. Then we will have to win or become extinct."

"You have given this a lot of thought Red Flame." said the Chief.

"I have Chief, every hour I ride alone across our country I think about it. That is why I said to Little Bear we need better rifles, repeating rifles like the bluecoats. Do you know that four bluecoats could wipe out our tribe? If one stood 50 feet to the north of our village, one to the east, one to the south and one to the west, with these new repeating rifles they would kill us all before we got to one of them. They can kill twenty or thirty of our people like that," he snapped his thumb and forefinger, "we can't match them until we get one of these rifles for each of our braves. Also, our ponies need to be well fed, to be able to outrun the bluecoat's horses. We need more food for all."

"And how do you propose that?" Asked the Chief slowly.

"Send your six best hunters to the hunting ground with extra ponies to hunt the Buffalo, we use the meat to feed our people and the skins we take to the trading posts to exchange for new rifles and bullets. As soon as we get the rifles we send out another six hunters and we do the same thing, but with the new rifles we can kill more Buffalo, more Buffalo means more food and more rifles. But firstly, we need to give those first six extra food for themselves and all the ponies they are taking, which means some of the tribe will be hungry for a few days, will they accept that?"

The Chief looked around at the others.

"I like what Red Flame says, he shows great wisdom for his young years, does everyone agree?"

They all looked at each other nodding except for Little Bear.

"Chief Sitting Bull has 8000 warriors, he will defeat the White man with or without these new rifles, I say we join him." Said Little Bear enthusiastically.

"My son, have you not heard a word of what Red Flame has said? I think sometimes you have your mother's brains. Think!" Said the Chief bruskly.

Little Bear stood up, annoyed and embarrassed by his father's words and left the Tepee without saying a word.

"Red Flame," said the Chief," will you go with our hunters to assist with the first killing of Buffalo?"

He paused a moment.

"Yes Chief, my rifle will help us kill more Buffalo and I can go for five days."

"Thank you. Your mother will be very proud. Your father would have been too."

"Just one thing Chief. If any of the young warriors should be attacked by any white men while we are away, they must remember to bury any dead. They must not leave bodies with Apalachee arrows in them because other soldiers will know who killed them, and they will come and take revenge on the whole tribe without hesitation."

"You have my word Red Flame. Let me know when you will seek the Buffalo."

"Yes Chief." He stood, nodded to the elders and left the tepee with all the others except Little Bear still talking about his words, and went back to his mother's tepee.

The next morning just after dawn when a fine mist still hung over the land, he opened the flap to his ma's tepee and was surprised to

19

see Little Bear and five young warriors waiting, all on their ponies and fully armed, each was roped to an extra pony.

"Are you ready to go Buffalo hunting?" Said Little Bear aggressively.

"Not really. I said we should feed all our ponies and ourselves before we left."

"Chief Yellow Bird said for us to leave today and to bring food back to our people as soon as possible."

"Did he? So much for listening to me, let's hope we don't run into any hostile whites. Give me time to tell my ma what is happening."

"Don't be long. We have been waiting awhile." Said Little Bear with attitude.

He paused a moment staring at Little Bear.

"Who's fault is that?"

He didn't like Little Bear at times. He turned and disappeared into the tepee.

Five minutes later he emerged with his repeating rifle, ammunition, his bow and a quiver full of arrows and a bag of oats which he placed on the ground in front of Laggon. He stood silently and watched the pony empty it, and only when it was finished he whispered something to Laggon and stroked the pony's head. He gathered up the empty bag and threw it towards the tepee.

"Don't I get a spare pony?" He asked sarcastically.

"No, the Chief said you will need to move freely to hunt and kill the Buffalo while we pick them up." Replied Little Bear.

"Good thinking," why hadn't he thought of that himself, "Ok let's go."

As they moved off the other warriors who he had not seen for many weeks moved closer to him in turn and greeted him, it was good to see some of them again, many of them were old friends from years ago, he smiled to them all despite feeling the full weight of the tribe on his shoulders.

They left the camp as fast as pulling the extra ponies would allow them.

After riding for several hours in what was known as safe country he moved close to Little Bear.

"I'm going on ahead to higher ground to scout for the herd as I don't have an extra pony, it will be much quicker that way. I will signal as soon as I see them. Ok? Just keep heading east."
Little Bear said nothing.
He pulled off to the north and then when out of sight of the others, he turned to the east as they were but being higher he could see the whole area for miles around. He continued for a few hours and was by now a good half mile ahead of them but could see them when there was a break in the trees behind him making good progress. All was well he thought to himself, find the herd and kill ten buffalo and return to the tribe, they should be finished in five days then he can start travelling again. Another three hours past until he saw a large dust cloud, it must be the buffalo herd on the move, this was good news he thought, the herd had moved west towards them so this should not take as long as he had expected. The herd were moving southwest diagonally across the path of the hunting party so he needed to let the others know to change direction to intercept the moving mass of food and hides.

Suddenly, there was a burst of rifle shots, repeating rifles so not from his fellow braves, he turned Laggon and galloped back towards the last position he had seen them, Laggon as usual moved swiftly over the undulating ground, between large beech trees and in no time he could plainly see the six hunters were still mounted on their ponies with their hands in the air, their rifles were laying on the ground in front of them. About fifteen feet in front of them, still mounted, were three white men who looked like bounty hunters, heavily armed and looking as though they knew how to use their weapons.
With every second he was getting closer; the whites didn't hear him until he was thirty feet away. He pulled up as they turned to see him, his rifle was trained on the middle man as he thought that he looked like the leader.
"Drop your weapons." He called out.
He was right, the middle one was definitely the leader, the man's rifle came up suddenly and fired at him but missed. Red Flame shot him in the chest, a man's largest mass, and as he fell backwards off

his horse Red Flame shot the man to the leader's right, again in the chest.

The third man was a lot slower than the other two and so Red Flame shot him only in the upper arm to make him drop his rifle. The man slumped forward and fell from his horse.

The hunting party cheered and all dismounted together and ran to the injured Bounty hunter, they got to him as Red Flame did. Little Bear was mad with bloodlust, he pulled out his knife from his scabbard and was about to cut the man's throat.

"Stop," Red Flame yelled, "not yet".

"Give me one reason why I shouldn't." Sneered Little Bear.

"Information, and I'm asking."

Little Bear let go of their capture but didn't like it. He pushed the bounty hunter head first into the grass and took two steps backwards watching him writhe on the ground.

"Little Bear, what did these men say to you before I arrived?" Red Flame asked.

"They appeared from nowhere, from behind those bushes, we thought they meant us no harm but then they pulled out their rifles and I remembered what you said about them having repeaters. We had to throw our rifles on the ground in front of us. They said that there was a bounty on all Indian scalps and we should prepare to die. Luckily for us they asked too many questions and you had time to save us. Thank you, Red Flame."

Little Bear sounded surprisingly sincere. The other five all echoed his thanks.

Red Flame dismounted and strode over to the white man, he was a skinny looking man missing most of his teeth from chewing too much tobacco, he smelt of shit and hadn't shaved or bathed for many days. Red Flame pulled him up on to his knees.

"Where have you travelled from?" He asked.

"St. Augustine".

"Why?"

"To make money."

"How? And if you want to live you will tell us the truth."

"Scalping Redskins, they are paying $20 for each scalp."

"Under who's authority?" Red Flame asked.

22

"We work out of Fort Marion but it was the President who authorized the bounty."

"When did it become Law?"

"One month ago. Can you help me with my arm please? It really hurts"

"No. You were going to scalp six of my friends without any mercy and you think we should help you?"

"I am sorry, really sorry." He didn't sound it.

"Of course you are. You know that if any one of us wants you dead, you will be. Live or Die. Were you going to offer my friends the same option? No, you weren't."

The man started to cry unashamedly.

"Please don't kill me, I'll do anything but don't kill me.... please." He sobbed.

"Scalp him," called out Little Bear from a few feet away, "he's a coward."

"Yeah. Scalp him. "Agreed a couple of the others.

Red Flame thought for a moment.

"Does your horse know his way back to the fort?" He asked the bounty hunter.

"Yes, why?"

"That may just have saved your life. Take your clothes off."

The man looked puzzled.

"Take your clothes off. All of them." He repeated raising his voice.

The man struggled to get to his feet, he was in obvious pain. Red Flame did not offer any assistance, he truly despised the man but maybe it was time to expose the injustice that was being played out by the Army and the Great White Father.

He called to one of the braves to quickly burn a stick so he could use it to write a note to the man's superiors.

The man slowly stripped off his jacket, then his trousers, his socks, his shirt and vest. He like most men did not like the humiliation of being told to remove all his clothing watched by another man, and only when threatened did he remove his under pants. The other warriors mocked him because of the size of his genitalia. Red Flame picked up the bounty hunters leather jacket and cut it into an eighteen-inch square, he took the burnt stick and wrote on it:

23

*THIS MAN ALONG WITH TWO OTHERS WAS GOING TO
SCALP FIVE APALACHEE BRAVES FOR A BOUNTY OF $20
EACH.*
*THE OTHER TWO UNFORTUNATELY WERE KILLED BUT
THIS MAN WAS SPARED TO PROVE THAT THE APALACHEE
DO NOT KILL WHITE MEN FOR THE SAKE OF KILLING.*
WE WANT TO LIVE IN PEACE WITH THE WHITE MEN.
RED FLAME. APALACHEE TRIBE.

The Man snarled at Red Flame when he read it.

"Ha. Do you think that will stop it? I'll be back out here soon again along with many others." The hunter had quickly regained his confidence considering he had come so close to death.

Red Flame thought momentarily. He grabbed the man's right hand and placed it palm down on the grass, he yanked his knife from its sheath and in one motion cut off the man's fore finger and index finger. The man screamed and clasped the bloody mess with his good hand.

"At least you won't be able to shoot or scalp any more Indians." Said Red Flame.

Red Flame tied the man's hands behind his back and hoisted him onto his saddle, and then tied him to it facing backwards and hung the newly printed sign around the man's neck, turning the horse back the way, it had come, he slapped its hind quarters and it took off at a gallop, the man bouncing up and down in obvious discomfort.

"I know you don't agree with what I just did but I appreciate you letting me do it." He said to the assembled braves.

"My Father thinks you are a wise man and I have come to realize he is right, I am sorry I doubted it. You saved our lives today and I will always follow you."

"Thank you, Little Bear." He said somewhat surprised. They hugged.

"Right let's pick up their repeater rifles and ammo along with their horses and get on with our job. That's three new rifles we didn't expect," handing one to each of three of the braves, "I saw the great

24

herd heading south across our path so we need to turn south east to intercept them. Are we ready? Let's go."

They moved off as one for several miles, before again taking up his position on the left of the others on higher ground until he spotted the herd again. From the highest point the lands opened up in front of him. The smooth undulating hills seemed to go on for miles, the colors of the grasses changing with the wind and the clouds moving across the sun. After seeing the herd again, he rode back down the hill to rejoin the others and soon they were among the charging buffalo. with the three new repeater rifles from the bounty hunters, within three hours they had six buffalo to prepare for the return trip. More than even he had thought possible at this stage of the hunt.

The hunting party decided to camp that night on the plains and get an early start so that by midday they could be on their way back to the village with a good supply of food and hides. Two days later they arrived home with nine buffalo on three travois, enough to feed the entire camp and enough hides to trade for five repeater rifles and ammunition. Plus, two new horses.

He was hailed as a hero when the camp found out that he had saved the six warriors from certain death and he had brought back nine buffalo for the tribe. That night a great party was held in his honor with much dancing and fire water. Little Bear even made a speech telling in detail of the incident and what a great warrior Red Flame was.

His Mother was ecstatic and told him so. Two of the young squaws showed him.

The next day as the sun was rising his mother was up early and made some food for him, they hugged and he left quietly before anybody was up and about, slowly he drifted past the ponies and sleeping dogs off into the morning mist, almost ghost like.

He travelled fully armed with his repeater rifle, ammunition, bow and quiver full of arrows, his tomahawk and shield, his knife and a lance, all this weaponry would slow him down in a chase but he would ditch the lance, shield and tomahawk if necessary.

He rode south east towards Florida again, the same route he had taken when he met David and Anne, he had been enroute to meet an old friend of his fathers in Newmansville who he had not seen in two years, he expected not to see his Mother again for about five weeks.

He kept off the main tracks as usual so as not to see too many other travelers, these troubled times were fired by many conflicting rumors about the Indian situation, some said the whites were again at war with all Indian tribes and others said that a new agreement had been signed by the President and the great chiefs just weeks before. He decided it was safer to stay out of sight unless necessary.

CHAPTER 3

He rode steadily for three days stopping only to catch the odd rabbit and to sleep.

It was early on day four that he heard a lot of gunshots about one hundred yards ahead of him. He was in a beautiful valley with Black Mangrove trees on both sides of his position and in front of him was a small rocky incline, he guessed that the shots were coming from the other side of that. He dismounted, grabbed his rifle and crouching down he moved forward until he could see over the rocks, there in front of him about sixty yards ahead, appeared to be a sheriff whose hand seemed to be injured and a very young deputy both pinned down behind a large rock to his right, they only had hand guns and seemed to be out of ammunition as they were not returning fire. The sun was reflecting off their badges. About forty feet ahead of him were four Mexican soldiers who had spread out forming a semicircle around the Lawmen and were really enjoying themselves, they were slugging back whisky as they fired at the two men. The sheriff and his deputy could only cower behind the rocks, it was just a matter of time until it would all be over, this was not a fair fight, this was more like a turkey shoot. What were Mexicans doing this far north anyway? Could it be that they had just lost their way or was it something more sinister?

He aimed at who he thought was the senior of the Mexican soldiers, a captain maybe, he certainly had the most gold braid on his jacket, who was sitting between and behind two good sized rocks, he was well hidden from the lawmen, he should be the first to be eliminated. 'Crack.' Red Flame fired, it hit the captain in the stomach, who lurched sideways and his whisky bottle dropped to the ground and smashed some ten feet below, the officer grabbed his stomach in pain but it was too late, seconds later he slumped forward dead.

The others didn't even hear his shot over their own so he was able to single out the next soldier that was in the most dangerous position to

27

the sheriff, 'Crack.' he fired again. A spurt of blood flew out the side of the soldier's head and he dropped to his knees and then on to his face. Now only two of the soldiers were still firing but it soon became apparent that it had gone much quieter, they looked at where the other two soldiers had been positioned and saw their blooded corpses, they both panicked, one stood up looking to the higher ground where Red Flame was, 'Crack', Red Flame shot him in the center of his chest, he dropped about twenty feet from his position in the rocks to the ground below with a scream.

One more to go, the last soldier must have seen his rifle barrel and shot at where he thought Red Flame was hidden, a bullet ricocheted off the rocks behind him. Red Flame paused, absolutely still, hoping the soldier would think he had been hit, give him a few more seconds he thought to himself one, two, three, four, five he counted. He stood up and knowing where the soldier was, aimed and fired. 'Crack.' He missed. His bullet bounced off the rocks also. The last soldier remained still for several seconds. Then he jumped up again and fired in the direction of where Red Flame was. Silence again. Red Flame stood up resting his rifle on a rock, looking down the sights he panned the area he knew the Mexican cavalryman was hiding. Then, he didn't know why, but he made the sound of a wild Bear as he did sometimes when hunting. 'Grrrr, grrrr,' he yelled. Immediately the soldier stuck his head up, probably out of curiosity. 'Crack' The soldier fell backwards with a hole in his forehead.

The sheriff and his young deputy cautiously peered around the rock, scanning the higher rocks knowing something was going on but not sure what, then they saw Red Flame armed for war, both stood up and raised their hands as though surrendering to him, they watched and waited for him to work his way down over the rocks still with their hands in the air until he stood fifteen feet away from them.

"You don't need to keep your hands up, I'm not going to shoot you. Are you both alright?"

They both let out a sigh of relief.

"Yes. Thank you, thank you." Said the Sheriff wrapping his neckerchief around his injured hand.

"Yes. Thanks to you." Reiterated the young Deputy who was the spitting image of the older sheriff.

"I thought we were a gonna there." Added the Sheriff putting his good hand out to Red Flame. They shook hands, he had a good firm grip Red Flame noticed.

"I'm Sheriff Davidson from Lancaster and this is my son William, he's also my deputy. These Mexicans just attacked us for no reason. They were hiding in those rocks and just opened fire on us, we dismounted but our horses bolted with our rifles and neither of us had much ammo. We soon ran out so without you showing up we would certainly both be dead."

"Why were the Mexicans so far north?" Asked Red Flame sounding intrigued.

"I think it's because their Government has offered a bounty." Said the Sheriff looking a little embarrassed.

"What for, Indian scalps?" Asked Red Flame.

"Yes, and now whites too."

"That's not good, it seems everybody was after the Redskins scalps, but now whites too? The worlds gone mad."

"Unfortunately, it seems that way. I'm sorry I didn't ask your name?"

"My name is Red Flame".

"Red Flame?" The father and son looked at each other in some sort of acknowledgement, "we are both honored to meet you, you are famous in these parts."

"I am? Why, what have I done?"

"There was an article and a photograph of you in the Madison Times a few weeks ago, hailing you a hero for saving the Editor and his wife from some cow hands who had robbed them, some really nasty men by the sound of it."

"So, David did write his story after all. They were a really nice couple, I hope they do well." Red Flame said smiling.

"They think a lot about you. Quite often they ask in the paper has anyone seen you or got any information about you and if they do then to wish you their best."
Red Flame smiled again.

"That's really nice of them. Where are you heading now?"

"We were on the trail of the McCain brothers, two mean bank robbers but their trail has gone cold so I think we will head back to Lancaster, I need to get this hand looked at by the Doc anyway. And you? Which direction are you heading in?"

"Well, I'm going that way too, can I ride along with you as I'm heading to Newmansville?"

"Certainly, you can, we would welcome your company. William, can you round up our horses and we will escort Red Flame back to town."

"Yes sir." William replied running enthusiastically over to their mounts.

"I will take the Mexicans ammunition if that is alright with you Sheriff?" Red Flame asked.

"Of course, help yourself. Take what you want."

Red Flame disappeared into the rocks and emerged a short while later leading Laggon with four rifles and several belts of ammunition which he had tied together with some twine hanging over his shoulder.

They moved off together with Sheriff Davidson in the middle, Red Flame on his left and William on the right. The Sheriff was eager to learn more about his background, about his father's murder and how his English was so good.

Red Flame wanted to know what it was like being the law in Lancaster, was it dangerous?

The forty miles seemed to fly past and soon they were in sight of the town limits.

"Well I suppose I had better leave you here, I tend to stand out in the white man's towns." Said Red Flame smiling at the other two.

"Nonsense. You are our guest and my wife would kill me herself if I didn't take you to meet her, after all you are the man that saved her husband and her son. Also, she's a great cook." Replied the sheriff. They all laughed.

"That's good. That makes all the difference." Red Flame replied still laughing.

"Definitely, you must come and meet her." Insisted William.

They rode on into the town together, Red Flame was aware of the well-dressed town folk's interest, some were pointing and some just nudging each other, they probably had not seen too many Redskins in the town before, not armed to the teeth anyway. The three of them stopped outside a small but immaculate house with flowers blooming in the front yard and spotless white paintwork and picket fence. It had a bright red roof, it didn't look real. As they were tying up their horses the front door flew open and a small buxom long blonde-haired lady with a bright light blue long dress ran out to her husband. Her dress whirled around behind her like a tornado.

"What's wrong? Are you ok?" She asked in a panic looking at the Sheriff's bloodied hand and then at Red Flame suspiciously.

"I am or should I say we are due to this gentleman, if it hadn't been for him we both would be dead." Said the Sheriff.

"What?" She replied looking horrified.

"This is Red Flame." The Sheriff said and gestured towards him. His wife nodded to him not knowing quite what to say or do. She looked scared.

"Let's just go inside and then we can tell you about it." He hugged her and kissed her on the forehead, she stepped over to William and hugged him, the three embraced as they strode up the two steps on to their verandah and into the house, he followed a few steps behind.

The inside of their house was immaculate too, bright green floral drapes and several vases of bright colored flowers with a couch and matching chairs in pale green, it was well taken care of and a world away from his mother's tepee. He pictured his ma in a home like this again. She loved the house she shared with his father.

Once inside she told all of them to sit down and immediately asked them what had happened. Between the father and son, they told her the story of their ambush by the Mexican soldiers and how they had run out of ammunition and if Red Flame had not come along at that exact time they would be dead. William stood up and was visually upset, his mother then stood and consoled him. After a couple of minutes William sat back down on the couch next to Sherriff Davidson and they hugged.

"Thank you so much Mister Red Flame and please call me Mary."

The Sheriff and William laughed, Mary turned to see why.

"It's just Red Flame Mary, not Mister Red Flame."

They all laughed together which eased the tension in the room, they weren't used to having a Redskin sitting in their spotless parlor, on a spotless couch.

"I'm sorry Red Flame, I should have known the name. You are the one we read about in the newspaper, aren't you? You saved that young couple, didn't you?" Enquired Mary.

"I just happened to be there at the right time. Like today."

"Your accent, how did you get that?"

"My father was from Scotland."

"That's right, it's coming back to me now, he was a Doctor and your mother was from the Apalachee tribe. Now I remember. Well welcome to our home, you have to stay for a home cooked meal and stay the night".

"That's very kind of you Mary but…."

"No buts about it, you will stay." She stood up and clapped her hands as though to say that's the end of it and no arguing.

"It's no good arguing Red Flame, once she's made up her mind it won't change." Remarked the Sheriff.

"She won't let you leave," William added, "she's like that."
They all laughed again.

"In that case how can I refuse?"

"Good," she stood up, walked over to Red Flame and embraced him, "thank you Red Flame. Now, would you like some tea or coffee?"

"Coffee please." Said the Sheriff.

"I'm asking Red Flame, not you. You will always drink coffee."

"Charming." Quipped the sheriff.

"Me too Mum, please." William added.

"I would love a coffee too please." Red Flame answered.

"Good," she said again, "I will get those for you and make a start on our celebration supper."

"What are we celebrating Mom?" Asked William.

"You both being alive William, that's what! And meeting Red Flame." She smiled at him and then disappeared into the kitchen.
There was a silence as both William and his father looked at each other and thought about the gravity of what Mary had just said.
William welled up again.

32

"Jesus Christ Mary, your right. We wouldn't have seen you again, we wouldn't be sitting here now." The Sheriff said and rising went to William and put his arm around the youngster's shoulders.

"It was not your time to die." Red Flame said quietly.

"I suppose not." Responded the Sheriff turning to look at him, slowly digesting Red Flames comment.

There was a silence for several minutes as each of them were alone with their thoughts, suddenly the silence was interrupted by Mary bursting back into the room bearing a tray with three coffees on it.

"There's your coffees, help yourselves."

They all thanked her and took a cup, the silence and their thoughts continued as they drank.

"Suppers going to be a while, why don't the three of you go to Doctor Allen's, get that hand looked at and stop in at the Saloon and have a proper drink." Said Mary.

"Good Idea," replied the Sheriff, "we don't need telling twice do we, let's go."

The Sheriff led the way out and they slowly strolled across the street past four more immaculate small houses, there was obviously competition between them to see who could keep the best bloomage going. It was only a short walk to the Doctors surgery; the Sheriff went in as he and William waited outside the hardware store next door looking in the shop window. The Sheriff rejoined them five minutes later and they all walked past his office which also served as a Jail, then there was a men's outfitters and then the Saloon. The horses tied up outside the Bar hinted that it was easily the most frequented of the local businesses, understandably as they offered rooms to travelers and other services to any gentlemen that required them. As long as they had enough money. It was also a smart looking two storey building painted in a burgundy color with cream trim and had the obligatory two swing doors. All the properties as far as he could see were newly painted and very well maintained. A prosperous town, and it showed. He didn't think the Sheriff would be called upon to administer any sort of justice too often here. As they walked together well-dressed ladies said 'good day Sheriff', 'good day William' and smart gents touched their hats 'Good day' seemed to be ringing out from all directions, several people acknowledged

33

him and he nodded back smiling at them all trying to look as friendly as possible, they were somewhat bemused to see an Indian war chief on their Main Street. What was the world coming too?

The Sheriff pushed the saloon doors open, everybody without exception turned to see who was entering, once satisfied, they then got on with their drinking or their card games convinced it wasn't anybody that might cause trouble. It was only when he appeared through the doors that a silence fell over the room, everybody stared.

The Sheriff led William and him over to the bar." Two beers please John, and what would you like Red Flame?" Asked the Sheriff.

"Just water please Sheriff."

"And a water for my friend please John."

"Yes Sir." John replied as he turned to the beer taps grabbing two-pint glasses. John was a smallish man with greased back black hair and a huge mustache and a winning smile. He wore a black waist coat over an immaculate bright white shirt. An ideal look for a barman.

Everybody seemed to relax again and the noise level rose once more, everyone seemed at ease with him being in 'their' bar, he wondered if it would have been the same if he hadn't been with the Sheriff and William.

The Sheriff introduced Red Flame to John and explained how they had met and the way he had saved both his and Williams lives. John stood with a puzzled look on his face.

"I have read about you," pausing a minute, "aren't you the Indian they wrote about in the paper, you saved some white folks lives?"

"That's the man." Interrupted the Sheriff before he could say anymore.

"Welcome to my bar Red Flame."

"Thank you, John. It's nice to be here."

They stood at the bar enjoying their drinks and chatting about the town and how it had changed over the years, how most of the old gunfighters had disappeared, there was still the occasional one looking to make a name for himself, but now it was the bounty hunters that were hunting for somebody that were more of a problem, and of course the odd drunk on a Saturday night, there would always be those. They all laughed together. John the barman joined in the conversation between serving other patrons. Lancaster seemed a nice place to live.

After an enjoyable hour chatting they headed back to enjoy Mary's supper, he thought he could smell it cooking from about fifty yards away, it smelt delicious and he was hungry.

CHAPTER 4

They had just finished eating their second slice of Mary's delicious apple pie when they heard somebody running through the street shouting as they ran towards the house.

"Sheriff, Sheriff come quick there's trouble at the Saloon, Sheriff."

The Sheriff and William stood up instantly, routinely they picked up their holsters and revolvers and rushed out the door. Red Flame followed two steps behind and grabbed his rifle from its sheath that was still tied on Laggon.

Both the Sheriff and William were one step inside the bar side by side when he came through the doors behind them. There, standing ten paces in front of them was a man all in black with two shiny holsters with a very nice sparkling revolver in each, waiting for them. The man looked mean, which he guessed was what the man wanted to achieve with the all black outfit, but he looked sober.

"Spread out William." He said quietly as he moved quickly past to the right of the Sheriff, about eight feet away. William moved away to the left of his father also about eight feet away.

"Do you remember me Sheriff?" The man called out, wanting everybody to hear.

"No, I don't. Should I?"

"My names Clancy. Looks as though I picked a good night to visit, you with a damaged hand and all. Do you remember me now?"

"What do you want Clancy?"

"You don't remember do you? I told you four years ago that when I got out of Jail I'd be back for you, and this must be your little boy. I remember him too. He used to follow you around like a sheep. Well, two Davidsons in one night. Well, what do you know?" He snorted with laughter.

The Sheriff started to sweat, it was obvious that with his heavily bandaged hand he could not outdraw anyone, let alone what looked like an experienced gunslinger and William looked like he would struggle with such a hardened man. He could be wrong though.

People were getting up from their chairs, card hands were being placed face down on the tables, people had lost interest in their games, drinks were left where they were as self-preservation took over. All scurried away from the line of fire to the perimeter of the bar still retaining that morbid sense of drama. They would all return to their seats after the show was over as though there had just been a short intermission.

"So, what do you want?" Asked the sheriff again sounding brave.

"I want to bury you in the cemetery, that's what I came back for……and your boy."

The sheriff turned sideways towards Red Flame with a very desperate expression on his face, almost seeking some inspiration.

"Mr. Clancy." Red Flame said softly.

"Well, what do you know? The Redskin speaks English. So now I can collect me an extra $20 bounty as well, now that's what I call a good night's work." He laughed as he looked around the room at the individual faces expecting them to appreciate his humor. Some smiled back through fear but others looked away.

"So, what's your name Redskin?" Clancy asked grinning confidently.

"You don't need to know my name, you only need to know that those shiny guns of yours are going to a good home." He answered with a grin on his face.

"What are you talking about?" Clancy's grin disappeared.

"Young William there," he nodded towards the young deputy, "he's just starting his career as a deputy and as you can see, he really needs some new hardware, and yours will do nicely. You can look at it as though you're helping to sponsor his apprenticeship for the many years he will help to protect the good people of Lancaster."

"You must be joking." Clancy's confidence suddenly dissipated along with his smirk.

"Haven't you heard, we Redskins don't have a sense of humor any more, ever since people like you started scalping us."

Suddenly Clancy's eyes were darting from his to Williams. Clancy had realized that the Sheriff was not a threat, Red Flame was an unknown quantity but holding a rifle, so slower to respond, and

37

William might just be better with a gun than Clancy had bargained for. Confidence was an easy thing to lose. Clancy turned just slightly to face William, probably not quite sure which of them he should aim for first, but then quickly making the decision to concentrate on Williams right hand as he would be the first to get a shot away. Which he should do.

Clancy's fingers twitched just slightly, implying he was about to draw on William. Red Flame suddenly cocked his rifle. The sound was loud in the silent bar and immediately made Clancy look towards him, his concentration now gone. Clancy's plan in that split second had changed but that was all William needed. He drew his pistol and fired. His shot hit Clancy right of center in the chest. Clancy dropped like a sack of potatoes.

Silence. Nobody moved for several seconds.

Then the patrons started whispering again, it suddenly got louder very quickly.

The father and son hugged, and the patrons clapped. Then they returned to their drinks and card games, the place was buzzing again within sixty seconds with chatter and laughter, how fickle people were he thought to himself. Clancy was still motionless on the floor, blood oozing from his chest. Nobody cared or even took any notice, someone would clear the mess away later, once they had finished drinking for the night.

He walked over to Clancy's body and undid the holster belt with the shiny guns and handed them to William.

"You earned them," he said smiling, "goodbye William, goodbye Sheriff, thank Mary for the lovely meal and hospitality." He didn't wait for a response, he turned and walked out of the saloon back towards the sheriff's house. He was just mounting Laggon when William called out as he ran down the street towards him, the sheriff stood in the open saloon door waving.

"Red Flame, where are you going? Dad wants to know if you are ok?"

"I'm fine tell your father. I have to leave William. When news of tonight gets out bounty hunters from across the state will be after my scalp, and neither you nor your father need them showing up in your town. Well done tonight, but practice with those new hand guns. Say

goodbye to your father and mother. I will see you all again I'm sure."
They shook hands, he waved back to the sheriff, slowly turned
Laggon and rode out of town.

He rode southeast for two days sticking to back tracks and
dangerous waterways and sleeping in trees so as not to run into any
bounty hunters or any white men for that matter. Laggon was always
nearby acting as his sentry.

He slowly rode down the old track approaching his father's best
friend Ewan Cameron's small holding with a wooden cabin in the
middle of it, it had not changed in all the years they had known each
other.

Ewan was also a Doctor, he and his father had been at school
together, then the University of Edinburgh where they both had
qualified and dreamed up the crazy idea of travelling around the
globe to the new world together to start a new life and to make a
difference to those that had already settled here.

Ewan didn't hear Laggon approaching and suddenly walked out
of his front door while talking to his wife about something else. As
he turned he saw Red Flame and his eyes nearly popped out of their
sockets.

"God in Heaven." Ewan yelled. The door slammed shut behind
him as he disappeared back inside. Thirty seconds later he
reappeared at the door with a double-barreled shotgun pointing
straight at Red flame.

"What do you want? Get away from here." Ewan yelled out.

"I see you have lost your eyesight as well as your marbles Ewan
Cameron." There was a momentary pause while Ewan's brain
absorbed Red Flames last sentence.

"Oh my god! Oh my god! Margaret come quickly, come quickly
women its Red Flame. Its Red Flame. He's here."

The door opened wide again and a tiny rotund lady with a reddish
complexion and with bright red hair ran towards him, her large skirt
blowing in all directions, her arms outstretched as if she was carrying
a large invisible ball, trying to drag him from his pony.

"Oh my God its Red Flame, its Red Flame, Ewan."

"I know that woman, I told you that. Leave him alone, let him get down himself. My God, stop Margaret, look at him," they both came to a sudden halt and stared at him, "my God my boy, you look magnificent. Doesn't he Margaret? Absolutely magnificent. Your father would be so proud to see you today." He was sure he saw a tear run down Ewan's cheek.

"Absolutely," echoed Margaret, "so proud."

"Get in the house out of this blasted sun, relax. Get some food women, can't you see he's almost starved to death." They all roared with laughter.

"I can see he hasn't eaten for weeks." Margaret added. They laughed together even louder.

"Get the whisky out women, the good stuff not that American rubbish."

Red Flame realized then how much he had missed his father's Scottish dry sense of humor and how much the two Scottish doctors were alike. He suddenly missed his father massively.

They entered the small house and he sat on the chair that Margaret directed him to.

"We have been reading a lot about you, you are a hero to many around here." Ewan said as Margaret handed them a large scotch each.

They spoke at length about what had been written of his exploits in the newspaper, they all agreed it had been exaggerated but it had all seemed very positive for the native Indians.

"I realize that some good had come from the articles but the publicity has also caused me much concern, in so much as it attracts trouble." Said Red Flame seriously.

"Naturally my boy. One goes with the other. It always has." Said Ewan.

"I have a dilemma Ewan. It is causing me many sleepless nights."

"You have come for advice from me my boy, an old fart like me? I am honored you would do such a thing."

"Thank you. Yes, I would like your advice because you are the only one that will tell me what you really think, like father," both Mary and Ewan sat back in their chairs expectantly, "the Great White Father is giving the tribes conflicting stories. He is saying that he wants the tribes to move on to a reservation large enough to maintain

40

their way of life, to hunt the buffalo when hungry but not cause trouble for the white folks who are seeking a new way of life, that want to purchase the lands, but at the same time it appears he wants to get rid of the great tribes completely. He makes promises but does not keep them and then he sends in the bluecoats to kill whole villages, children, women and warriors. I have met with the Chief of ma's tribe, he has listened to my arguments about going to war and I am surprised he still backs my peace plans, but it won't last long now, in fact I think we will have to go to war soon, very soon. The white man now is scalping all the Indians they can round up and the Government is paying them $20 per scalp to do it. The tribes can only take so much. Bounty hunters are flooding into the south to make money. I believe we will lose the war but it is best to die with dignity than with no dignity. What do you think?"

Ewan thought for a moment nodding his head.

"I think you are right my boy, but not an all-out war, you can't compete with the cavalry's numbers and weaponry, you must do it by stealth. Hit and run and hide. It's what the tribes have always done best, better than any army I can name, why change now? You are bringing this situation to people's notice with your good publicity but I doubt anything will be done about it quickly. America is being built on greed and power, ever since Washington and his likes invested money in the Indian lands in Ohio some one hundred years ago, they have wanted the Indians gone. I don't think that will ever change, there is no discipline here, which you need to have, there's no law to speak of therefore people just do what they want. I think that once all the native tribes are gone the whites will turn against other whites, they just lust blood, any blood. It's as though if you have something that I haven't got, then I will just take it from you. Everybody here has a gun and consequently they will use them. It was for this reason alone that your father and I discussed returning to Scotland many times, he feared for you and your mothers' futures, and if it wasn't for our patients, we would have both long gone. I feel we could be having this same conversation in another fifty years or one hundred and fifty years and your people, the Apalachee will be surviving on a pittance, if they are still around at all then."

Red Flame nodded in agreement.

"I think you are right. I worry that I will never have a family of my own, no children, no peace. I just can't see it happening. Everyone I meet now on my travels I unfortunately expect to have to kill because they want to kill me for a bounty, its easy money. A person can't live like that for long." Said Red Flame thoughtfully. Ewan nodded eagerly again.

"No, they can't. All that stress." He added seconds later. Mary left the room and headed for the kitchen. She was upset, probably by all the talk of war.

Apart from his mother, Ewan and Margaret were his nearest and dearest since the killing of his father and he had never hesitated in asking their opinions or advice on any subject so he was perturbed to hear their opinions on the Native Indian-white man war that was raging at its worst so far. He really could not see a future for his own Native Indian people.

He missed talking to wise men such as Ewan and his father, men who could charm and guide with humor but also with their intelligence and honesty.

"Food woman. We're starving. Where are you?" Ewan suddenly shouted out laughing. Margaret appeared with enough food to feed the 5000 and it was delicious.

The conversation of war was forgotten and Margaret and Ewan started recollecting events with his parents which resulted in much laughter and a few tears but a good time was had by them all, and soon the whisky took its toll and all were asleep by midnight.

The next morning, he awoke early and was sitting on the verandah when Ewan appeared with two coffees which he placed on a small wooden table in front of them.

"Did you sleep well Red Flame?"

"Like a log Ewan. And you?"

"Good. Yes, me as well."

"Margaret's meal was superb, as usual."

"Aye, she's a fine cook. She loves to see you, you're the bairn we never had, she thinks of you as ours, you know that don't you?"

Red Flame just smiled.

"Thank you, Ewan." They both stood and hugged each other.

"I don't envy you Red Flame. Yes, you are a fearless warrior, no doubt about that but there will come a day when you will have to decide whether to embrace the white man or kill him. An act probably of war will determine that for you and I cannot see you becoming a white man to submerge yourself within their culture to live an unhappy existence, that is not you," Ewan paused momentarily, "I can honestly see you going to war in retaliation to an act of war by the white man, you will cause them many deaths and you will become even more famous than you are already, perhaps infamous is more the word they will use but, eventually they will win, as we have already said, they have to, numbers, better arms, better supplies," they sat in silence for several minutes looking at each other. Red Flame nodded, "I think you have already resolved yourself to the fact that you, Red Flame, will take on the might of the white man and you will test him every inch of the way. It is I feel a battle that you owe to your people and also to show the white man that given different times and different circumstances history should and could have been written a different way," Ewan gave him time to think, "Red Flame, I think if your Father was alive today he would have said to you that this is not what he and I came to America for, this country is still uncivilized, and I'm not sure it ever will be, all these guns everywhere, I know that he was very disappointed with the American politicians and their Generals and their barbaric treatment of the Native Indians, whatever their tribes and he would say you have to do what you think is right. Just you, forget the old chief's, times have changed, just you!"

He sat, thinking for several minutes.

"Whatever happens, as you say, I will not and cannot win, I suppose as long as I tell my people that then I will not be lying to them, no false hopes, just the truth."

"That's right, it's a no-win situation," Ewan looked at him sympathetically, his expression said it all, "you're going to die sooner than you think, old age is not an option for you."

Red Flame nodded slowly in agreement.

"I know." He said.

They both stood up and hugged each other again. Then Margaret came out and wrapped her arms around both of them. They kissed each other.

He walked over to Laggon and mounted.

"Thank you both for your hospitality and your valued advice. If you need me anytime." He said quietly looking away. Not wanting them to see his tears.

"We know, we know, we will be in touch." Said Ewan.

"We love you," called out Margaret, "God speed."

He turned Laggon and headed north. He waved as he left without looking back. Tears rolling down his face.

He rode for over two days heading back to the village, stopping only for short breaks, with each mile he got angrier, over and over he ran through Ewan's words trying to establish a plan in his mind, why are these white men taking over their lands, why are they killing innocent people, running through the same words, he felt he already knew the outcome but having someone as intelligent as Ewan confirming it made it ten times worse. Why weren't more white men intelligent like Ewan, someone that could reason, without fighting, thinking first.

As he turned north east two white men flagged him down, they had been hidden in some trees, one looked mean with shaggy beard and dirty clothes, the other not quite so bad but still dirty looking, maybe they were trappers, or scavengers more like, they just hadn't caught anything for a while, but he was not in the mood for idle chatter. He was still considering Ewan's observations and he really wanted to get home and discuss their thoughts with his Ma, that was why he had let his guard slip, he should have smelt these men a long way off. Any other good scout would have.

"Yes, what do you want?" He snapped, stopping ten feet away from them.

"We are just being friendly." Said the dirty looking one uneasily.

"I'm sorry, but I am in a hurry."

"No need to be like that," the other man said sounding calm," we mean no harm."

Red Flame already had his rifle in his hand laying across his legs, his preferred way of travelling. He thought for a moment, no need to get uptight, relax. He felt his heart rate going down. Perhaps they didn't mean any harm.

"What's your name Redskin?"

He didn't like the man's brusque tone.

"Why?"

"I just like to know......." The man shrugged.

"You want to know my name so you can get the reward for my scalp, right?"

The men's facial expressions changed and they immediately went for their guns.

He didn't care, his rifle came up before either of theirs and fired twice. They both died instantly. His anger was intense. They deserved that he thought.

He picked up their rifles and the horse's reins and lead the horses away.

CHAPTER 5

Early the following day he could see his mother's camp circle in the distance but he knew instinctively something was wrong, there was too much smoke rising from the tepee's, way too much smoke. He moved on quickly pulling the two scavengers' horses behind him.

Blooded bodies of predominantly women and children were strewn everywhere, there were a few dead warriors who had tried to defend the camp and many tepees still burning. Terror struck him, where was his mother, he jumped from Laggon and ran into the remains of her tepee. She was lying on a bear skin with her niece tending to her wounds, they both turned towards him in shock as he burst in.

"Ma, are you Ok?"

"Yes, I'm fine thanks to Little Wolf." She smiled acknowledging her young niece.

"What happened?"

"Bluecoats attacked us at sunrise, just hours ago, they just rode in setting fire to our homes and shooting anything that moved, children, they killed children, women and anyone that resisted them. They scalped people."

"Where is Chief Yellow Bird?"

"I don't know, in his tepee I expect."

"I will be back."

He ran to the remains of the Chief's tepee and looked in, the Chief was sitting, looking up to the sky in some sort of prayer.

"What happened?" He asked.

"They just attacked, no warning, no nothing. It was that Captain Hancock's troop from Fort Dade."

"Captain Hancock? The one that came for peace talks last year? Bastard. He is going to die." His anger had now taken him over, his blood was boiling. All he could see was a red mist.

"What?" Asked the Chief.

"They are all going to die." He shouted back.

"How, when?" Asked the Chief totally perplexed.

"Starting now. Where is Little Bear?"

46

"Probably in his tepee."

Red Flame turned and ran to Little Bears tepee and opened the flap. Little Bear looked up, but cradled in his arms was his young three-year-old son. Dead. Little bear was crying unashamedly.

"Red Flame, what are you doing here?"

"It is time Little Bear. We cannot let this happen again. I intend to kill all the Bluecoats that did this, or die trying. I need all your ammunition though."

'I will come with you."

"No Little Bear. You should stay with the tribe, you are needed here now. We cannot win this war, we will surely die. I just need to show the white man that we are not going to let this continue without a fight for as long as I am alive, I will fight them."

"I am with you Red Flame. What do I have left?" Little Bear looked down at his dead son.

Red Flame looked at Little Bear, before him he saw a broken man who also had had enough of all the killings.

"Right. Let's kill as many soldiers as we can." He ran back to his mother's tepee.

"Ma, I am going after the Bluecoats that did this and I promise I will not return until they are dead. If I don't return you will know that I failed."

"No Red Flame, you can't kill them all."

"I'm going to try ma. I will return within two weeks. Please take care. Thank you, Little Wolf for all your help with ma," he nodded to his niece, "take care ma."

"You too son."

Because of the cavalry attack and him losing his temper he had even forgotten to tell her about Margaret and Ewan. Next time.

He and Little Bear ran to their ponies and saddled up, Red Flame had two extra repeating rifles bound within his blanket and twenty extra arrows, they moved off quickly after the Bluecoats together. They followed the trail towards Fort Dade until the ground grew more undulating and then they headed for the highest ground hoping to see the troops dust cloud ahead, but nothing.

After riding flat out for three hours, they stopped to give their mounts water and a rest.

"Are you sure you know what we're doing?" Little Bear asked suspiciously.

"No, I don't, but I know it has to be done, I am not giving up my life so white men can carry on killing our mothers and children, we have to stop them. Or die trying."

They rode hard for the next four hours until eventually they saw the dust cloud that the forty or so troopers were causing as it rose sixty feet up in to the air as they made fast time back towards their Fort, he reckoned it would take them, if they stopped for the night at sunset, until late the following afternoon to get there.

They pulled up and walked their ponies to rest them while he explained his plan to Little Bear, there was no rush, the soldiers would still be there in a few hours.

"We need to slow down now as I expect them to make camp for the night, don't you?" He asked. Little Bear just nodded thoughtfully.

"Probably another hour or so." Added Little Bear enthusiastically.

"We can sneak in and kill two or three guards tonight, then tomorrow when they are on the move again we will crisscross their path at the rear and take out two at a time. I will cross from the east, take two with bow and arrows and then ride on to you who will be watching my rear from undercover, so if any of the others see me or hear anything and come after me, you can give me covering fire. I will then take a longer route back to the east and we repeat. I would like to get twelve or fifteen of them before they realize what's happening. Does that make sense?"

"Yes, that is a good plan, I thought we were just going to attack them. Which scared me."

"No, we can't, too many of them. This way we might be able to take Captain Hancock alive. I think we keep riding until they stop. Let them bed down for the night, they will position sentries and then we go in and kill some."

"They will realize in the morning what we have done, and they will come after us."

"Agreed. What do you think of this idea?" he asked," they will position guards every hundred yards in a circle around the camp like

48

they always do, we will take one at a time and instead of leaving the bodies for them to find in the morning, like we usually do, we will hide them. They will just disappear. Well that's the plan. What do you think?"

Little Bear said nothing for several seconds while he ran through it in his own mind.

"It's a good plan. I suppose the further the bodies are from the camp the safer it will be for us." Little Bear eventually said.

"The river is close by here, we could dump them in there, they would travel downstream hopefully for miles. We would have plenty of time to finish the job." Added Red Flame.

"Yes, that's better, much better. Great idea."

"Ok, but if it is fast flowing enough we might get away without weighting the bodies down, we should go and have a look."
They mounted their ponies again and slowly headed towards the Bluecoats camp which was being established on an open grassy area in a small valley, as soon as they saw movement from within the camp they dismounted and waited for darkness to fall.
The captain had chosen a good location for a one-night stopover, a large open space surrounded by high sycamore trees and many smaller beech trees.

They turned west, away from the camp and found the river 300 yards away, it was flowing very fast. So fast, that they could just dump the bodies in the river, no need to weigh them down, which would have taken more time. They returned to where they could see the camp taking shape and waited patiently until there was little movement from within it.
He tied Laggon to a beach tree and slowly maneuvered himself the 150 yards through the undergrowth until he was only fifteen feet away from the first sentry. He waited and watched without moving. The guard was more interested in lighting a cigarette than he was protecting his fellow soldiers, he was not paying any attention to the area outside the camp. Red Flame inched his way through the bushes towards the sentry and only when he could hear the sentry breathing he jumped up and brought his tomahawk down onto the top of the sentry's head. He took the dead man's weight as the sentry dropped to the ground, so as to not make any unnecessary noise and then he

stamped out the still burning cigarette. He crouched down and hooted like an Owl to Little Bear who appeared immediately and picked the soldier up, slung him over his shoulder and disappeared back into the undergrowth. Red Flame moved off in the direction of the next sentry who was well hidden in a large thicket about a hundred yards away and it took him awhile to sneak around behind the sentry who was obviously nervous about being on duty on his own in the darkness, as he kept turning around, staring into the blackness and fidgeting with his rifle, then walking around the thicket again. Red Flame waited for the sentry to get back to his starting point and grabbed him. He didn't make a sound until he repeated his Owl hoot to let Little Bear know he was ready for sentry number two. Again, Little Bear appeared almost immediately, picked up the sentry and disappeared into the woods again. Red Flame moved on to find the third sentry who should also be about one hundred yards away, he hoped.

This fellow made life easier for him to find, he was smoking like the first sentry, a little red light was glowing in the darkness but it might as well have been a fire, it was so bright in the surrounding blackness. This guard also had a smoker's cough, he could be heard from about twenty-five feet away, surely these men shouldn't have been smoking while on duty, obviously not a very well-disciplined troop. Red Flame spared him from getting lung cancer.
He did his impression of an Owl again and Little Bear took away number three.

The sentries were so far all about fifty yards from the first of the small tents which were all neatly lined up in rows where all the lucky troops or as he thought unlucky troops, were sleeping. He estimated they would have positioned probably eight sentries, maybe nine. Now to find number four. It took him ten minutes to locate the next, he was smarter than the others, he had climbed about eight feet up a tall sycamore tree and was not moving a muscle, just scanning the surrounding ground area. Red Flame almost walked directly under him but then smelt him, a mixture of body odor and nervous perspiration. He looked up, the sentry was directly above him. He took his tomahawk from his belt, looked up again to see which way the sentry was looking and took two steps the opposite way and threw the weapon at the man's head, thud was the sound the impact made, the man dropped from the tree like a stone. He found his tomahawk and let out the Owl hoot for Little Bear again. Four more he thought to go, he just hoped that it wasn't the time for the changing of the guards.

It took them almost an hour and a half to find and kill the remaining four, but they did it.

Little Bear had returned from the nearby river where he had dumped the bodies of the eight sentries', hopefully they would be washed well downstream by the fast-moving current by first light. Little Bear looked exhausted with all the heavy lifting and carrying he had done.

Early the next morning, before the sun was fully up, the camp went into panic, all eight sentries had disappeared without trace, soldiers were running through the trees in all directions trying to make sense of it, but they couldn't. An hour later after an intensive search of the area, the remainder of the company mounted up and headed off towards their Fort, this was the first sight he'd had of Captain Hancock since last year, the man he really wanted to take revenge on. He was small and slightly built and not what Red Flame had remembered, but he still wanted to kill him painfully. He still had the vision in his mind of what these troops had done to his mother and family and it would just not leave him. He estimated he had maybe eight hours before the troop arrived at the Fort to complete his task. There were twenty-five troops still alive he estimated, he would have to kill twenty-four before he could get to Captain Hancock unless he ran out of time, in which case he would go directly after him.

As the troop moved away Red Flame and Little Bear immediately began to initiate their plan of crisscrossing behind the soldiers and taking out two at a time, he knew as long as his aim was true he would manage to get through the bulk of the remaining troops. He circled to the west side of the trail while Little Bear went to the east staying well hidden among the dense trees but close to the fast-moving troops.

Red Flame emerged from the trees about twenty feet behind the troops but by the time he had set his bow and arrow to fire they were

51

about thirty-five feet ahead, he stopped in the middle of the trail, aimed and fired. The arrow hit the trooper on his left who was riding slightly behind the one on the right, who slumped forward and dropped to the ground, the troop were making so much noise, the horses hooves pounding the ground, their spurs jangling, some talking to each other, and the wind howling through the trees it wasn't any wonder that not one noticed or heard anything. He positioned the next arrow on his bow, they were now forty-five feet ahead, and fired, center of the man's back again, the trooper to the right slumped forward and fell to the ground. He quickly rode on into the trees where Little Bear was waiting for him. They nodded to each other in a very self-satisfied way.

They rode together until they had caught up with the troops again, the mounts of the two dead soldiers were continuing to follow the rest of the group but gradually dropping back, he certainly did not want either horse to take off at a gallop past the troop. He rode back into the center of the track again about twenty feet behind what were now the last two troopers, loaded his bow and fired, exactly the same as he had minutes before with the same result, he reloaded his bow and fired again. Now there were four dead troopers. He continued into the trees and immediately began the chase to catch up with the rest of the troops again. Little Bear was watching his every move in case he had to cover him with rifle fire if something went wrong, it hadn't yet but there was still a lot more killing to be done.
After an hour using their crisscross tactics there were fourteen dead troopers but as Red Flame aimed at number fifteen the soldier turned slightly, probably just to check on those behind him and the arrow struck him in the shoulder, he screamed as he fell from his mount and panic broke out amongst the remaining soldiers, all moving in different directions, horses turning in circles, trying to regain their composure, expecting an all-out Indian attack. Red Flame rode on into the trees and out of sight as the troops waited, scanning the trees to see where the arrow had come from. It was only then that the remaining troops seemed to realize that half of their troop had disappeared. As one trooper rode back in Red Flame's direction a shot rang out and the trooper fell to the ground. Little Bear had done his job. Red Flame loaded another arrow and rode towards the troops

as they were still running around like headless chickens and with cover from the trees he fired, another soldier dropped to the ground. Another shot and one more Trooper fell to the ground, Little Bear was still covering him well.

After what seemed like several minutes the remainder of the troop moved off following their Captain who was frantically bellowing out orders. From what he could hear Red Flame expected them to be making a run for the Fort.

Both Red Flame and Little Bear followed and despite being on opposite sides of the track and unable to see each other maintained the same sort of distance behind the troopers, as he rode Red Flame made the decision to concentrate on getting the Captain as soon as possible as the track would eventually open up to the flat lands where he and Little Bear wouldn't have any cover, they would be completely exposed. He decided to take the risk and cross the track to tell Little Bear of his plan to take the Captain one on one and hoped that none of the soldiers would see him. He moved to the edge of the tree line and could see the troops were not even worried about what was happening behind them they just wanted to get to the safety of the Fort. He waited out of sight in the thick undergrowth and then guided Laggon to the right and onto the track and on into the trees on the opposite side, he could see Little bear about twenty feet ahead of him still making good speed despite having to dodge the trees and overhanging bowes. As soon as Little Bear realized Red Flame was behind him he pulled up so they could talk.

Red Flame quickly suggested his plan of him getting in front of the troop and where the trees ended but still offering him cover, he would shoot the Captain. Little Bear would give covering fire from the rear and then Red Flame would do the same from the front, getting the remaining troops in a crossfire. Little bear agreed with the plan and Red Flame took off at a gallop to pass the troopers and get in position at the end of the tree line which was looming quickly. He galloped for an hour and passed the soldiers even though he was in dense forest, the troops not hearing any more shots began to slow down, once he got to the last group of trees he stopped and dismounted, he took his rifle from its sheath and laid it on the ground next to where he planned to avenge the slaughter of his village and kill Captain Hancock. He looked back down the track to see how far away the troop was, only about two hundred yards he thought and that gave him less than thirty seconds to prepare himself.

He took one arrow from his quiver, checked it was straight and positioned it on the bow and waited, 10 seconds, 9..8..7..6..5..4..he stepped out from the trees onto the track, he was now in full view of the captain and the trooper beside him who was luckily the signaler and carrying only his bugle as they galloped directly towards him. The captain's eyes were wide open in disbelief that one Indian would stand alone in front of a Troop of cavalry charging towards him, little did he know that it was only about a third of the troop at this time. Red Flame took aim and fired, the arrow hit the Captain in the middle of the chest who fell backwards into the path of the following troopers who's only saw the captain when their mounts stamped on him. Red Flame threw himself onto the ground next to his rifle, cocked it and starting firing at the fast-approaching remaining troops. He shot the bugler. He could hear Little Bear had already started shooting at the rear of the troop, two more troops dropped to the ground as two managed to get past him going full speed towards the Fort which now was only about four miles away, he spun around and tried to pick them off but missed. He turned back and shot three more troopers, he stood up motionless and counted how many troops were injured or dead, he counted nine. It had been a good day, only two had got away from the original forty and they would be back from the fort with reinforcements soon, very soon.

Red Flame and Little Bear walked towards each other checking on the Bluecoats bodies, were they dead or alive? Suddenly Red Flame stopped in his tracks, did he feel right killing all these men? No, he didn't. But then he thought about his mother and nieces and friends and changed his mind. Someone had to make a stand and let people know what was actually happening to the native population. He would write to David and Anne and tell them the truth, they would listen.

He looked at Little Bear who was jubilant, running towards Red Flame, he stopped and hugged him.

"Thank you, Red Flame," tears running down his face, "thank you."

"This is just the beginning Little Bear, this will go on for probably our lifetimes. However long that is likely to be."

Little Bear stepped back and looked at him as though he had just realized what Red Flame was implying, the Bluecoats would not take this lightly, they would be back to hunt them down no matter how long it took. Days, weeks, months or maybe years it could continue.

"So be it," Little Bear smiled, "so be it. Today we became heroes to our people, I thank you for that Red Flame."

Red Flame said nothing. He wasn't interested in being a hero. He carried on collecting all the rifles and ammunition that was strewn across the grass.

CHAPTER 6

The next afternoon they rode back into their village, it had been cleaned up considerably, tepees had been repaired and all the dead had been buried. Some children were playing and even some of the dogs had returned. Several ponies had been rounded up and new pens had been erected to house them, if you had not seen this village before the massacre you would never have known such an atrocity had ever taken place, apart from the smaller number of tepees.

Several people cheered as they rode in, he stopped outside his mother's tepee, she must have heard the commotion and ran out to greet him.

"Red Flame, your safe?"

"Yes ma, I'm safe." He replied smiling at her as he dismounted.

She flung her arms around him and pulled him into her bosom kissing his face and rubbing his back.

"I thought I'd never see you again. Did you catch any of those evil men?"

"We did ma, all but two I think."

"All but two?" Her mouth was wide open in shock.

"Two got away," he reiterated, "I missed them both."

"Only two, what did you do to the others?"

"We killed them, including Hancock," he answered, "but only just before they got back to the fort."

She led him by the hand into her tepee, all the smells of his youth came flooding back helping him relax, it was good to be home for however a short time it would be. She poured him some water and cut off a piece of roasted venison that was hanging from the roof and handed it to him.

"Thanks ma, I really miss you, and your cooking." They both laughed.

"Thank you, son," she replied tearfully, "I miss you too."

Just then Chief Yellow Bird burst in, wrapped his big arms around Red Flame and hugged him.

"Thank you for bringing Little Bear back to me, he has told me what you did to those troopers, you are a great warrior Red Flame, you have brought great dignity back to the Apalachee tribe and I thank you for that too."

"We have to discuss the future though Chief, the future of our tribe, the Cavalry will come after me, not Little Bear because they will only find my arrows, Little Bear used a rifle but I wanted them to know it was me. I'm just worried that when they come back and don't find me they could take it out on the rest of the village." He said thoughtfully.

"We will move the village up country for a while and see what the Army does."

"I think that's a good idea, but I think that they will initially send troops from Fort Dade again, so I will ride to meet them and hopefully they will run back to the Fort giving us more time to move away."

"On your own? How do you think you can stop them? Asked the Chief pessimistically.

"On my own, yes. I think it best not to involve Little Bear or anyone else at this time. I do not know how many I will be able to stop, but I have to try."

"When will you leave?"

"Tomorrow, at sunrise." He replied.

"Alright, I will leave now so you can spend time with your mother," the Chief said and acknowledging ma with a polite nod he turned, "thank you again Red Flame". The Chief said as he left the tepee.

His mother moved towards him and stroking his face with her hand she looked into his eyes.

"You are truly your father's son, he would be so proud of you." She said quietly turning away with tears streaming down her face. He stood behind her placing his hands on her arms.

"He would be very proud of you too ma." She turned to face him again and they hugged.

"You are leaving again so soon?"

"Yes ma, I have to."

"May your God be with you Red Flame." She had never asked him or even hinted before if he had decided on following his father's

Christian faith or the Indian spiritual way. Now was not the time to answer. They sat and talked mainly about his father again and their past good times for hours until it was time for sleep.

It was a beautiful bright morning as he left the village and headed back towards Fort Dade, there was a crispness in the air and the visibility was good, the grass and trees were brilliant shades of greens again and he should be able to see any dust raised by horses a good mile away. He immediately headed for the higher ground so there were trees between himself and the main trail that the cavalry would have to follow because of their chuck wagon, which they always brought along for expected larger battles, but he had to remain vigilant as the Army had hired many local Indian scouts lately for the prime reason of travelling ahead of their patrols to warn of any Indian war parties that might be in wait to ambush them. Apart from stopping once so that he and Laggon could drink fresh water from a local stream, he rode for seven hours without seeing anything that moved, until he saw the sun reflecting off something that was moving towards him in the distance, he could not make out what it was but it was just the other side of the trees about five hundred yards in front and to his right. He pulled up and slowly moved through the trees, he watched as whatever it was got closer. It was primarily blue in color. As it got closer he realized it was a Pawnee scout wearing a blue cavalry tunic and it was a brass button that was reflecting the sun, not a good thing to wear he thought when you are trying to remain invisible, a real giveaway.

The scout was moving quite fast so he knew the troops could not be far behind. He moved slowly further into the trees and waited. Slowly taking his bow off his back and an arrow from his quiver he waited. He was now only six feet from the tree line that edged the main trail, the scout was only one hundred yards away, he waited, poised to shoot, and he waited, no scout came past. He edged closer to the trail so he could look back along the trail, he was now getting concerned. Nothing, the scout had disappeared.

Had he been spotted? He didn't think so. He could not hear anything over the southerly winds blowing noisily through the leaves. The scout must have decided to cut through the trees and get to the higher ground which is exactly what he would have done if he was scouting. He scoured the trees in case the man was using the trees for cover, in which case he would literally bump right into him any second, he waited without moving a muscle for about thirty seconds. Where had he gone?

He turned Laggon and moved back along the path he had just taken but in the opposite direction, he was now looking at the plush green grass with the sun on it and the hills behind.

He felt slightly anxious as he felt a bead of perspiration run down his back. Was the scout watching him he wondered?

Suddenly the scout rode passed him, literally ten feet away, it was astonishing to him that the Pawnee hadn't seen him, after all Laggon was pure white and although he was hidden behind trees he fully expected a good Indian scout to have spotted him. Luckily this scout was not very good. He moved out of the trees as the scout was quickly moving away from him, he let the arrow go and it hit the Scout in the middle of the back and he fell to the ground. Red Flame did not like the Indian scouts that were employed by the Army and had no compunction in shooting him, even in the back, as he felt they were helping to wipe out their own people for the almighty dollar or worse, a bottle of whisky.

He dismounted and bent down to see if the scout was dead. He wasn't, but it was only a matter of time, blood was gurgling in the man's throat.

Red Flame picked up the man's rifle, he also took two of the scout's arrows, these could come in handy sometime if he needed to kill anonymously. He tied the loose pony to a tree as he did not want it finding its way back to the approaching troopers as they would then know that their man had been ambushed and probably killed. The pony had lots of fresh grass and would eventually be found, probably by a passing Indian war party.

He turned Laggon and continued following the trail for two more hours on the high ground until he saw a huge red dust cloud approaching, it was the Cavalry troop travelling at speed and heading directly towards him. It was difficult to see just how many there were at this distance and he was surprised that they had not started bedding down for the night as the sun had begun to go down and he knew they liked to get settled before dark. He would wait and watch, his plan was to strike at night when the majority were in their tents sleeping with just a few sentries posted around the camp perimeter, so this concerned him slightly. Hit, run and hide is what Donald had told him. That was exactly what he was going to do. As they got closer, he could see that there were the regular forty men to a platoon with a chuck wagon, good, now all he needed was for them to settle for the night, if they were going to. It suddenly dawned on him that they wouldn't set camp on the trail with the trees on either side, it would be too dangerous for them, they would not be able to fight off an ambush so they would probably continue until the trail widened considerably or there was a break in the trees. That would take hours. They couldn't go to the higher ground because their campfires would be seen from miles around and certainly would attract the interest of any local war parties. He decided just to wait and watch.

Almost an hour later they slowly rode past him, about fifteen feet away, he sat on Laggon motionless, watching. The noise of the jangling spurs, the thumping of the horse's hooves on the grass and the constant chattering among the soldiers was almost deafening, he waited until they were just out of sight and then he moved off behind them but still hidden among the trees. They rode until it was almost impossible for him to see them ahead but luckily, he could still hear them, then, it went quiet, so he knew they had stopped and were beginning to set up their camp for the night. The Officer in charge was obviously inexperienced in this type of warfare, he had set the camp up on the trail itself which meant the tents were only six to eight feet from the trees that were on either side of the camp, little did the troops know that this would make his task much easier.

He pulled well into the trees, dismounted and squatted on the ground, opening his pouch he ate the piece of venison his mother had given him before he had left the village. He rested for two hours just lying on the ground, by now it was dark and he could plainly see two campfires burning, one at each end of the camp. The fires were illuminating the trees with an orange hue and he could smell the food that was being dished up to the troops, it smelt good. Really good.

His plan was to attack the front of the column hopefully driving them back in the direction they had come from and away from the village. He could still hear some laughter and chatter from the tents, he would wait until there was silence.

An hour later all was quiet, he placed his quiver on his back, he still had eighteen arrows left, picked up his bow and rifle and slowly walked through the trees towards the campfires. He scoured the trees as he got closer looking for any sentries that had been posted. He saw two immediately silhouetted against the first large campfire both deep in conversation, they were standing talking together in the middle of the trail about forty yards away from him. The trees were rustling in the warm breeze that had got up in the last couple of hours so he couldn't make out what they were saying. The troops had set their tents in the narrow trail, firstly a group of eight tents in two rows of four then a large camp fire with several men sitting on logs just smoking and chatting, then the chuckwagon where the cook kept all the rations for the trip and also stored all the extra ammunition, then ten more tents in two rows of five with about five feet between them, all the guide ropes on one side were pegged down amongst the trees. There was a smaller campfire burning at the far end with nobody sitting around it, it was probably to deter any animals from getting too close to the chuck wagon and the troops horses which were tied to lines attached to some of the trees. He couldn't see any sentries at the far end of the camp, that didn't mean there weren't any though. The moon was behind thick cloud and unless you were close to the fires it was pitch black, he took this as a sign that the spirits were watching over him.

Indians of all tribes had an aversion to fighting at night, they figured that if the spirits couldn't see them then how could they watch over them. Despite what his father had told him about Christianity, the good bits and the bad, he still believed to a degree in what his uncles had taught him in the tribal village about the various spirits and their meanings and until he could disbelieve either, he tended to go along with both as it suited him.

There was no sign of the cook. He was probably in his tent asleep as he would have an earlier start the next morning than the rest of the troops as he had their breakfast to prepare.

Red Flame felt as long as he stayed away from the fires he would not be seen.

He moved back into the trees and gingerly crept passed the two sentries who were too busy talking to notice much else, he stopped opposite the large campfire with three troops still sitting on logs, they were quietly talking about women and gambling and could not see him standing in the trees literally twelve feet away from them. He would wait until they made their way back to their tents before starting his attack.

He stood motionless for nearly one hour, just listening to them, until they eventually stood up and wandered back to their own quarters, he was just about to move when he heard something moving in the trees about five feet away from him to his right, he froze. Was it an animal attracted by the smell of the food he wondered? Now was not the time to get into a fight with a bear, he'd probably come off second best any way. Suddenly he was able to make out the silhouette of a man, a tall man, a tall thin man, it was a trooper just taking a piss before hitting the sack, how the man had not seen him was a miracle he thought. He waited again, the trooper finished, shook himself and strolled back to his tent. What had he been thinking about the spirits? Someone was definitely watching over him.

Red Flame looked at the fire, it was still burning well and there were some good sized sticks still very much alight, he placed his rifle and bow next to the tree he had been standing behind and crept to the fire keeping on the opposite side to the sentries so they would not see him, he selected three burning sticks, pulled them from the fire and moved around to the back of the chuck wagon where the ammo was stacked and threw one stick on to the top of the munitions boxes, he quickly turned and threw the second onto a tent and again with the third. The tents ignited immediately. As he moved back to where his rifle and bow where he had to pass the fire again and he noticed more good-sized burning sticks, he grabbed two more and threw them at tents in the direction of the sentries and ran back into the darkness of the forest.

He waited to get his breath back, bow in hand, an arrow in position ready to fire at the first sign of movement. Seconds later a trooper ran from his burning tent yelling 'Fire, Fire'. Red Flame let the arrow fly and the man went silent, he reloaded as another appeared yelling for help, he fired again, more silence.

The sentries by now had seen the flames and were now running to the tents closest to them, he fired another arrow, one sentry dropped silently, he reloaded and moments later fired again, the second sentry fell to the ground.

As no bullets had been fired the troops must have just thought it was a fire and so were not overly concerned, certainly an imminent Indian attack hadn't even crossed their minds, until one realized the wagon was ablaze and the ammunition would soon blow. One soldier bravely tried to climb up the side of the wagon to douse the flames. Red Flames arrow hit him in the side and he dropped to the ground.

Other troops began running around in a blind panic, some going to check their horses that were still tied to a line but as soon as the troops were away from the fires and the burning tents they were in darkness and couldn't see very much. As soldiers ran past his hiding place in a frenzy it was easy for him to shoot another three troopers before he had to run to the back of the trees as he knew the chuck wagon would blow up imminently, sending thousands of bullets in all directions. As he moved quickly away from the wagon and main campfire, he decided as the troops were so close but were still not aware of his presence, or even the arrows that were in the troops laying on the ground he should continue firing. He knelt down and reloaded his bow and fired, another soldier went down. He reloaded again, another fell and then another fell face down on to the trail. Suddenly the wagon blew, 'Kaboom' sending 1000's of bullets flying and cracking in all directions, zipping past him, hitting troops and trees around him. He now picked up his rifle and started shooting at troops that were still running around, the soldiers naturally thought the firing was coming from the burning wagon.

Some troops were still scurrying around with buckets of water dousing tents and the burnt-out wagon trying to get the flames under control, he managed to shoot three more while the pandemonium continued, that made a total of nine troopers killed by arrows, he didn't know how many he had shot by rifle or how many had been cut down by the exploding ammunition. He thought the cook must have gone up with the wagon. He wasn't sure.

Suddenly a figure appeared and was shouting commands, he was the Officer in charge, and Red Flames next target. As the man walked between the burnt-out tents he stumbled over a trooper's body, the officer bent down thinking to help the trooper up and pulled out the arrow from the body, Red Flames arrow. The Officer stood up and holding the arrow aloft.

"Indians. We are under attack." He shouted.

Red Flame shot him where he stood, the Officer slumped down to his knees and stayed in that position, it looked almost surreal but spiritual at the same time, as though he was praying. It caused him to loose concentration momentarily. Troops were now running to their horses, pushing and shoving each other in a bid to get to their mounts in an attempt to get away from the invisible 'Indian' enemy. Most didn't even bother to find their saddles or rifles, just mounting and galloping off towards the fort, some still only wearing their pants. Fear and confusion had grasped them all.

He managed to shoot three more as they tried to leave the camp. Within minutes there was silence, apart from the crackling of the fires and the burnt-out wagon. Silence, his favorite sound.

He stepped out from the protection of the trees and stood in the middle of the trail, he looked north, nothing except a few tents silently smoldering and several bodies on the ground, he turned and looked south, a few more tents and their contents smoking and more bodies lying on the ground and the wagon which was now burnt to a crisp, just a few glowing embers and the remains of the metal wheel rims left. Because of the darkness he could not count how many dead soldiers there were, that would have to wait until dawn.

He inched his way back into the trees and found Laggon, he lay down next to him on the ground and went to sleep, safe in the knowledge that if anyone got too close his trusted pony would soon let him know.

The next morning as the sun rose he walked slowly through what was left of the trooper's camp. There were twenty-nine dead or almost dead troopers including the Officer who was still kneeling in the same position, some were shot by him and others had multiple bullet wounds from the exploding wagon and others with arrows stuck in them. He immediately had a pang of conscience again and felt sick, but only until he thought again about how the same Cavalry had slaughtered nearly all his mother's tribe. There was too much to do than to worry about his conscience.

He foraged through the nearby trees and found two stout branches and constructed a travois, he placed all the troops rifles on it and secured them with twine. Then he rounded up all the horses that were still attached to the line tying one to the next. A string of twenty-two in two rows of eleven. As he was about to leave he saw the dead officer's tunic on the grass, he picked it up and threw it on to the travois.

He mounted Laggon and pulling the crudely constructed travois and twenty-two horses in a line behind him, he set off back towards the tribe's village, he stayed close to the trees on the higher ground. It was very slow going but he didn't see a soul for the full twelve hours duration of the journey which was just as well, it would have taken too much time to release the travois and the horses from Laggon, and so he was relieved to see the village in the distance.

As he entered the children ran towards him yelling and cheering and the dogs started to bark, the adults suddenly appeared outside their tepees as they always did when a warrior or stranger arrived at camp and congregated in a crowd around him and then his mother's tepee. He jumped down from Laggon and embraced his mother.

"You smell of firewood." She said smiling.

"I'm sure I do, it was a big fire."

They both laughed together.

"You can tell me all about it over supper."

"I promise I will." He said jokingly.

Just then the Chief appeared, pushing his way through the crowd.

"Welcome back Red Flame. How went it?" He quickly asked.

"Good. I managed to get some rifles and horses."

"Did you kill any soldiers?"

"Yes, I did."

"How many?"

"A few."

"How many?" The Chief persisted.

"About twenty-nine, but I am not sure."

"Twenty-nine," the Chiefs eyes almost popped out, "that's great Red Flame. Very well done." The Chief said with a big smile on his face.

Red Flame looked at his Mother, she wasn't sharing the Chiefs enthusiasm for death.

She knew her son did not like killing for the sake of killing but knew that what he did was out of necessity for the tribe's protection and their reputation. She smiled sympathetically at him. He returned the smile.

"When are you moving the village?" He asked the Chief curtly.

"Tomorrow we head west, across the Mississippi river to join our brothers the Choctaw. But tonight, we celebrate your victory." Everybody within ear shot cheered.

The next morning, he helped with the taking down of tepees and the loading of the travois', tying the tribe's ponies to them and generally making the tribe ready for the long march to the Choctaw lands. By late afternoon he was saying goodbye to his mother again, something they both had got used to, but both still found very hard to do. He watched as the tribe slowly melted from sight into the early sunset. They would travel for a few hours before setting up a temporary camp for the night before the long slog westwards. As soon as they disappeared he called Laggon to him and they set off in the opposite direction.

CHAPTER 7

He rode until after sunrise, he didn't see or hear anyone, it was so peaceful. He could see in the distance where the lush green flatlands ended and met with the grey rocky range hills, he rode on and scoured the rocks and ravines until he saw what he was looking for. A small opening with what looked like from this distance a small clearing of grass in front, insignificant to most but he had stayed here several times before when he needed to think and get away from the world, or whoever was after him. He took Laggon as far as he could ride him and then dismounted, he didn't want to risk injury to his best friend. They scaled the rocks together for a while until they got to the opening, Laggon immediately started eating the fresh grass in front of the small opening, it was a cave which was about eight feet in diameter, he needed to check that it wasn't already a residence for a bear or a cougar, he took off his bow and pulled an arrow from his quiver, he moved away from the entrance and circled back to the side, he looked in and then ducked back, he couldn't see in properly, it was too dark, he looked in again half expecting a bear to come charging out at him, nothing happened. He entered throwing small rocks inside and shouting war cries, making as much noise as he could hoping if there was an animal sleeping inside they would show themselves. The cave was empty. He felt safe here.

Laggon was busy feeding on the small grassed area in front about fifteen feet below the cave entrance but quite hidden by large rocks from the trail.
He made up a fire for the night and to warm up the pieces of venison that his mother had given him when he left the village, she always gave him venison, rain or shine she always had venison for him. He smiled to himself at the thought of her cutting it up into manageable pieces for him, he hoped she was safe on the tribe's long journey west into Choctaw country. He just hoped that the troop that would be heading towards his village now because of his actions, would be slowed up enough for the tribe to reach their friends.

He grabbed his two almost empty water bags and climbed higher up into the rocks looking for small pools of water, he needed enough for Laggon and himself, he soon found enough in a natural pool and headed back to the cave, before entering he placed one bag in front of his friend and the other he took up to the cave to keep it cooler. He feasted on hot venison and cold water, sitting with his back against the cave wall and looking out over the wonderful vista and the sunsetting in the west, he could see for miles, he would have plenty of time to ready himself if anybody should be travelling the same trail or Bounty Hunters specifically looking for any Indians so they could claim their $20 reward. As darkness engulfed the area he slowly dozed off.

He was awakened early the next morning by Laggon sounding distressed, he grabbed his bow and quiver and stood so he could see his pony below him, it was a cougar that was lurking around near to the cave entrance, only yards away, the cougar was pacing back and forth more interested in the pony as an unexpected meal, he armed his bow and fired, the cougar dropped to the ground, now he had a choice of menu, Venison or Cougar. A good start to the day he thought. He climbed down to where Laggon stood just to reassure him that all was well and to thank him because it now appeared as though the cave was probably the Cougars, and with him being asleep he would have been easy prey for the adult male cat. Red Flame dragged the big cat into the cave to keep it cool and away from insects and other predators. He would cut it into smaller pieces later. He lay down on the grass in the sun next to where Laggon stood and spoke to him of his worries, how could his tribe survive, would the tribe's way of life survive, would the Buffalo survive, then he dozed off again.

He awoke a couple of hours later, Laggon was still looking at him closely, almost nose to nose as though expecting the conversation to continue, he picked up the water bag that was lying on the grass and climbed back above the cave entrance to find another larger water pool, he sat in it, splashed water over his face, filled the water bag and made his way back down to where Laggon stood, placing the full water bag in front of him again.

He went back into the cave placing more sticks on the fire, he sat again against the cave wall and checked his rifle was clean and none of his arrows were damaged. It was now midday and the sun was at its hottest. He took one quick look out of the cave, nothing was moving for miles around so he started skinning the cougar and cutting small pieces off so they would cook quicker and then placed them on sticks ready to place on the fire later when it was darker.
He had not relaxed like this for weeks and he was enjoying every minute. Just doing nothing.

By the time he decided to move on he had spent six nights in the cave, the rest had done the two of them good, he felt stronger and more alert, he had cleared his head, he felt he could take on the world, today he thought was a good day to leave the safety of the cave.

After some berries and cougar meat he set off with the sun on his back, following but not on the trail. The barren gray rocks soon disappeared and the lush green forests again filled the landscape. He rode for over four hours until the sun was directly overhead. He could see the trail suddenly veered to the left over a small rushing river with trees on three sides, this would be an ideal place for an ambush, he laughed to himself as he thought he would have to remember this spot for future reference.

Suddenly a loud 'Crack,' something hit him on the forehead and then he hit the ground hard. Then nothing.

It was dark when he eventually regained consciousness, his head was pounding, his vision blurred, but at the moment he opened his eyes he immediately closed them again, something didn't sound or feel right. His hands were tied behind him around a tree. He could hear voices, speaking English, men's and ladies. He could smell food and smoke and hear the sound of a campfire crackling away.
He listened, one man was asking for money, who was he asking? A lady responded saying they had not got any more. He slowly opened his eyes slightly again. There were two men sitting on a log

with their backs to him, there was a dark-haired lady sitting on the other side of the fire and a blond lady standing behind her looking directly at him.

"He's alive, look, he opened his eyes," she yelled pointing at him excitedly, "he just opened his eyes." The ladies both sounded English.

The men jumped up, turned and walked over to him and were looking directly at his face.

"Are you ok?" Asked the blonde.

"Yes, I'm fine." He replied.

"Are you English?"

"Not really."

"You sound it."

"Did you say he was English?" One of the men asked. He was a scary looking man with just one black front tooth and his face was badly scarred.

"Yes, he sounds it." The lady answered.

The two men looked at each other in excitement.

"It's him, it has to be." Said the other man who looked more normal.

"What's your name?" One of the ladies asked.

"Red Flame."

"Yippee, it is him. We're rich, were rich," the two men grabbed each other and started dancing around the fire as though they were mad, "it's him, we found him."

The two ladies stared at each other in amazement not knowing what all this meant.

"We don't need your money anymore, we are rich," one of the men said, "we're rich."

"How. Why?" The blonde lady asked.

"That's Red Flame. He's got a $500 reward on him if he's caught alive, and we just caught him".

"Why didn't you tell us that when we paid you to help us find him," the blonde asked, "what did he do, kill someone?"

"Yes, he's killed hundreds of Cavalrymen."

"Have you?" She asked sounding shocked and looking straight at him.

"No, not hundreds. That's a lie."

"Are you calling me a liar Redskin?" Asked the larger one toothed man.

"Yes. I am."

The man lunged forward and kicked him in the ribs. Red Flame grimaced but did not utter a sound.

"Not so big now are you, eh?" Said the smaller man sneering.

"Leave him alone, that's not fair." The darker haired lady said.

"Don't tell me what to do Lady." He moved over to her and squeezed her cheeks together between his thumb and forefinger.

"Ouch," she said as she turned her head away, "that hurt." The two men laughed.

"Now get the grub," the man yelled, "now."

The girls looked at each other nervously. They both immediately started gathering plates and cutlery and spooning what looked like beef stew on to each plate and handing one to each of the men, which they snatched without any acknowledgment. The men ate feverishly demanding second helpings before the ladies had even sat down to start theirs. How had these ladies got tied up with these two who looked like fur hunters he wondered, they certainly were not compatible but they weren't their prisoners either.

After an hour the men went and laid on their sleeping bags a few feet from the blazing fire while the ladies cleaned up the pot and plates. Suddenly the blond knelt down next to him with a plate of beef stew and offered him a spoonful, and then another.

"You must be hungry," she asked, "here, take some of this," as she continued to offer him spoonsful of the stew, she asked, "how's your head? You are very lucky that Jim is a lousy shot, otherwise......," she shook her head, "I shudder to think."

"I'm fine thanks but I appreciate the stew, it's very tasty. Was he just after my scalp? Which one of them is Jim?" He asked.

"I think so. He's the big one. I'll get you some water." She stood and walked over to a large pot and scooped out some water with a wooden ladle into an old tin mug and kneeling back down again offered it to his mouth, he swallowed several times, he was thirsty.

"What are you doing with these men?" He asked.

"We hired them to find you."

"Me. Why?"

71

"So, you could help us find our sister, she's been missing for over two months. We read about you in the paper and Sheriff Davidson said you were the man to help us."

"How is the Sheriff?"

"He is well and said if we did catch up with you to send you their regards."

"They are nice people." He replied thoughtfully.

"Yes, they are," she paused, but it was clear she had a question she was desperate to ask, "is it true what Ed said, have you killed hundreds of Cavalrymen?" She asked quietly.

"No, not hundreds," he paused momentarily, he could see she was concerned, "but a lot."

"How many?"

"I don't know. But a lot."

She stood up and stared at him with a look of disgust, almost a snarl, and walked back to the fire and sat back down on the log next to her sister. A minute later she turned and stared at him again, almost in disbelief, still with that look of disgust on her face.

He tried to smile but couldn't, her look said everything that needed to be said.

The two Ladies sat and chatted whilst drinking coffee for about an hour, he couldn't hear what was being said but neither looked back at him.

The two men were asleep on their bedding rolls and snoring away in harmony.

He took a deep breath and rested his head back on the tree trunk. Firstly, he thought to himself, could he untie the rope securing him to the tree, yes, no problem. Secondly, was Laggon close by, he scoured the surrounding area, first left and then right, yes, he was standing way back in the trees as he always did, never more than fifty feet away. Thirdly, was he going to help the Ladies or should he just carry on with his journey, he would certainly stand out riding with two attractive white ladies and would they want his help after their last conversation? He decided to sleep for a few hours, hopefully his headache would ease, get free, and then just follow the four and see what happened, at least for a couple of days as these two men are going to be very upset when they realize in a few hours' time that he had gone. Their financial status had just changed dramatically, $500 was a fortune to lose, especially overnight. He was concerned about how the men would react and consequently the welfare of the Ladies.

At about four in the morning he slipped the ropes that had held him to the tree for many hours off his wrists, he had been working on them for over an hour, it felt good to feel his blood circulating back to his fingers again.

He slowly and silently raised himself to a standing position, he needed to get his legs moving as they had become numb and if required to make any sudden movements he would be in trouble.

Slowly the feeling returned. He stood absolutely still, he could now make out the two men still snoring away on their bed rolls, the Ladies were inside their bed rolls fast asleep, he could just make out the colors of their hair. The campfire was almost out but still giving enough light for him to move around the small camp without tripping over anything or anybody. He moved towards the men, they had their rifles and boots next to them, one had a huge hunting knife in its sheath next to his head, a sensible move he thought to himself.

He carefully picked up the two rifles and gun belts and went to walk towards where he had last seen Laggon when he glanced back at the hunting knife, he could not resist, also it would show the blond that he did not kill everybody he met. He smiled, he liked her. He withdrew the knife from the sheath and placed it upright in the ground less than an inch from Ed's head. Ed should get a shock in the morning when he woke. Red Flame stealthily moved over to where he knew Laggon would be waiting, being careful not to step on any twigs or branches as in the quietness of these trees they would certainly wake everyone within a twenty feet diameter, every little sound was amplified in the woods. Once he had greeted and petted his friend he led him away from the camp. They walked for maybe half a mile, it felt good to get his blood circulating again properly.

Two hours later he returned to the campsite area and was sitting about twenty-five feet high in a huge oak tree with its limbs covered in Spanish moss overlooking the camp he'd been a prisoner in for what had felt like many hours, he watched as firstly the ladies moved, yawning and stretching. Then the men, Ed opened his eyes,

73

and screamed. All four of them jumped up, Ed's eyes were fixed on his own Hunting knife sticking out of the ground. Then they all turned and stared at the bare tree trunk Red Flame had been tied to.

"No, no. He's gone," Ed yelled looking everywhere expecting Red Flame to suddenly appear, "our rifles, he's taken our rifles. Oh shit, oh shit. And our revolver's, they are all gone. They are all gone. Shit," he yelled again, "you didn't tie him up properly, you hopeless Bastard." He yelled at Jim.

"But you tied him up Ed." Said the dark-haired sister.

"Shut up," he shouted back, "who asked you?" She looked away terrified.

"Hang on Ed, it's nobody's fault." Said Jim, trying to re-establish some normality.

"We lost 500 dollars and its nobody's fault, you're kidding me. You useless piece of shit."

"Wait a minute Ed...."

"Shut up, just shut up you," he pointed at Jim, "don't say another word you, or else."

Jim now looked scared. Obviously, Ed had a temper. Everything went quiet. Nobody said a word for a few minutes, there was an uneasy silence while nobody made eye contact with anybody else, the tension was mounting. Ed just walked around in circles looking down at the ground.

"So, are you still working for us to help find our sister or not?" Asked the blond.

Ed looked at her, a filthy look, he turned away saying nothing.

"Well? Are you or not?" Asked the darker one.

"Don't you speak to me like that you hore."

"How dare you speak to me like that you, you......."

"Oh, shut up." He kicked the water pot that was lying on the ground. It flew towards her, but missed.

"Ok, that's it," the blonde turned and walked towards the dark-haired lady, "we're leaving Ella, let's get our things together."

"That's what you think Lady," Ed snarled as he strode towards her, "you let that Redskin get away, did you cut him loose so he would help you look for your sister?"

"Don't be ridiculous." The blonde replied packing her bed roll.

"Don't be stupid. As if she'd do that." The other lady said.

"Did you call me stupid?" Ed asked.

"Yes." She replied without thinking, kneeling on the ground concentrating on packing her own things away.

Ed strode over to her and as she looked up he slapped her hard across the face, so hard that it sent her sprawling on to her back. She raised herself up onto her elbows and stared at him with a look of disbelief across her face.

"You have been asking for this since we met and now you're gonna get it." He tore at her blouse exposing her breasts and then threw it into the nearby bushes. She screamed. Her eyes wide open looking towards the blonde for help. The blonde leapt forward and tried to grab Ed but he just shrugged her off and she went flying into the bushes.

"Jim, keep her off me. Why don't you have a little fun as well?" He said with a smirk.

"Why not indeed? Replied Jim returning the grin, eager to get back into Eds good books.

Ed was now standing over the dark one undoing his pants and pushing them to the ground. He stood towering over her, showing himself to her, obviously proud of his manhood.

Jim was slower to react, he seemed pensive, maybe embarrassed, or just maybe not so proud of his manhood.

"For Christ's sake get on with it," Ed yelled, "don't you want to fuck her?"

This galvanized Jim into action, he then grabbed the blond and threw her to the ground and like Ed he tore her blouse off her back. She screamed trying to cover herself.

"No, no." She yelled. Not believing this was actually happening to her.

Ed had already got the dark ladies skirt up around her navel and was ripping her panties off. She didn't say a word but was noticeably shaking, it was as though she was absolutely petrified.

Jim followed suit and already had the blonde's panties in his hand, swinging them around above his head as though they were a lasso laughing and yelling with excitement, the two men didn't even notice Red Flame until he was just six feet away from them, he coughed, one of those I want to be noticed coughs.

Both men scrambled to their knees and tried to stand, Jim fell sideways back to the ground but Ed was up staring at him. Red flame motioned with his rifle to Jim to stand. He laughed at them both, standing with their dicks hanging out.

"Well Ladies, what do you think of your brave men now?"
Both ladies were still lying on the ground, completely exposed to the elements, sucking in air trying he guessed to make sense of the last few minutes.
Suddenly Ed yelled loudly.

"Rush him Jim." Ed took a couple of steps forwards. 'Crack" Red Flame's bullet hit him in the middle of the chest. Ed dropped to the ground.
Jim was not so quick, he only managed one step before the second of Red Flames bullets hit him squarely in the chest. Jim dropped like a bag of rocks.
Red Flame walked over to each man and kicked them in turn in the ribs, they were both dead.
He turned and faced the ladies, they still looked terrified, he walked over to where some of their clothing lay and threw them to who he thought they belonged.
He waited, looking at the blonde, almost inviting her to say something, she stared back as she redressed herself.

"I suppose your waiting for me to thank you?" She wasn't smiling.

"No, that's up to you. But, once what happened here this morning gets out the bounty for me will go up another hundred dollars, more bounty hunters will try to track me until they find me. Do you think that is fair? Do you think I was wrong in what I did?"

"Well yes. Yes. No," she paused seemingly confused, "no you weren't wrong."

"Yes, you said, you thought I was wrong? You would have preferred that I rode away last night, not knowing what was likely to happen this morning. Well now I almost wish I had. There is nothing I can do to make you understand is there?" He turned and walked away towards Laggon.

"Red Flame," the dark-haired sister called out, "I want to thank you for saving us today and I am sorry that this will cause you extra problems." She turned and glared at the blonde.

76

"Thank you for that." He smiled at her and nodded, then he turned and continued walking away. He could hear the two ladies talking in raised voices. He continued into the trees.

"Red Flame, Red Flame wait," it was the blonde shouting, "wait. Can we talk?"

He was furious with her attitude but also concerned about leaving two ladies out here on their own. He stopped and turned around to face her.

"I'm sorry," she said matter of factly, "I am sorry, I really am. I didn't mean…., I was just so……., so annoyed when Ed said you had killed a thousand soldiers, I couldn't believe it." He stared at her expecting more, it didn't come.

"So, what do you expect me to say?"

"That your sorry maybe? I don't know. Oh……., I don't know." He was about to say but I'm not, but didn't. 'When in doubt say nothing' is what his father had told him and it had always worked in the past.

"So, what do you want to do know? Are you continuing your search for your sister? Do you want my help? You need to tell me because if not I have things to do."

"Like killing more soldiers?" She replied sarcastically.

"Martha!" Ella said in shock.

"Actually, yes." He replied.

"I knew it."

"You know nothing about me or what I have done," he paused, stern faced he asked, "I will ask just once more before I leave. Do you want my help?"

"Yes. A thousand times yes," shouted Ella, again she glared at Martha, "what's the matter with you? Tell him yes." There was a silence. Ella tutted at her sister and raised her eyes to the sky.

"Yes, I want you to help us." Martha answered eventually. Again, there was another uneasy pause.

"On one condition." He said quietly.

"Oh, here we go again, how much do you want to be paid?" Martha said sanctimoniously. Ella glared at her again.

"I don't want any of your money, why would I? I have nothing to spend it on. I would ask just one thing, if we pass near my village, I would like you to come and meet my mother and the few remaining members of my tribe. You can then ask them any questions about why I have a bounty on my head and if you still do not understand why I have done what I have, then you are free to just leave. That is all I ask, and also for your anger and sniping to stop until then. Are we agreed?"

"Yes. Agreed." Said Ella.

They both looked at Martha.

"Yes, I apologize for my manners Red Flame." She said and nodded, still sounding as though she begrudged having to say it.

"One other thing. What I say goes. Ok?" He added.

The sisters looked at each other, and nodded.

"Agreed." They both said together.

"Right, let's get going. Gather your things, load your horses, tell me all the information you have about your sister as we ride. Ok?"

"OK." Came the collective answer.

"What about them?" Ella pointed to the two bodies on the ground.

"I will move them into the ditch."

"We are not burying them?" Asked Martha sounding shocked.

"No."

"Why not?"

"They do not deserve to meet their God, that's why."

"Why not, doesn't everybody?"

"They were going to scalp me. They were going to rape and then maybe kill you both, and you are questioning whether they deserve to meet their God?" He raised his hands in disbelief, "you can't waste your sympathy on people like that, you will meet many more like them here, you really shouldn't trust anyone until you know them. Hopefully time will change that."

"Ok." She agreed, unwillingly.

He watched as the two ladies gathered their belongings together and secured them to their horses. He headed over to the two bodies and dragged each one in turn over to the nearby ditch. Only their bones would be there by sunrise once the animals got their smell.

The ladies watched, but didn't say a word. That's the way he hoped it would remain.

Within an hour they were heading north west again, they were still on the main trail which he didn't like, this is the route most people used and where it was easy to run into trouble, any bounty hunters, Indians or bandits could be waiting in ambush. Once he had got all the information about the sister they had he would separate from the ladies until it was time to make camp for the night, it would be safer for them all. An hour later he explained that he was moving to higher ground so that he could see any would be ambushers and other travelers heading their way, at first, they weren't happy about parting but soon accepted it.

"Remember one thing," he said trying to reassure them, "I will be watching you at all times, if you need me to come to you look towards the sun, I will be there, just wave. If I see something to worry about I will let you know. Ok?"

"That sounds good." Martha said."

He turned Laggon from the track and rode off through the woods until he was in a good position to watch the ladies and the road ahead, for almost five hours they rode until it was time to change direction, so he dropped back down through the trees until he was riding alongside them again.

"Do you want to stop for a while, are you thirsty or anything?"

"Yes please. Can we stop soon please?" Asked Ella.

"Of course, about an hour ahead when we turn south slightly there's a nice small lake, it's very quiet and out of the way where we can water the horses and rest awhile. I need to bathe myself." The sisters both laughed. They continued riding together, the three of them all chatting about their sister's disappearance and how this was not like her to go off somewhere without letting either of them know. How the sisters had spoken to David and Anne at the Madison paper and how they thought Red Flame was the best, a real hero and how he would help them find their sister. Between laughing and details about their past, time passed quickly, suddenly Red Flame raised his hand.

"Stop." He said. They all stopped dead.

"There are white men ahead," he looked down studying the tracks, "two white men ahead."

"How do you know that?" Asked Martha.

He raised his fore finger to his lips, listening.

"You go ahead," he whispered, "two white men, maybe soldiers about forty yards ahead, they have stopped so probably sitting down resting. Act surprised when you see them. I will be there too, but out of sight, only tell them about your sister and how you are looking for her, have they seen her? Do not mention me, you understand?"

"Of course." Said Martha off handedly.

He peeled off to his right into the trees taking time to watch them move slowly along the trail and then themselves into the trees, he dismounted and followed behind on foot but twenty feet to their right, slowly he thought and then there they were. Two soldiers sitting with their backs against tree stumps just idly chatting and smoking. The cavalry always shoed their horses the same, that was the giveaway. As they heard the horses approaching they went to jump up but sat back down again when they saw the two attractive ladies coming through the trees slowly towards them. The Soldiers rifles were still in their sheaths on their horses that were a few yards away drinking at the water's edge.

"Well, "said the older looking one, drawing on his cigarette, "what have we got here?"

"Hi," said the girls, "what are you doing out here?"

"Never mind that, what are you two ladies doing out here?" Said the other soldier.

"We are looking for my sister, she went missing some weeks ago," said Martha, "and you, why are you here?"

"We are looking for Indians. We get a bounty for every scalp. $20, not bad eh?"

"Indian scalps?" Ella paused, "any one in particular?"

"Yes. Red Flame is his name. You don't want to meet him out here on your travels, he'd kill you without thinking about it. There is a $500 bounty for him dead or alive. But never mind him, come and sit down here with us." He patted the ground next to him.

"I'm ok thanks." Said Ella.

"No, I insist. Sit." His expression and tone changed. He patted the ground again.

"We are ok. We are only stopping for some water for us and the horses. But thanks." She smiled, albeit a nervous smile.

"Why don't you want to sit with us?" The other soldier asked.

"Because we can't stop. As I said we are looking for my sister, she's been missing for over a month."

80

"Well if you're nice to us we might help you look for her." Said the first soldier smirking at his friend.

"And if we don't?" Asked Ella.

"You will be nice to us."

"I don't think so. We just want to get on our way." Ella said.

The soldiers started to get up.

"As we said, you will be nice to us."

"No, we just want water, then we will leave," there was a note of desperation in her voice, "we just want to go."

"Well that's a shame. Get off your horses and come over here. Now."

Martha looked petrified again. She was glancing at the bushes surrounding them looking for Red Flame. He didn't appear.

"Get off your horses," the trooper yelled, "get down now."

The ladies immediately obeyed, fear written across their faces.

"Don't hurt us, please," said Martha, "anything, we will do anything, but don't hurt us."

Red Flame realized that she could only take so much of this aggression, she had reached her limit, surprisingly Ella seemed more relaxed.

The two soldiers looked at each other and laughed raucously.

"Well, we didn't expect to have such a good day, did we?" The older soldier said. Again, they laughed to each other.

Martha was falling apart, she burst into tears.

"No, no not again. I can't do this." She turned to Ella despairingly.

Ella just stared in disbelief.

"Please don't hurt her, she's been through enough." She pleaded.

The soldiers laughed.

"We can help her relax. No one can hear you out here Lady."

Both ladies were sobbing uncontrollably by now.

"Shut up crying," the first soldier shouted, "now....... "

"Now...or what?" Red Flame asked, standing six feet behind the soldiers.

They spun around, startled, staring at him.

The ladies breathed a sigh of relief when they saw him and smiled through their tears.

"We were just having some fun with these Ladies."

"I thought you were," he replied. He laid his rifle on the ground in front of the two men and turned to the Ladies, "they were just having some fun. They mean you no harm."

The lady's facial expressions changed to horror, they thought for a split second that he was serious.

He heard his rifle being cocked behind him. He turned quickly towards the soldiers.

"How stupid are you Redskin, now we can earn another $20 bounty as well as having a fuck."

Red Flame drew his knife. The soldier pulled the trigger. Click. Nothing. He pulled the trigger again. Click. Nothing. Red Flame threw his knife under armed. It stuck in the first soldier's belly. The soldier slumped to his knees dropping the rifle. Red Flame immediately stepped forward and withdrew his knife from the soldier's stomach.

The other soldier took several seconds while he took in what had just happened, he then jumped up and ran at him screaming abuse but Red Flame had ample time to reposition himself and thrust the knife into the oncoming soldier's midriff. The soldier stopped and fell onto his back, groaning and holding his stomach which was bleeding profusely. Red Flame yanked his knife from the second soldiers' stomach, wiped the blade on the grass then picked up his rifle and proceeded to refill the chamber with the bullets he had removed discretely while out of sight a few minutes earlier.

Both ladies were now sitting silently on the grass not knowing whether to cry or laugh.

Ella looked at him and mouthed 'Thank you.' He nodded to her and smiled back.

Martha, with no sign of emotion on her face looked blank, totally drained, she just sat looking at the trees swaying back and forth without saying a word. He was getting worried about her mental state.

Red Flame called Laggon to him and then walked him into the lake until the water was up to his chest, splashing the pony all the time as they walked along the beach away from the two bodies that lay motionless. He beckoned to Ella to follow him, she

82

acknowledged him with a wave. He continued walking and splashing Laggon as the pony kept playfully nudging him along.

After a few minutes he looked back to see the ladies walking with their own horses in the water a few feet from the beach, they were both laughing as they splashed each other. They walked in the lake for over a mile and then he stopped and waited for them to catch up. They were all soaked. The girls sat down on the beach while he gathered some branches and kindling and lit a fire to dry off some of their clothes. He pulled over part of a downed tree trunk and the three sat around feeling the warmth of the fire and talking about their pasts and the girls told stories about how their older sister had always looked after them. Nothing was said about soldiers and killing and because Martha now seemed a lot brighter Red Flame suggested they camped there overnight and get an early start in the morning, he would catch something for supper and Martha offered to get some coffee going. He felt it would be safe for the ladies after all they were well hidden from the trail which was about two hundred yards away hidden by thick foliage and forty to fifty foot-high trees.

That evening they enjoyed a good supper of fresh fish from the lake, and again they sat around the camp fire enjoying the balmy night and each other's company chatting about anything and everything. He had really enjoyed their companionship and hoped the feeling was reciprocated.

The next morning, they set off west towards the Mississippi river as that was the last known direction their sister was seen heading for accompanied by an unknown man, he was said to be smartly dressed, but that didn't mean a lot but better that way than a fur hunter.

The ladies were following the trail while he had headed to the higher ground as per the day before, this enabled him to see the ladies and if anybody was approaching them from the west. They rode for nearly five hours until he saw a dust cloud on the horizon moving quickly their way, he turned Laggon and moved through the trees until he was within ear shot of the ladies.

"Ella, Martha come over here quickly," he beckoned them into the trees until all three of them were out of sight of the trail," there are many horses approaching us from the west so best to dismount and stay still. I am not sure who they are but there are quite a few of them, maybe a troop of cavalry. They only had to wait several minutes for a troop of about twenty Mexican soldiers sped past their position, more Mexicans he thought to himself, why were they so far north again? The noise of spurs jangling, horse's hooves and the soldiers yelling to each other was deafening for a minute or so, then silence again. Just as he liked it. He walked to the edge of the tree line and looked east, the Mexicans were making good time. What were they here for he wondered again, a long way from the border, must be a raiding party, they liked to rob and kill white settlers as there was still a dispute going on between governments about who owned what territories and it was said that they got a bounty for scalps, any scalps, and the Indians would always be blamed for it. Or.....maybe they were just looking for supplies?

A few minutes later there was gun fire, a lot of it, from the east, the Mexicans must have been ambushed or they had ambushed somebody themselves.
"Wait here, I'll be back," he said to the girls, "I won't be long." He looked at Martha's face, she looked terrified again, he glanced at Ella who was looking directly at him, she shook her head.
He decided immediately he couldn't leave them, not even for a short time, Martha was just too fragile.
"Ok, let's go together." They mounted up and took off along the trail for a few minutes and then he led them back into the trees until they could plainly see the Mexicans had circled eight wagons of white settlers, Indian style, and were attacking them. At least the settlers had managed to form some sort of circle, albeit quite small, only about one hundred feet diameter, but it had improved whatever chances of defense they had. The Mexicans wanted primarily the settler's horses, their rifles, any supplies and of course the women.

Red Flame watched for a second, the Mexican in charge, a Captain in all his finery was on his horse stationary about thirty yards from where the three had hidden themselves among the trees, watching his troops surrounding and firing at the wagons. Settlers had positioned themselves in and under the wagons including the wives and older children but would be no match for the Mexicans

84

who were seasoned soldiers and quite professional in their ways of warfare. He had never seen or heard of them attacking a wagon train using Indian tactics before, this might work against them as they all needed to be circling at the same speed, and they weren't.

"Do you want to just wait here, have your rifles ready though, just in case." He whispered.

"Yes, ok we will." Said Ella.

He dismounted, took off his bow, quiver and rifle and ran closer to the Mexican officer. He stopped. Carefully loaded his first arrow and fired. The Captain disappeared over the side of his horse. Dead. The Mexicans were not used to fighting this way, they were really strung out and seemed unable to shoot straight whilst riding. Not one settler appeared to be injured. He loaded another arrow and fired at the closest trooper as he passed by. He too died instantly. Then another. Because the soldiers were concentrating on the settler's gunfire they did not seem to notice their fallen comrades lying face down in the grass with arrows sticking in their backs.

He reloaded. Fired again. Another trooper dropped to the ground. Then another. Then one of the Mexicans did notice a fallen comrade and realized they were being attacked from the rear and their commanding officer was already dead.

"Indio's, Indio's." He started yelling at the others and pointing to their fallen comrades that lay on the ground. While the confusion continued he was able to bring down two more soldiers with his bow and arrows and then he started using his rifle which was much faster. He suddenly heard rifle fire from where the girls were, they had joined in the fight. He smiled to himself, the ladies were actually firing at the Mexicans. He wondered if the girls were actually aiming for the soldiers or were they just making the right noises. The remaining soldiers fled, there were only five left that were still able to ride. They wouldn't be back. It was a long way to Mexico.

A cheer went up from the settlers, patting each other's backs, kissing their loved ones, and small children hugging their parent's legs.

Red Flame waved the girls forward towards the circled wagons, the settlers cheered them both when they emerged from the trees, he remained in the trees out of sight, it might not be a good idea to show himself just yet, one of the settlers might shoot first before knowing he was with the two ladies.

The girls got to the wagons and were immediately mobbed, people shaking their hands and patting their backs. Then it went quiet, they were being asked about the arrows he guessed, then they both waved and beckoned him to the wagons. Hopefully Ella and Martha had explained what had happened and it was just him that had used his bow and arrow to bring down the first of the Mexicans. He cautiously and slowly emerged from the trees, he had his bow and quiver on his back again and his rifle in its sheath so as not to look as though he was ready to fight again. The people all started to clap and cheer as Laggon walked into the wagon circle. He dismounted, all the men shook his hand, some of the ladies threw their arms around him and most of the children just stared at him. So, this was a red Indian?

There were two of the settlers that needed medical attention and so the wives started sorting through their medical supplies and bathing any wounds, the man in charge of the settlers came to Red Flame in tears. He was a tall man in his forties, his face, clothes and boots were caked in dust. The tears running down his cheeks carved tracks on his face. It had been a long tough journey for them all.

"I can't thank you enough, we owe you everything," the man put out his hand to him and said," I'm Jim, Jim Callahan." They shook hands.

"Here, here," several people said still standing around them. Intrigued to be this close to a real live Indian, who was friendly too.

"Hi Jim, my name is Red Flame."

"How can we ever thank you?" Asked Jim.

"A cup of coffee would be great."

Jim and the others nearby laughed, more with relief than how funny it was. The leader called two other men to him and suggested that now they were in their overnight circle they may just as well set up camp for the night and get an early start in the morning. This was met with a chorus of more cheers.

"Ok everyone, get the fires lit." Yelled Jim to all in the surrounding area.

Everyone seemed to run in all directions, even the children. Two men ran into the trees and emerged pulling dead branches and smaller tree trunks for the fires and then proceeded to cut them up.

The women folk disappeared into the backs of the wagons and reappeared carrying pots of all sizes and metal tripods that the pots would hang from when cooking or boiling water and a clattering of utensils.

Other men were tending the horses, removing their bridles and tying them up to the rear wheels of their wagons. Children of all sizes and shapes hustled about carrying bags or boxes which he surmised were filled with various food stuffs. All this activity reminded Red Flame of a highly organized army of ants, every one of them had a job to do and they just did it without question.

Ella and Martha wandered over to him as if they were going to say something but he interrupted them.

"I just have one thing to do while I remember, excuse me." He said.

They turned to watch him stroll out of the wagon circle, he went to each Mexican body in turn, checked the pulse of each and if they were killed by an arrow he yanked it from the corpse. He then dragged the dead bodies into the trees. He felt it was not good for young children to remember this sight, especially as in the morning with all the animals that hunt the woods during the dark hours the bodies would be even more morose. He then gathered the remainder of the Mexican troops horses and started tying them in pairs to the rear of some of the wagons. It was then he noticed two young boys following his every move, each one was wearing short trousers which still only reached their calves, long socks that were around their ankles and no shoes, they reminded him of his early school days. Each time he stopped to pick up a Troopers rifle and place it in its sheath, they stopped, he moved on, and they followed. He turned and smiled at them, they hesitantly smiled back. He waved them forward to him, they eagerly ran to him and he gave them each a horse to lead back to the wagons. When they returned to him, after tying up the horses there were nine children all wanting their own horse to tie to a wagon. The children grew in number and followed him like a swarm of bees, everywhere he went, they followed chatting to him like long lost friends. He was different to their fathers, they were fascinated, he didn't wear many clothes and he had long hair with feathers in. A novelty. He hoped they would remember this day and know that not all Indians were bad despite what they would probably be told by some white folk. He glanced over to the wagons where they were being watched from and laughed at by many of the children's parents, and his two lady friends. Martha looked very happy, he was pleased.

"So," said Jim, walking towards him as he wandered back into where the fire was now blazing away, "you will stay the night and eat with us?"

"If that's alright with Ella and Martha, then I would like that."
Both he and Jim turned to the Ladies for their response.

"Of course, we'd love to." Said Martha momentarily looking to check with Ella who nodded eagerly.

"Excellent," replied Jim, "that's settled then."
Jim's wife then introduced herself to the sisters and offered to show them where they could 'get cleaned up' before the festivities started. They wandered off to one of the wagons and disappeared inside.
Red Flame sat on one of the logs that had magically appeared next to the fire, immediately another of the wives with a beaming smile handed him a mug full of hot coffee. He took a gulp and then another.

"That's the best coffee I have ever tasted."
She sat down next to him and introduced herself as Helen and then pointed out her husband David, who was gathering more wood for the fire and her daughter Elizabeth, one of the swarm of little bees.
Just then Martha appeared from the rear of a wagon and sat close to him, very close. She placed her right hand on his knee, she then nodded to Helen, almost as though she was saying he's mine, stay away. Perhaps he was imagining it.

"You were amazing today, very brave." Martha looked straight at him.

"Oh," he was taken aback, "no, I just did what anybody would do in the circumstances."

"I don't think so." Said Helen.

"Nor do I." Added Martha.

As they sat discussing where the settlers were heading and what they were hoping to find when they got there, more folks joined them sitting around the fire grabbing a coffee as they passed the boiling pot, along with a larger swarm of bees all sitting on the ground quietly staring at him. The parents joined in with the conversation, each sharing their hopes and dreams, not only for themselves but also for their children. Each had a different story but he was amazed that they had not been told of the dangers they might encounter on their 2000-mile journey from east to west. They knew nothing about having to ride through Indian country where the buffalo herds were and the Indians hunted. Dangerous lands because different tribes had different relationships with the whites. Some traded and helped with the planting of the new settler's crops, others killed them mercisly. He spent time advising on the safest route they should take and answering any questions they had about the impending Indian war, they all listened intently and thanked him afterwards. All this time although listening, ladies were fussing over foods, dicing this and that and adding to the huge cooking pots, some already steaming away over the flames while other pots were lined up awaiting their turn to be added to the heat of the fire.

When it was time to eat, a concoction of chicken, rabbit and vegetables were offered and what a feast it was, enjoyed by everyone, particularly him.

It was two hours later, after all the children had been ushered to their beds that most of the adults congregated around the fire, a bottle of whisky appeared and every one was soon laughing and joking when suddenly, William, one of the younger men asked him a question that silenced the crowd.

"I believe there is a ransom out for you Red Flame, a bounty?" Silence, everyone turned to look at him.

"There is, yes." He stared straight at William.

"Oh, I'm sorry, I didn't mean anything by it. It's just I cannot believe what they say about you is true." Several of the others said "William?" as though he shouldn't have asked such a question to someone who had earlier saved their lives.

"What do they say?" Asked a weedy looking man at the other end of the log who he hadn't yet been introduced to.

"Well," replied William, "that Red Flame has killed many Soldiers."

Nobody said a word, they just stared at him. The silence was loud and awkward.

"Is that true Red Flame?" Suddenly asked the weedy man he didn't know.

"Hey," said Jim sensing the tension, "whatever you did in the past, you saved all our lives, and we owe you everything."

"Hear, hear." Shouted a few of the others.

Red Flame paused momentarily. Martha was watching him closely waiting for his response.

"I will explain what I did and why."

"You don't need to do that." Said a man sitting on the log opposite.

"But I do," said Red Flame, "I'm sleeping in your camp tonight, with all your children, I am eating your food and so I think I owe you an explanation. I would want it that way if I was you."

"No Red Flame, you don't owe us anything," said Ella, "we all here owe you our lives, that's enough for me."

"Hear hear." Some said again in unison.

"Thanks Ella. But I think it might help some folks sleep better tonight if I tell you how and why there is such a big bounty on me. It is actually very similar to our situation here, I returned to my village less than an hour after a troop of Cavalry massacred them, nearly 250 men, women and children were dead, many were even scalped. Some of the women raped. My family, all except my mother were dead. At that moment I decided I wanted those soldiers to die too. So, they did. They then sent more troops to punish me and whoever was alive, so I killed them too."

There was a silence for several seconds, some of the ladies held a hand to their mouths in disbelief, some men shook their heads, one man he didn't know just stared at him, a weasel of a man with long dank greyish hair. Red Flame felt his eyes boring into him, he would have to watch this man. This man meant trouble.

Martha walked towards him holding out her hands, she grabbed him and kissed him on the forehead.

"I'm so sorry you had to go through all that." She said quietly.

"Me too." Said another of the wives.

"You have been through a lot in your young life." Said Jim walking over to him and shaking his hand, then all the men stood, in a line, except the weasel and shook his hand, some of the women hugged him. Some had tears rolling down their face.

"Is it coffee time yet.?" Asked Ella trying to bring some levity to the situation.

Many of them laughed.

"Yes of course, I'll get it." Called out one of the ladies.

Ella looked towards him and smiled.

"Thank you." He mouthed silently.

The frivolity continued for about an hour or so longer and then everyone drifted off to their respective wagons including Ella and Martha who had been offered a stores wagon to sleep in. A lot more comfortable than the beach from the night before.

Red Flame gathered up some blankets some of the ladies had wrapped around them against the evening chill, that they had just left by the fire after the celebrations. He made his bed and laid down on them looking up at the stars as they swiftly moved across the sky. He started counting them but by the time he got to number eighty-seven he was asleep. Laggon stood about ten feet away from him. Watching.

An hour later he woke, something was telling him to move, he lifted one blanket and laid it on the ground, he then rolled the others into a cylindrical shape and laid that on the ground too, he then covered them in the blanket, to all intents and purposes it appeared as though he was sleeping under the top blanket. He moved over to one of the wagons furthest from the fire and crawled underneath it. From here he had a view of the whole campsite and all the wagons.

A short while later a shadow of a man appeared from one of the wagons carrying a revolver, as the lone figure got closer to the diminishing light from the fire, he could see it was the Weasel. The man crept to within two feet of where 'Red Flame' was supposedly sleeping and fired a bullet into what he assumed was Red Flames head. 'Bang'. The man immediately started dancing a jig, hollering and shouting.

91

"I'm rich, I'm rich I just shot the Indian. 500 dollars. I'm rich, Yahoo." Men and women appeared immediately from their wagons. Some bleary eyed but all armed with some sort of firearm. Jim walked over to the Weasel, grabbed the revolver from him and hit him flush on the nose, the weasel fell backwards on to the ground with blood running down his face and shirt. His nose was broken.

"You bastard," yelled Jim, "you bastard. Get out of here." Another man came over to the Weasel and kicked him in the ribs.

Martha appeared near the stores wagon, took one look at the bundle of blankets she thought was Red Flame and screamed, a second later Ella rushed to her and consoled her. Everyone appeared to be in shock at the Weasel's action, men were comforting their wives who in turn were consoling what children had appeared.
The weasel appeared surprised that he wasn't being hailed a hero.
Weasels wife joined the melee and started calling him all the names under the sun, telling him to leave her and their children and leave the camp. Weasel painfully stood up and put his hands out to her.

"But we are rich, I did this for you and the children."

"You Liar, you did it for yourself. You killed the man that saved your family when he was asleep. You coward."

Martha by now was kneeling on the ground inconsolable. Nobody noticed Red Flame crawling out from under the wagon.

"Hey, I'm Ok," he called out, "sorry, I needed to put some clothes on." He turned to the weasel and just stared.

Fear was written across the weasel's face. Fear is a strange animal, you are either consumed by it or inspired by it. Weasel was consumed by it.

Jim ran to Red Flame and put his arm around him, a protective arm like his father used to. How he missed that. He decided in that instant that he would go back to Tallahassee when he could and find the murderer of his father. His father deserved it. So did his ma.
Jim was crying again, obviously a very emotional man, but this time with joy.
Now Martha had hold of him kissing his face, then Ella joined in.

Others came up to him, some just touching his arm, some patting him on the back while others shook his hand.

"Can we get some coffee please?" He asked. People laughed again.

"Yes, more coffee please." Was now the cry amongst the crowd as some settled back down on the logs chatting away, others put more wood on the fire and a couple added more water to the pot. Nobody was ready to go back to bed yet.

Weasel stood on his own, his head bowed, about twenty feet from the log circle bemused and belittled. He wandered off to the darkest corner of the camp and started to cry. He was ignored by all.

Red Flame, coffee mug in hand made his way to where Jim and his wife were sitting and sat down.

"Jim, can I ask you a favor?"

"Of course, anything."

"Can I leave Ella and Martha to travel with you until tomorrow afternoon?"

"Yes, that's not a problem," he replied, "why, are you leaving?"

"Well, we are entering Choctaw country and they can be a little bit of an unknown quantity, usually they are a very peaceful people but if they feel threatened they can be very aggressive so I am going to their village just to tell them that you are just passing over their land and do not intend to settle on it or hunt their herds. Also, I might find out more about Ella and Martha's sister, if anybody knows anything, they will. Then I will meet up with you again tomorrow afternoon where a stream crosses the trail, that's about forty miles away."

"That's fine Red Flame, we will look after them until you return," they both stood and shook hands, "when are you leaving?"

"Right now."

"Take care then."

"You too Jim. Thanks for everything." He waved and smiled to Jim's wife.

He turned and looked for Ella and Martha. They were both sitting by the now well burning fire watching him closely. He waved and strolled over to where they were and squatted between them.

"Are you ok Martha?"

"What's going on?" She asked hesitantly

"I am leaving, just for tonight. I will be back tomorrow afternoon."

"No, you can't leave us alone here, please."

"No, I'm not Martha, Jim has said you can both travel with them until I get back tomorrow, then we will find your sister."

"What are you going to do?" Enquired Ella.

"I'm going to the Choctaw camp to make sure they know we are only travelling across their land to get to the other side, we do not intend to settle on their lands. Otherwise, we could have some more trouble. I will see you both tomorrow at the river crossing. Ok?" Reluctantly they both nodded, "don't worry. You will be safe." He hoped that was the truth.

He stood up and walked over to Laggon, mounted and rode off into the darkness. At least now he wouldn't need to worry about somebody killing him while he slept.

The next morning as the sun was rising he walked, with Laggon beside him into the Choctaw camp, many of them he knew from his boyhood days when the two tribes used to meet up for festivals and sports days, they all welcomed him warmly, his fame had preceded him, he knew that by the way some of the young squaws looked at him. If only he had more time he thought to himself. Several of the warriors called out his name and waved. The Chief appeared walking towards him, he was still physically imposing, over six feet tall and very wide, despite his age he looked as though he would still go into battle if he had to. He walked quickly to meet him, they hugged like the old friends they were, others gathered around listening.

"It is wonderful to see you again Red Flame after all this time. How is your mother?"

"Ma is fine thank you. It is great to see you again Chief and your family, you look well"

"Yes, we are. Thank you," the Chief replied, "is this a social visit or something else? I'm surprised you have the time to socialize if it is," the Chief said roaring with laughter, "we have heard of your exploits with great pride. You have made the White Chiefs in Washington take notice of us again, which is good but you must

94

watch your back Red Flame, many will be after your bounty. It is a large bounty."

"Yes, I know Chief, I have experienced the bounty hunters firsthand several times."

"Red Flame," the Chief said looking and sounding serious, "is it true that you killed all the soldiers that massacred your village?"

"Most of them, yes Chief."

The Chief grinned from ear to ear and raised his hands to the sky. Those that had gathered around them cheered.

"I am sure glad you are one of us Red Flame," the Chief laughed again, "now come sit at my tepee with me, join me for some food and drink. How can we help you today?"

As they sat talking the Chiefs daughter, Spotted Elk entered with all sorts of food for them both. She kept smiling at him. He wished he could spend the night there, but he couldn't.

"I have been helping two white ladies to find their sister who has been missing for two months now, and we came across a small wagon train of about eight wagons heading towards the ocean, but they were being attacked by a troop of Mexican soldiers."

"More Mexicans? We have come across several of their raiding parties lately. What did you do?"

"I had to kill most of them."

"Well good, well done," the Chief said sounding surprised, "so what do you need from me?"

"Firstly, I wondered if you had seen a white lady with a man travelling across your lands recently, and secondly, I came to ask if you would allow this wagon train to cross your lands, they are going to the ocean on the west coast, they have no intention of settling anywhere near here or hunting any of your animals."

"How do I know they won't build on our lands, many have said this before and then they do settle here and we get in trouble when we try to move them off."

"I will stay with them until they are on the other side of your lands Chief."

"Do I have your word on that Red Flame?"

"Yes."

"Then they can cross in peace. Regarding the other matter, I have not been told of any white couple being seen nearby, but Yellow

Hawk is out leading a scouting party now, he would be the one to ask."

"If I see him I will ask him. Thank you Chief."

"Look," said the Chief pulling his waistcoat back exposing his formidable chest and pointing to a two-inch diameter indentation just above his right nipple," that's where your father took out the bullet after one of my battles with the cavalry, he did a good job don't you think?"

"Very good."

"I will always be indebted to him for saving me, and you are definitely your fathers son. Now go quickly, catch up with Yellow Hawk, he doesn't know you are friends with the wagon train settlers, and find the missing white lady." He smiled and stood up. Red Flame rose, they hugged again.

"Thank you Chief." He quickly left the tepee and went to Laggon, mounted and waved back towards the Chief and his daughter.

"Come back safely." The Chief yelled. The onlookers waved and called out to him.

He rode back in the direction he'd come from hoping that the war party hadn't already started an attack on the advancing wagon train. He pushed Laggon harder than he could ever remember doing before, time was of the essence and they kept up a gallop for over two hours, Laggon didn't falter, then he saw the large dust cloud of the wagons, they had also made good time and no sign of Yellow Hawk yet. Then out of the corner of his eye he saw the raiding party galloping out of the trees towards the fast-moving wagons, they were only two hundred yards ahead of him but he would not catch them before they attacked. He snatched his rifle from its sheath and fired in to the air, the trees that surrounded the trail amplified the sound and the raiding party stopped to see who was attacking them from the rear. The whole party pulled up and turned together seeing him galloping towards them. Yellow Hawk immediately rode away from the rest of the war party to meet him. The others followed behind. The wagon train stopped.

"Red Flame," the young war chief said smiling," what are you doing here. Have you come to help us?"

"No Yellow Hawk, I have just left your father. I went to ask for safe passage across your lands for this small wagon train and he has given that on condition that I do not allow any of them to settle on any of your lands. They are all heading to the west coast and I will make sure they get there and there will be no hunting of any of your animals either."

"Oh, ok," the young warrior sounded disappointed, "we will have to pick up the trail of the Mexican troops that were spotted near here yesterday then."

"I'm sorry Yellow Hawk," he grimaced, "I got them yesterday, with some help."

"All of them?"

"I'm afraid so, well almost." The braves all looked at each other and burst out laughing.

"You got them all? How many were there?"

"About twenty-five. A handful got away."

"If it was anybody else but you that told me that I would call them a liar, but after hearing about your other victories I believe you."

"Thank you," they smiled at each other, "oh, by the way, have you seen a single white lady travelling with a white man recently?" He asked.

The young chief looked around him at his braves, as though asking them the same question.

"No, but we did see a white woman with three fur hunters, she did not look as though she was enjoying their company, if you know what I mean. They were heading north west. Nasty men these fur hunters. They have long rifles too, so be careful."

"Thank you, Yellow Hawk, I will. Take care yourself." He turned Laggon towards the wagon train which had stopped about one hundred yards away, the settlers just watching nervously and waiting.

"My best to your Mother." Shouted the young chief as he and his braves waved and turned back towards their village and rode off. He is going to make a good tribal Chief when his father retires Red Flame thought to himself as he galloped towards the wagon train. He couldn't wait to see Martha again.

Jim was driving the lead wagon as usual and was waiting to greet him.

"I thought you were in trouble there, or should I say we were in trouble, we heard the shot just after the war party came into view. What happened? We thought we were going to be attacked again." Red Flame was scouring the others in the wagons behind Jim, where was Martha? He couldn't see her.

"Sorry to interrupt Jim, are the girls ok? Where are they?"

"Third wagon back, but they are both ok." He smiled reassuringly at him.

"Good. Um, oh yes, I went to see the Chief of the Choctaw and he gave us permission to cross his lands as long as none of you decide to settle on them or hunt his animals."

"His animals? But surely they are not his……."

"In Indian eyes they are his animals, they were promised these lands and all the animals on it by your President and guaranteed that no whites would hunt on it. That treaty has been broken so many times that the Chief is now threatening war against any whites that do it again, even crossing their lands will have a war party after you, as you just saw."

"You stopped them?"

"Yes, luckily."

"Thank you, Red Flame, but I don't think luck had anything to do with it." They smiled.

"By the way, I have to travel with you until we have crossed these lands."

"That's great." Said Jim excitedly.

"Are you sure Jim, we don't want any more trouble. It seems to follow me around."

"Don't worry. Ernie left this morning, we gave him a horse and some water, he headed off east. His wife told him to leave and never comeback. I think they had marital problems long before this episode." Ernie must have been the man he called the weasel.

He rode on to the third wagon, he saw Ella who waved and smiled at him and then behind her popped up Martha from inside the wagon whose facial expression said it all. She was as excited to see him as he was to see her. He tied Laggon to the wagon and jumped

98

up onto the seat next to Martha who was now at the reins. He looked forward to Jim who was still stationary looking back at him and nodded, Jim raised his hand and yelled, "Wagons Ho." They all moved off together marveling at the sun as it began to set behind the landscape.

A short while later they stopped to make camp. Exactly the same happened as the night before once the wagons were in a tight circle. Men rushed into the nearby woods for firewood, the ladies carried out pans, utensils and boxes of food, children fed the horses and a couple of men dragged logs to the unlit fire for all to sit on. An hour later the fire was raging, with a large number of kettles and pots were bubbling away and all were relaxing around the fire. Laughter filled the hot stifling air. He sat between Ella and Martha.

"I'm just going to feed Laggon," he said as he stood and walked away, "be back for the food and a coffee in a minute." Those that heard him laughed. His mention of coffee seemed to make them all laugh. Perhaps an Indian drinking coffee was funny. He hadn't thought about it before.

"Him and his coffee," Martha said, "it will be the death of him." They all laughed again.

He strolled over to where Laggon was nuzzling up to a lovely jet-black pony and stroked his neck and thighs, suddenly he heard several horse's galloping close by, he froze, he watched as two fur hunters rode passed his position looking for the opening into the circle. He moved around Laggon so he could get a better view of the men, they both looked like seasoned fur hunters, both carrying long rifles that gave them a good forty to fifty feet advantage when firing over the regular Winchester rifle.

They both had their rifles across their saddles ready to fire. Both had bushy beards and neither of them looked as though they had washed in days, both were pulling an extra horse which was laden down with different furs.

"Howdy all, Ladies," said the first man, who was well overweight as he took off his hat and nodded without taking his eyes off the ladies, "we bumped into an old friend of yours this morning, Ernie something or other, he said that the Redskin Red Flame was travelling with you, is that right? You know he's got a big bounty on him?"

Nobody said a word.

"Why?" said Jim suddenly, "who wants to know?"

"I do," the fur hunter said cocking his rifle. The man stared at Jim. Everybody nearby felt the tension.

Just then right on que Laggon galloped past the entrance to the circle, about twenty feet behind the two fur hunters, but with what appeared to be no rider.

"What the……" Yelled the other fur hunters as he spun around to see Laggon rider less disappearing westwards up the trail. Just then Red Flame pulled himself up onto Laggon's back, he had been riding by holding on to Laggon's mane and supporting his weight with one leg over the pony's back. To anybody on the other side it looked as though Laggon had no rider, but Red Flame made sure the hunters saw him as he sped off into the night.

"There he is, that's him," he heard one of the hunter's shout, "quick, get after him."

He galloped off knowing he was already out of their rifle range and no hunters would catch him particularly pulling an extra horse. The hunters took time to turn their horses around and set off after him. At least they were leaving the camp, everyone would be safer now he had left. He was already out of sight.

He headed west as quickly as Laggon could safely see the route ahead, it was almost dark in the shadows of the large beech trees but quite bright because of the full moon when in open areas. After about a mile the trail opened up before him, high trees on his right that went on for miles but the ground fell away to his left with just a smattering of small bushes in front, and to his left were the start of the hills.

The obvious thing for him to do would be to hide in the dense forest and wait for the two to pass and then open fire, but these two looked experienced and they would be expecting that, so he quickly dismounted and tied Laggon to one of the trees in the woods, grabbed his rifle and ran cross the trail which was about forty feet wide at this point and positioned himself under one of the larger bushes. Across from him were the woods, to his right was the trail opening up from twelve feet to forty where he was hiding, with more small bushes, behind him the ground fell away steeply into the darkness. He took a deep breath and waited. No one in sight. He flexed his fingers to keep them as supple as possible. Still no one in sight. Maybe the two had decided to wait until morning and then track him. They would be more than capable of doing that, but unlike most Indians they weren't worried about fighting at night. No, they were just travelling slower that was all. Suddenly the moon reflected off something metallic about sixty feet away, probably a rifle barrel, moving very slowly along the forest line, stopping periodically and scanning between the trees. Slowly a man on a horse pulling another became more visible, the man was getting closer. The sound of his horse's hooves getting louder. Where was the other man? He looked away to the right, nothing.

He had expected them both to come thundering along the trail together and he would pick them off one after the other. They were smarter than he gave them credit for. He tried to turn his head further to the right but immediately he heard the bush and the dead wood he was lying on start to crack under his weight and now the ants were biting him too. The first man was now about twenty feet away, Red Flame knew he had to shoot this man soon before he spotted Laggon in the trees. He waited, another ten feet he thought and then he would fire.

"Anything?" Suddenly a voice whispered from behind him. How had the second man got behind without him seeing or hearing anything. The second hunter must have gone down the hill behind him and then come back up again. Clever tracking. He suddenly felt nervous.

"No, not yet. I think he took off. We will get him tomorrow." Said the hunter only a few yards in front of him and getting closer all the time.

"Ok, another 100 yards then we can pitch camp." Said the man who was now on Red Flames left only a short distance ahead of the one nearest the woods who was just about level with Laggon. The ants were now swarming all over him, biting as they went.

"No, there is nothing here." The first hunter said.
Red Flame had a clear shot at the first man, the moon did the man no favors. It was the bigger of the two hunters who had done the talking

at the wagon circle. He slowly cleared his face of the ants and took aim.

'Crack.' The man dropped from his horse.

The second man's horses were spooked by the rifle sound and spun around causing him to momentarily loose his sense of direction.

Red Flame rolled out from under the bush and looked to his left, luckily, again the man was silhouetted in the moonlight. The hunter was fighting to regain control of his horses, but incredibly the man was able to aim his rifle and fired first, but Red Flame was still flat on the ground and the bullet went over him. He fired almost immediately. 'Crack'. He cleared his eyes again. The man seemed to sit motionless in the saddle, frozen in time.

'Crack'. Red Flame fired again and this time the man fell sideways and hit the ground with a thud.

Red Flame rolled on to his back and exhaled. He swatted ants from his legs and arms. That was close he thought to himself, too close. The hunters were better at their jobs than he had expected. He lay motionless looking up at the stars getting his breath back. What a lovely night he thought, why that flashed through his mind he did not know. Suddenly there was a loud shriek and the first hunter was charging at him brandishing a huge skinning knife, he looked huge because Red Flame was on the ground looking up, the man's chest was pumping out blood and he was definitely in a lot of pain. Red Flame fumbled for his rifle in the grass as the man got closer, now only about eight feet away, he couldn't find it, then he felt the stock, then the trigger and with one hand lifted it and pointed it and fired. 'Crack'. With only inches to spare. The man fell backwards.

This time he didn't hang around to admire the heavens, he jumped up and felt the man's pulse. He was dead. He ran to the second of the hunters and leaning over the man he felt his pulse, he was still alive, surprised because he had two bullets in him, Red Flame quickly stood up and shot him again. Tough men these hunters. Then his shoulders dropped, he relaxed. He wiped his face wearily. His heart was pumping.

It had been quite a while since the last time he had come so close to death. He slumped back on the ground and looked skyward, the stars were like meteors zipping across the black sky, in his father's world they were stars, in his mother's they were good spirits, he didn't know or mind what they were but they always looked amazing. He lay still until his heart rate dropped to normal. He then strode over to the trees and untethered Laggon, he gathered the two fur hunter's horses, leaving all the furs beside the trail with one of his arrows. He expected a Choctaw war party would find them and his arrow would let them know that he had left the furs for them. He started back towards the awaiting wagons.

Martha was standing alone at the entrance to the wagon circle, waiting, she waved madly and called out to him to him as soon as she saw him approaching, Ella came running hearing Martha's shouts, then the rest of the camp appeared clapping again. As he dismounted Martha rushed to him and kissed him on the lips, he was not expecting it, but liked it. As she went to back away he pulled her forward and they continued for what felt like several minutes. Then they looked at each other soaking in what they had just done.

"Red Flame," said Jim running towards him, "are you ok?"

"Yes, thanks, I'm fine".

"They looked mean hombres, we were worried about you. Where are they?"

"About a mile up the road."

"Are they likely to be coming back?'

"No Jim, they are dead."

"Dead. You killed them?"

"Well yes, they were going to kill me. What did you think they were going to do to me?"

"I don't know, I really don't know." Jim answered honestly, he couldn't comprehend what bad men did in these times and particularly in these lands where anything could happen. Was this man that naive? These men would have cut his balls off and scalped him.

"My bounty has just gone up again." He said, to no one in particular.

"Now I understand this ridiculous bounty thing," said Jim, "it's all wrong Red Flame. All totally wrong."

"Food Red Flame, I kept you some, I thought you might be hungry after dealing with those thugs." Said Helen, Jim's wife, interrupting them both.

"Yes, please Helen, I'm starving."

"Good, there's plenty of it."

As he sat down on the log with a full plate of food, Martha joined him on one side and Ella on the other. Everybody seated themselves around the fire again which gave them all an orange glow and everyone seemed to be in a good mood and laughing. It was a good night to be alive he thought to himself.

CHAPTER 8

The next morning, he had fed Laggon and re- logged the fire before the settlers were up, they started their daily chores immediately, sorting through their preferred breakfast foods, feeding their horses and getting their kids dressed.

"Good morning Red Flame," called out Ella walking towards him, "did you sleep well?"

"Yes, thanks Ella, did you?"

"Like a log."

"Good, we have a long day ahead of us." As he turned back towards the fire a reflection on the hill behind where Ella was standing caught his eye. He stood concentrating, wondering what it was.

"What's wrong?" Enquired Ella.

"There's something up there on the top of that hill." He replied slowly, still trying to make out what it was.

"Where, I can't see anything."

"There. Can you see it." He pointed to the north.

"No," she said scouring the hills, "I can't see anything."

"There," he pointed again, "you can see the reflection now, see."

"Yes, yes I can now."

It was a small group of riders galloping down the hill towards them, still about half a mile away, but making good speed, he couldn't make out who they were, friend or foe, but they were certainly in a hurry. He watched and waited, if he could not make out who they were then they definitcly wouldn't be able to identify him. Were they Lawmen?

Then after a minute or so he saw it was a part of the Choctaw war party he had spoken to the day before, they were all carrying their rifles which meant thcy were either ready to fight or they had just been fighting, it was the reflection off one of their rifles that had attracted his attention.

What did they want, why were they in such a hurry? He took Ella by the arm and led her back to where Laggon was still tied, he slowly removed his rifle from its sheath and held it down by his leg so it wasn't quite so obvious. Were the Choctaw coming to cause problems, had he missed something, maybe one of the settlers had done something they shouldn't have, maybe they had broken the agreement he had made with the Chief?

"Where is Martha, do you know." He asked.

"She said she was going for a short walk a while ago."

"What? Where did she go?"

"I don't know, she left a few minutes ago."

She must have gone while he was in the woods collecting kindling for the fire. He slowly turned through 360 degrees scanning the hills and the dense woods, searching for any sign of movement through the tall thin birch trees but because there were so many it was impossible.

It was also totally impractical to take off in one direction as she could just as easily appear within seconds from another.

"Ella, round up everybody and get them armed and tell them to get behind or under the wagons. There might be trouble." Just then he saw Jim walking towards the fire, "Jim," he yelled, as he pointed to the incoming war party, "get everybody armed quickly and out of sight. I will be back when I know what is going on." Untying Laggon, he mounted and rode straight towards the incoming war party. Within several minutes he was face to face with a very worried looking Yellow Hawk.

"Red Flame," he said breathlessly," there is a troop of Mexicans right behind us, they ambushed us at Little Creek and killed four of our braves and now I think they are looking for the patrol they lost a few days ago, the ones that attacked your wagon train. The ones you killed."

"Ok," he looked back past the young braves and could see the Mexican patrols dust rising into the sky, he still had ten minutes he thought until they got to within shooting distance.

"Shall we take them head on or retreat to the wagons where we will have the settlers to help us? Which would you prefer?"

"I don't know Red Flame, what do you think?"

Between themselves and the circled wagons was about 300 yards of very dense birch trees, where they were now on the hill they could see over the trees and clearly make out the wagons positions below and the settlers scurrying about getting organized for an impending attack were clear to see. The Mexicans will have this very same view when they get to this position in a matter of minutes. He turned to the young chief.

"We have a total of fourteen men, we can form a V with five braves in each of the V," he held his arms out as though he was welcoming somebody, "five on one arm," he motioned to his left arm, "five on the other," he pointed to his right arm, "and the other four behind the wagons, here," he motioned across his chest, these men must move around a lot and will take all our ponies inside the wagon circle so the Mexicans think we are all in there. They will not be expecting us to be in the trees, we can catch them in a crossfire while the other four under or behind the wagons can fire straight ahead into the woods as soon as they hear gunfire. Everyone understand?"

A few hesitated looking towards Yellow Hawk for some sort of guidance.

"You four follow me, the rest follow Red Flame, let's go we don't have long before they get here." Yelled the young chief panicking slightly.

"That way about thirty yards Yellow Hawk," Red Flame said pointing to his left, "rest follow me." He shouted to the remaining braves. He moved thirty yards to his right, the other eight braves followed him in single file and once they were among the trees he told the last man to dismount with his rifle and lay on the ground, he grabbed the reins of the man's horse and moved further into the trees about another twenty yards and then did the same to the next man, then again to the next and once more and finally once they were almost out of the trees he stopped for the last of the five.

He then rode out of the trees with the remaining three braves calling out to the startled settlers not to shoot, he didn't want any itchy fingers on triggers as they appeared. He led the three and the horses into the center of the wagon circle and quickly pointed to where the three men should position themselves under the wagons lying on their stomachs with rifles ready. He released the ponies hitting several on the rump to make them spread out just as a young brave who had followed Yellow Hawk appeared at the tree line with their five ponies, he handed their reins to Red Flame and ran back into the trees to take up his position.

"Keep low." Red Flame called out to him as he disappeared back into the trees. Red Flame let the five ponies loose into the wagon circle and then took up position next to Ed.

"Jim, when we open fire get your men to fire straight ahead into the trees, not to the sides, we have friends in the woods lying on the ground firing at angles to get the Mexicans in a crossfire. Aim between five and seven feet high. Ok?" He yelled.

"Ok Red Flame." Jim then started calling out the same instructions to his men.

Red Flame knew from experience that Yellow Hawk would let the majority of the raiders past the first few of his men before opening fire so none could turn to get away. It seemed like an eternity.

Suddenly a crescendo of noise erupted from within the trees, Red Flame immediately fired followed by the three braves lying near him and then Eds settlers joined in, the noise was deafening, he wondered if anybody could survive the hail of bullets entering the forest. Sixty seconds later a Mexican appeared from the trees coming straight for them, his red tunic standing out against the darkness of the tree's. Red Flame shot him in the chest, the soldier dropped to the ground. Another appeared a few feet to the right of the first but a good shot from one of the settlers brought him down. Then another, but he stopped at the tree line, he was already badly hurt but his horse's momentum must have carried him forward, he slowly slumped to the ground. The firing continued for several more minutes but gradually decreased in number and volume until absolute silence.

"Red Flame, we have got them all." Shouted Yellow Hawk from somewhere in the woods.

"Stop firing," shouted Red Flame to the settlers and the three braves next to him, "stay low but stop firing. Can you hear me Yellow Hawk?" He shouted.

"Yes, I hear you." Still deep in the trees.

He motioned to the three braves to follow him but keep low and spread out.

"Yellow Hawk, we are entering the woods, can you hear or see us?"

"We can hear you Red Flame but can't see you yet." The undergrowth between the trees was about three to four feet high in some places so walking through it was tiring and awkward.

"We are walking slowly through the trees towards you, do not fire unless it is at a red uniform. I will keep talking so you know where we are. There are four of us walking towards you. I count at this time six dead Mexicans on the ground and two dead horses."

"Two more Mexicans here on the ground Red Flame." Said the brave immediately to his left who was about sixteen feet away.

"Another one here." Yelled another brave way over to the right.

"Two more here." Shouted a voice way off to his left.

"We have eleven bodies now and still walking."

"Two more here." A voice yelled from a good distance in front of him and the three still walking forward among the trees.

"We have thirteen now and still walking." He noticed several of the patrol's horses were just standing motionless among the trees almost as though they didn't know quite what to do next, looking lost.

"Two more here, no, three more here." Came from another invisible source.

"We have sixteen bodies and still walking."

Suddenly 'Crack' a gunshot, so loud as the sound ricochet off the trees, everyone he could see around him crouched down peering through the trees to see any movement.

"It's Ok, one of them moved, I thought he had a gun. One more body here." The voice said apologetically.

"Seventeen bodies and still walking, lots of rider less horses. Still walking." They were, he thought about three quarters of their way through the trees. As they continued to walk more braves stood up and joined the line as it progressed towards the far tree line, there must be only another four braves he thought left to make up the original fourteen.

"Still walking." He shouted again.

"Two bodies here." A voice ahead of them shouted.

"Still walking nineteen bodies so far."

"Two more here." Another voice. Closer this time.

"Two more." Yet another voice.

"Still walking. That's twenty-three bodies. Anyone know how many were in the patrol?" Shouted Red Flame.

"I would say that was about it." Said the young war chief who was suddenly standing right in front of him. Red Flame looked to his left, there were six braves in a straight line, he looked to his right, again six braves in a straight line and with himself and Yellow Hawk all were accounted for. Yellow Hawk stepped forward and hugged him.

"That was amazing, thank you Red Flame, you certainly saved our lives and the settlers too."

"No, we did that together, all of us. But first, let's just double check there are no Mexicans faking it. You know how cunning these rats are. Let's just spread out and walk back to the wagons and count as we go again."

This time Yellow Hawk led the count, after all it was his war party.

"We have two, we have seven, we have nine, we have thirteen, now we have sixteen, now twenty," five minutes later, "and now twenty-three. All dead." The braves cheered and let out whoops of pleasure. They walked out into the clearing and all the settlers were waiting to cheer them. Men, women and children ran towards them and shock hands, hugged and even some kissing went on.

"Right everybody, get the coffee and food going, we need to show all these brave men a good welcome and thank you party." Shouted Jim, and at that very second, the fire sent burning embers way up into the sky almost in celebration and people disappeared in all directions to get Jim's welcome party organized. The braves stood in amazement not knowing what to do or how to help, could they help? No, they were told emphatically, sit down and relax. Yellow Hawk sent four of his braves into the trees to collect the Mexicans horses and secure them to a line strung between two trees. They would gather any rifles and ammunition later after they had been fed and watered.

That day and night the party ran on and a good time was had by all, Indians danced with settlers, some played pots as make shift drums and a couple of settlers played guitar and one of the wives played the fiddle. Everybody clapped and sang along if they knew or didn't know the words. This night made a big impression on Red Flame, one that he would remember for the rest of his life and that was that different peoples could live together if they really wanted to. It was a shame the Big white chief wasn't there to see it himself because he might have believed it too.

When Red Flame awoke the next morning, the Choctaw had already rounded up their own ponies and the Mexicans horses and tied them to a line, all the captured weapons were bundled neatly together and laid on the grass. One of the wives standing by the fire shouted that coffee was ready for serving and breakfast would be a few minutes later, everyone without exception converged on the fire pit like a flock of curlews all chatting away and laughing.
Martha and Ella appeared from their wagon still clearing their eyes and stretching, seeing him they walked over to him smiling.
"Did you sleep well Red Flame?" Asked Ella.
"Yes, thanks Ella, and you?"
"Absolutely, we were both shattered last night, all the excitement I suppose."
Just then the three of them were surrounded by the war party all eager to talk to him.
"We just wanted to thank you again Red Flame, that was a great plan you came up with yesterday, I thought about it last night, it was brilliant and you thought it out so quickly, we usually take days to plan something like that. We would have all been killed by those Mexican runts, us and the white settlers, so thank you again." The other braves all agreed quite vocally patting him on the shoulders and back.
"Well, I have to thank you and all your magnificent braves because, without you I shudder to think how this would have turned out, we would not have been able to withstand their attack without you, so thanks to you all." He looked at each brave in turn, nodded and smiled.
"We have tied the Mexican runts horses to that line," the young chief said very matter of factly pointing to the horses, "and stacked their rifles and ammunition just there by the trees." Again, he pointed in the general direction.

"Thank you. But no, you should take them. You deserve to have them and really the settlers don't need them, so please take them." Red Flame insisted.

"Are you sure about that."

"Definitely, take them!"

"Well we could certainly use them, their rifles are a lot newer than what we have been using, but I don't wish to offend our new friends." Said Yellow Hawk speaking very maturely Red Flame thought for such a young war chief.

"You won't, please take them, we owe you all so much." Said Martha reassuringly.

The chief smiled at her, he liked her that was obvious and Red Flame felt a pang of jealousy, a feeling he had never experienced before and he didn't like it.

"There, how can you argue with that, they want you to have them." He quipped trying to hide any hint of his feelings.

"Ok Martha, we will take them, only because you said so. I hope we meet again soon."

"Me too." Replied Martha rather coyly. They looked at each other and smiled.

"Right," said Ella," let's get some breakfast." As she made her way back to the fire pit. They all turned and followed her. Red Flame breathed a sigh of relief, he was pleased that the slushy stuff was over.

An hour later the war party was ready to leave, there was a lot of shaking of hands and hugs
again, and the settlers seamed genuine as they stood and cheered as the war party left the wagon circle and disappeared over the hill.

Immediately Jim started shouting orders to the others about not losing any more time, time was of the essence. Get the horses hitched to the wagons, put away all the cooking utensils, douse the fire and get aboard your wagons. After ten minutes the wagons were rolling west towards the coast and out of Indian country, not that they had anything to fear from the Choctaw anymore, particularly now after the friendship they had formed.

Red Flame and Laggon rode about three hundred yards south of the moving wagons but as high as they could get above them enabling him to see a full 360 degrees around them, if anyone should approach from any direction he would see their dust cloud and make some sort of decision on what action to take to deal with it. For five hours they rumbled west without stopping except to water the horses and a quick gulp for everybody that needed it.

After nine hours they were again looking for a suitable safe place to spend the night when he spotted a rider approaching from the north, by the way the man was riding he guessed it was an Indian riding at speed, then he recognized the rider, it was one of the war party braves, he galloped forward to intercept the young brave and within minutes they were standing six feet apart.

"Yellow Hawk sent me to warn you that the white lady you are looking for is with three fur traders about a day ahead of you, that's all, but these men are evil, they are heading north west but he says to warn you to beware, he thinks we have had several run ins with these men and they are dangerous, very dangerous. Do you want us to help you?"

"Oh," he had not anticipated this and was taken aback, Yellow Hawk was obviously concerned for his wellbeing, "tell the chief I will be careful not to take these men lightly. But thanks."

"He also says you do not have to stay with the wagons until they cross our lands. You are free of your promise to our Chief. Also, he thanks you again for saving us."

"Send both Chief's my best wishes and also thanks to you for being the messenger, take care." He waved to the young brave and turned Laggon back towards the wagon train and galloped off towards it.

"Trouble?" Enquired Jim as Red Flame approached him.

"No, its good news really," Red Flame said turning Laggon so that he was riding alongside Jim's wagon, "the Choctaw Chief now says that I don't need to stay with you until we clear their lands and that the girl's sister has been spotted about a day ahead of us heading north, so I think we ought to leave you at first light to go after them, depending on what the girls say."

"Well that's good news for you but not so good for us, we feel safer when you are with us but that's us being selfish," Jim laughed as he said it, "we are setting up camp as soon as we find a suitable site. Perhaps we could get together and have a little talk later tonight, I have a few questions I'd like to ask you, if that's Ok?"

"Of course, anytime, I'll see you later on." He turned Laggon around and headed towards the third wagon in line where he knew Ella and Martha would be on the seat driving the wagon. He felt a pang of disappointment to be leaving Jim and the others, he had made some good new friends.

They both instantly waved as soon as they caught sight of him moving towards them, their smiles lifted his spirits.

"We were worried when we saw you galloping towards that Indian up there on the hill, we thought there might be trouble coming." Said Martha.

"No, no quite the opposite," he paused momentarily, "firstly the good news. We can leave the settlers any time we want to, they are free to cross these lands on their own without me escorting them. Secondly, and I'm not sure if this is good or bad news," he paused again, "the Choctaw have reported that a white lady, who they think could well be your sister, is travelling with three fur traders only a day ahead of us travelling that way," he pointed towards the north west.

"Wow, that is good news." Said Martha excitedly.

"Are these men helping her or what?" Asked Ella hesitantly.

He paused while he thought of a suitable diplomatic answer.

"I don't know to be honest, that's why I said I didn't know if it was good or bad news, I don't believe these men are helping her. These men have a bad reputation, they are mean and nasty, as the Indians that have fought them in the past will tell you. They probably will not treat her like a lady, they will not be nice to her." An awkward silence fell over them whilst the ladies digested his words.

"Do you mean……...?" Asked Ella after a minute.

"Is she their prisoner?" Interrupted Martha.

"I'm not sure, but that would be my guess. I think we need to catch them as soon as possible. I'm afraid they could be using her."

"Using her for what?" Asked Ella. Then it hit her what he was insinuating. She covered her mouth with her hands as it all sunk in. A look of total shock in her eyes.

"Oh my God, they wouldn't, would they?" Martha asked staring at him in disbelief.

"It's not uncommon around here as you have seen for yourselves, there are a lot more men than women, and there is no law as such for protection."

Ella just stood with tears rolling down her lovely face. Silence, even the birds had stopped their calls and the trees their whispering as the two sisters stared at each other for what seemed like minutes.

"Libby, poor Libby." Ella whispered. More silence.

"We go after them at first light, Ok?" He said shattering that silence.

Neither sister answered, they just nodded their heads and looked straight ahead to where Ed was now organizing the wagons to circle.

A short while later the settlers were well into their chores, the fire was burning, various pots with steam spiraling upwards into the evening sky, the horses were fed and watered and every one was beginning to relax. As Red Flame sat on one of the logs surrounding the fire Jim sat down next to him.

"Are you alright to talk now?" He asked.

"Of course, what's up?"

"I really just wanted to pick your brain about homesteading when we get to our destination, your people have roamed and made a living from these lands for 100's of years, and I really wanted to learn from you what were the things to do and the things not to do. I don't want to upset the Choctaw or any tribes for that matter, I believe we can all live in harmony and I want to cultivate that."

Red Flame just looked at Jim and thought for several seconds.

"I'm so pleased you asked that. Most settlers arrive here, start building a property, kill all the buffalo they can and then get upset when the local tribes get annoyed. Indians kill animals when they are hungry and need to eat, but they use everything from that animal's carcass, fur for clothing, meat to eat, sinew for rope and bow strings, bones for tools, large birds for meat, feathers for arrows, nothing from any carcass is wasted. The whites kill Buffalo by the hundreds,

115

they strip their coats to sell to the fur traders and then leave the carcass to rot where it fell which leaves many tribes starving, and that is when they take up arms to fight back. Most settlers don't bother to plant crops or if they do they plant the wrong ones, the ones to cultivate in this soil that are usually successful are beans, squash and corn. You see, we believe that land cannot be owned, it belongs to the animals, the birds and the spirits, how can a man own it. The white man buys small plots of land and from that day it is his, but nobody owned it before, he seems to need to own it, different philosophies but who is right? My father thought that both of them had a point, but agreed to disagree, he was a white man and so he bought a white man's house, my mother on the other hand, although she lived in that house while my father was alive, thought that nature and the land was gods only, and so no one should own it and lived that way of life after my father was killed. Who knows? Neither would ever agree and it still is a dividing factor between the Big white chief and the Indian nations."

"How was your father killed?" Enquired Jim.

"He was murdered."

"Really? By who?"

"I don't know yet but I will find that out after I find Libby, that's Ella and Martha's sister."

"Good! You must. You cannot let whoever it was get away with it." Red Flame nodded in agreement. He knew Jim was right.

They continued to talk well into the night about different things, different perspectives and it was only when Martha came up to them to say she was going to bed that they realized the time, and how most of the others had already disappeared into their wagons.

Red Flame liked Jim, he had since their first meeting just days ago, he was intelligent and would argue his point if he thought he was right but quick to admit if he was wrong too. He liked to think that they were alike in that respect and how if only there were more like them, these ongoing land problems could be solved without all the blood shed that was happening now on a daily basis. He thought back to what Donald had said at their last meeting, was it a blood lust thing that the Whiteman had brought to the Indians land and nothing was going to stop them from exterminating the tribes? Not if they thought like Jim. Only time would tell.

Red Flame said goodnight to the few stragglers that were still sitting around the fire chatting and headed over to Laggon to share some water and then bedded down under Ella and Martha's wagon. There was not a sound, absolute silence. The trees around them were swaying in the moonlight, but no sound, just the way he liked it. He was asleep in minutes.

Several hours later his sleep was disturbed by Laggon pawing at the ground a few feet from his head trying to attract his attention, he thought it was because of the fact that several of the settlers were up preparing breakfast and Laggon felt a little intimidated by all the movement and noise around him, neither were used to it. Red Flame rolled out from under the wagon, stood up and stretched. He stroked Laggon to reassure him that all was well.

It was going to be a lovely bright morning and he wanted to get on the trail as soon as possible, he thought he would give the girls some extra time so he strolled over to the ladies already pouring coffee for those that were really desperate for that first shot of caffeine. His mother and father always had a coffee pot on their stove and so it was quite normal for him just to pour a cup anytime of the day, just second nature and he had acquired the taste. The two girls soon joined him on the log and grabbed their own coffees, several of the settlers milled around them saying how sorry they were that they were leaving the wagon train and hoped they would soon catch up with their sister. Jim had passed on the news to them all about the girl's sister, and some were visibly upset that they were leaving. The settlers didn't know how apprehensive he was about this whole thing, he just hoped he wasn't going to lead the girls into a complete nightmare.

CHAPTER 9

Less than two hours later they had left the wagon train and the main east to west trail. The terrain was now hillier, there were still some wooded areas with less tree coverage but not enough to make him feel any easier. They could see further into the distance which also meant they would be seen sooner than he wanted. They rode side by side to start with and kept up a strong pace, he knew that the fur traders would be a lot slower, it was the nature of the beast, they would still be looking for signs of animals they could trap, sometimes stopping to set traps and even going back to check on them awhile later. Yellow Hawk had said that the traders were a full day ahead so he felt they would be safe together for at least five hours. His problem was that he didn't want to literally run into them, these men were known to be vicious and with the bounty on his head they would not hesitate to kill him, also what would they think up for the girls, he shuddered when he thought about what that implied.

They stopped once, several hours later at a small river to water the horses, it was here that he noticed for the first-time fresh tracks at the water's edge, six horses had stopped for water in the last few hours. Four were being ridden and two were pulling travois. He didn't tell the sisters, no need to frighten them yet. Then he immediately split up from the girls, still maintaining visual contact with them but out of sight of anybody else, at least that was his plan. He maintained the same speed as the sisters but he was about 350 yards west of them trying to keep as many treed areas between them as he could. As each hour passed he found himself getting more anxious, the 'what if's' grew more in number, 'what if' the fur hunters had already set camp for the night so they could return to check on their traps, 'what if' he or the girls had been spotted already, these men were good at their job, 'what if' he was in fact being followed by them, 'what if' they weren't going to stop for the night and so it went on. As the sun started to set, he decided to make camp as he really was concerned about getting to close to them at night, these men often hunted at night and so he would rather be a good distance from them just in case they wandered into their camp by chance. He preferred to catch up with them during the day light hours. He rode down the hill to meet the girls and explained why he thought it best to find a safe camp now rather than wait until it got dark. At first Ella wanted to continue the search and voiced her disappointment but eventually she agreed and they set about finding a safe position to start a small fire. He wouldn't bother if he was on his own, but the girls were frightened of stray animals and they thought the fire a necessity, the fire concerned him as some of these fur traders were as good at tracking as many Indians, they could smell meat on a burning fire from about half a mile away depending on the wind direction, he could.

If these men came close by checking their traps, they would be looking for whoever was doing the cooking. He would have to be concerned about where he slept that night.

They started gathering some kindling and soon had the fire ablaze and the coffee pot boiling, Martha produced some food that the settlers had given her for them and in no time, they were relaxing around the fire. He was constantly on edge, several times he got up and walked around the perimeter of the camp, listening for any abnormal bird sounds, they were usually the best at alerting others that something was moving nearby. Nothing, just silence.

They continued chatting mainly about Libby and how this disappearance was so totally out of character for her, how she was the brainy one of the three and could get herself out of any predicaments she found herself in. This was why they were so worried. They finally laid down on the moist soft grass, the girls in their bed rolls, him on a blanket. In no time the girls were asleep but he laid awake thinking of all the permutations that could develop, finally he stood up and walked around the camp again, looking and listening for what he did not know. He untied Laggon and led him about fifty yards away and retied him to a tree out of sight of the camp. He took his bow and quiver full of arrows and made his way quietly back to the fireside. He looked skyward and chose an oak tree covered in Spanish moss that was close by but sheltered from the light of the fire. He climbed twenty-five feet high and straddled a

119

good-sized bough and put his head back on the trunk, he closed his eyes and waited, and waited. Then he dozed off.

He awoke with a start when he heard Martha cry out. It took him a second or two to realize where he was. Martha's muffled cries made him focus quicker. The fire he had lit earlier was still shedding enough light that he could make out several figures moving about below him. A tall thin man was standing behind Martha with his left arm around her waist and in his right hand he held a large hunting knife pressed to her throat. He couldn't see the man's face. She was standing motionless, probably scared stiff.

Ella was being held by another man, she couldn't move either. He was behind her and had his arms around her in a bear hug. This man was closer to the fire and so was more visible, he was thickset with a large bushy beard as so many of these trappers had, they did not like to shave because any type of soap had a fragrance that could be smelt from a distance by animals and good trackers alike.

Dirt was more effective than soap out in the wild to mask smells.

A third man was searching the area for tracks, sometimes on his knees searching the ground and then standing up looking towards the trees, disappearing from the warm glow of the fading firelight and then reappearing as he started a new search. This was a monster of a man, maybe 6'7 or 6'8 tall and almost as wide. He also was heavily bearded. He was dressed just like the others, animal skin clothing, animal skin hat and fur boots. The hunter was looking for him, in the trees and in the grass for any tracks he might have left. He hadn't left any. The man was getting frustrated and started kicking out at anything that was lying about.

The monster stopped in front of Ella and raised his huge hand and gently caressed the side of her face. His hand appeared to be twice the size of her head. Red Flame certainly did not want to get into a scrap with this man, at least not while the other two were there.

"Where did the Redskin go?" The big man asked Ella in a deep southern drawl.

"He left last night." She replied.

"Liar." The man said as he smacked her around the side of the head. Red Flame flinched with the ferocity of the man's slap. He thought she would be unconscious. She wasn't, but was dazed and blood was pouring from her mouth.

"Are you going to lie to me again?" Asked the man monster, "because I wouldn't."

"He went just after sunset, back to his village." She mumbled through the blood in her mouth. The man shook his head. He paused and then he punched her right in the face. If the tall thin man hadn't been holding her she would have gone flying into the surrounding bushes.

"Liar, your lying to me. Where is he?" The man yelled.

This time Ella couldn't answer, she was unconscious. Streaky, the tall thin man let her drop to the ground. She collapsed like a straw doll.

The big man turned to Martha who was now sobbing loudly, she was petrified, gasping for breath.

"Where is the Redskin? I'll ask just once more."

"He's............he's gone."

He moved to within six inches of Martha's face, staring into her eyes. Intimidating.

"I know he's gone. But w-h-e-r-e has he gone?" He growled.

She stood trembling, he was looking right at her, she was looking down at the ground.

"I don't know."

The monster stared at her for what seemed like minutes. Red Flame was cursing himself for not having his rifle with him, the bow and arrow was slow to reload, too slow to take on three armed men. He quickly decided that if the monster was to strike Martha, the man holding her with the knife would probably let her drop, if he didn't the knife would still be at Martha's throat so then he couldn't take the risk of firing, but, if the trader did let her go, he would fire one arrow to take out the big man and then decide the best plan as to how to deal with the other two later. He slowly stood up balancing on two hefty boughs, one foot on each side of the main trunk, his back supported by another bough, he adjusted his stance ready for the shot. The monsters bearded face was still only inches from Martha's face.

"You lying bitch," the monster said, "you dare to lie to me."

He slapped Martha so hard the noise echoed throughout the trees, she slumped forward out cold, the other man released her, she dropped to the grass. Immediately Red Flames arrow flew into the monster's neck with a thud. The man slumped to his knees and then flat onto his face. Red Flame readjusted his footing to reload his bow, he lost sight of the melee that was happening below him around the fire. The whole area went dark as one of the men kicked dirt on to the fire killing the flames. Suddenly bullets were flying everywhere, into the trunk of the tree above his head and below his feet, the branches, the leaves so much noise he daren't look to see what was happening, the two trappers had figured out where he was hiding by the angle that the arrow had hit their hunting partner and they were just firing in the general direction but he knew they could get lucky. Then silence again.

He waited and listened. Still silence. He slowly peered around the tree trunk, nothing, just enough light to see the monster's body still lying on the ground, the two men and the girls were gone, they had disappeared. Were the remaining trappers just waiting for him to appear or had they taken off somewhere. He waited, straining to hear the slightest movement below. Nothing.

He waited maybe three minutes, still nothing. He removed his quiver with twelve arrows left in it and under armed threw it about twenty feet away to his right. The quiver landed amongst some bushes, not overly loud but enough for a good tracker to hear and locate where the noise had come from. He paused again. No rifles were fired, no sudden movement of men rushing through the undergrowth to get to where the noise was. Nothing. He positioned his bow over his shoulder and very slowly climbed down from the tree, stopping every few feet, his heart was pounding and the sweat was dripping down his face. He finally reached the ground but standing behind the tree, the opposite side to where the fire was still barely smoldering, he realized that the two men would probably be somewhere on the other side of the fire unable to see him until he approached the remaining embers. He slowly walked in the opposite direction to the fire still trying to remain hidden by the tree trunk and after taking twenty steps he turned east and moved around in a circular pattern that would eventually bring him around behind the fire and with any luck behind where the two fur traders were still hiding. He knelt on one knee, listening again and slowly scanning the trees and undergrowth against the diminishing light of the fire for anything that didn't look as though it should be there. He waited. He watched. Nothing, for about an hour he didn't move. Eventually he stood up, he had to accept the fact that they had got away and he had wasted valuable time because he was scared of rushing. He walked straight to where the monster had hit the ground, he knew he was dead by the size of the blood puddle that over the time he had wasted had now become a pool. Turning the lump of a man onto his back he relieved the body of a huge knife and a hand gun, it was fully loaded. He stuck it in his belt. He threw what was left of their water on to the fire. Everything went totally black. He couldn't see anything or anybody which meant they couldn't see him either, and that suited him fine.

Slowly he found his way back through the bushes to retrieve his quiver and then onwards to where he had left Laggon, his mind turning over and over trying to come up with a plan to get the girls back, but these were not your average cavalrymen or white settlers, these men were part animal, not only could they hunt like an animal they had no compunction in killing like an animal.

If he could separate them he knew he would win in a one on one hand fight but the two together would be too strong for him, also if he did get one, the other would probably kill the girls just out of spite.

What if he allowed them to catch him, no, that wouldn't work, they just might kill him straight away, no questions asked and they would still have the girls.

He decided it was too dark to attempt tracking them now, he would be better to have a rest and start at first light.

As the sun was rising he was scouring the nights campsite, he quickly found some footprints, two sets only, so each man had carried one of the girls which helped him as it made the prints deeper, also it showed that they left the site immediately, there were no signs of them hiding or planning to ambush him, they weren't going to hang around. They wanted the girls and with Red Flame killing the monster it meant they both got a larger share of the spoils, no love lost there then. He probably ruled them with a heavy hand anyway.

He followed their footprints northwards for two hundred yards which led to where they had tied up three horses to a tree, the horses were gone and it looked as though one of the girls was either riding or thrown over the saddle of the third horse which must have been the monsters, the hoof prints were a lot lighter. One man had the other sister on his horse with him, his was the heaviest, the other trader was on his own. They had not taken the girls horses which surprised him, they had left in a real hurry. They would normally sell them to other traders.

They were still heading North probably back to their own camp where Libby must be alone with the other two horses and their cache of furs.

Again, his mind was working twenty-four to the dozen, would they set an ambush for him knowing he could track them or would they proceed to their camp and head off quickly hoping he wouldn't catch up with them? He couldn't remember having to go up against a more cunning enemy, he had always been good at coordinating a plan but now he was disputing himself. How had he dozed off in that tree, he had already thought it a possibility the traders would be out hunting and just might come across them, that was why he was in the tree, but to fall asleep, he couldn't believe he'd been so stupid.

He just hoped the girls were Ok.

He followed their tracks for over a mile until he came upon their camp which was now deserted and looked as though they had hurriedly packed up and left leaving a lot of old clothing and cooking utensils strewn over a wide diameter around a still burning fire pit. The trader's tracks were now easier to follow as the men were pulling two travois laden with furs and causing deep ruts in the trail. They must realize that it would be easy for him to follow or was this just a ploy leading him into an ambush. He painstakingly kept crossing from one side of the trail to the other and into the woods so as not to become predictable if he was being watched.

For eight hours he followed their clear trail, it was almost as though they must have immediately broken their camp on returning with the girls last night and headed straight off heading north, but it was obvious to him that they knew he would eventually catch up with them, so what were they planning?

It was as though they were making it as easy as possible for him to follow them.

He dismounted and led Laggon off the trail and into some large bushes and trees on a small hill, they walked together to the highest point where he climbed to the top of a high Birch tree to give himself a better view of the surrounding landscape and see if there was any sign of movement along the winding trail, nothing moved. He scanned for several minutes and then retreated back to the ground. Mounting Laggon he galloped to the furthest point he had seen from the tree, the tracks were still plainly visible from several yards away, still travelling as a group and so no one had dropped back to intercept him, which he thought had also been a strong possibility. He rode on for one hour then two, slowly staying in the trees but able to clearly see the tracks, no sign of any deviation. For two more exhausting hours he moved forward, his eyes were stinging from straining them and his head was pounding, the concentration was getting to him, he was having to blink more to focus, then suddenly the tracks disappeared off the trail. He stopped, his eyes peeled, straining to listen for the slightest give away sound. He dismounted slowly, so as not to disturb Laggon, he reached for his rifle and took it from its sheath and eased the pony back into the cover of the undergrowth.

He slowly knelt down and looked for the tracks, where were they? Considering how easy the trail had been to follow for all these miles, how could that many riders just vanish. Which direction had they taken after leaving the trail. His mouth was dry, exceptionally dry as he tried to find that little bit of moisture buried somewhere in his mouth. He gulped. Crouching down he ran to the other side of the trail, he surveyed the ground around him, nothing seemed out of place. Had they used an old Indian ploy of sweeping the ground with a branch or even to drag one behind the last rider masking any of their tracks? He looked up from the ground to see if there were any broken branches or snapped twigs or even flattened grass. Nothing looked disturbed. He crossed back to where Laggon was grazing and conducted another search. Again nothing.

He then walked thirty yards further into the trees, moving slowly and cautiously in case one or both of the traders were lying in wait, then he turned west and walked back to the trail in a thirty-yard diameter half circle, there was nothing out of the ordinary. He turned back and retraced his steps but continued in the same thirty-yard diameter half circle back to the trail. Nothing. He slowly strolled back down the trail to where Laggon was, turned again into the woods but walked sixty yards in and repeated the walk back to the trail and then retraced his footsteps until he reappeared on the trail. Two hours he had spent looking for the missing tracks. No sign of any tracks what so ever. Did he try again moving ninety yards into the woods this time or did he cross to the other side of the trail and repeat at thirty yards. He paused momentarily thinking. He crossed to the other side of the trail and repeated the whole procedure again. Still nothing. When he got back to Laggon he was in two minds to continue the search or just continue on the trail. Think he thought to himself, five horses with two travois would measure maybe thirty yards so another forty yards on horseback would only take three or four minutes, maybe he just hadn't gone far enough into the trees. He decided to walk one hundred and twenty yards this time before repeating the circular walk back to the trail, another two hours lost by the time he had retraced his steps but he continued on to rejoin the trail as before. He was now losing heart, but then out of the corner of his eye he spotted a newly broken branch, only a small one but about seven feet off the ground, about shoulder height for an average mounted person, he looked back to gauge where Laggon was and then turned back to face the damaged branch. He very slowly walked past it a couple of feet and looked straight ahead, nothing, he took another two paces and there, same sort of height from the ground was another dangling small broken branch. He walked slowly to it, again this was very new, just hours old, he walked past it still looking ahead, then he looked down, six inches of a travois rut stood out like a sore thumb, the branch they had used to cover their tracks had missed it. He breathed excitedly, at last he was on to something. He picked up his pace in excitement and strode forward, there a few yards ahead was another broken branch, another few yards and there was a full hoof print. They had got careless. It had been just a matter of time until they felt encouraged enough to discard the big branch they had used to sweep away their prints. He marched on, more evidence almost every few yards and then right in front of him laying across the narrow track was the actual branch the hunters had used for sweeping. All their tracks appeared again and, just like before, they were easy to follow.

He ran back through the trees and undergrowth to where Laggon was waiting and led him back to where the prints had started again, he mounted and followed them and he would until the light faded, that would give him about an hour until sunset.

Sunset came and went, he was so excited about finding the tracks that he just wanted to keep going, he was now walking and leading Laggon by the reins, he knew the Traders would not be expecting him to track them in the darkness because they were aware of the Indians fear of night fighting. He should see their camp fire long before they saw him. Or so he hoped.

Onward he moved stopping periodically to check there were still the same number of horses on the move, that one man hadn't stopped to ambush him while he was concentrating on the tracks, it had happened to him before, but luckily for him that man had been a lousy shot.

It was almost dark, the moon was moving behind the clouds, the light was beginning to fade fast so he moved into the trees but parallel to the trail, this he thought would be about the time the traders would be setting up their camp for the night so he was constantly viewing the tree line for any telltale smoke trails, Laggon walked slowly between the trees enabling him to swivel constantly looking in all directions for anything that might just give him an advantage.

Fifteen minutes later he stopped dead. There, in the distance about three hundred yards ahead of him and further into the forest he caught a slight orange glow reflecting off a silver birch tree, he slid off Laggon and pulled his rifle from its sheath, crouching down he made his way closer towards what he thought was a fire. Perhaps it was the last of the sun going down, no it was too late for that it had to be a fire, moving further into the dense forest he could plainly see a flickering fire, no sound yet. He stopped again and kneeling down he waited, no noise at all. He moved on, his eyes fixed firmly on the now obvious flames illuminating quite a large area, no other movement to be seen or heard. He was now only fifty yards from the fire, there were three what looked like handmade tents made from various animal furs and skins pitched in a semi-circle each with the door opening towards the fire, always a good idea as it keeps the wild animals from entering while you sleep. He was rushing, he needed to slow down. All their horses, he could see five, were tied to a line just to one side of the largest tent, he moved slightly to his left so he could get a better view of the darker side of the camp. There were several trees together and between two of them a naked lady was tied by the wrists in the standing position, her head was slumped forward and knees slightly bent as though she was sleeping or unconscious. Could this be Libby? Something closer to him caught the fire light again, it was another naked body, another lady also tied in the same manner between two trees, she was blonde, it was Martha. It was Martha! He stood up in shock, his blood boiling he stepped forward and then something hard hit him on the side of his head. It was a rifle barrel.

"Don't move Redskin, or I'll blow your bloody head off." It was Streaky, the tall trader he had seen the night before.

Red Flame didn't move. He could smell this man, why hadn't he noticed it earlier? All his experience meant nothing, he had moved way too quickly. Probably desperation.

"Drop your rifle." The trader said gruffly.

He let his rifle go. The man's own rifle was still pressed hard against his temple.

"Walk towards the fire. Don't try anything or I'll put a bullet in you."

The man moved the rifle from his head and pushed him hard in the back with it.

"Keep your hands up where I can see 'em. Go. Hey Shamus," He shouted loudly, "look what I caught me. Shamus, look at this. A Redskin."

As soon as they got into the camp he was able to see that Shamus wouldn't be interested at this particular moment in a Red Indian, he had a naked lady spread eagled face down over one of the travois which was piled with animal skins and he was shagging her loudly, his hands were forcing her shoulders down and he was looking to the sky in satisfaction, the lady was crying and then it hit him, it was Ella. If he could he would have plunged a knife straight in Shamus's heart. Red Flame felt his muscles scream with anger.

The man behind him with the rifle pushed him in the middle of his back.

"Keep moving," he pushed Red Flame a second time, "Shamus," he shouted again, "what do you want me to do with this?" Red Flame realized Streaky was referring to him.

Shamus just glanced over, totally disinterested.

"Just scalp the Indian." Shamus replied but not sounding concerned, he had obviously been at the whisky bottle for a while. He continued shagging Ella and getting ever more vocal.

"Shamus," shouted Streaky, "I think we have a 'wanted' poster for this one, I think we should just check first, if we haven't then I'll just take his scalp. Ok?" Shamus didn't answer.

Ella moved her head to glance over and saw him standing there in the fires glow. She had given up on any hope of getting out of this.

"Get down on your knees and put your hands behind your head and don't move." Said Streaky. Red Flame dropped to his knees and raised his arms. He listened. He tried to eliminate the rantings of Shamus and concentrate on the sounds from behind him, he heard a saddle bag being opened, a rustle, the sound that papers make when held, the saddle bag being closed and the trader walking back towards him. The man walked around Red Flame to get closer to the fire so that he could read the bundle of 'Wanted' posters. Streaky was having trouble sorting them out whilst holding his rifle in a usable covering position, posters in left hand but using his right hand to sort them and hold the rifle. He looked at about twelve different posters and the pictures of the wanted men until he suddenly grinned, the fire light glinted off his front teeth, he bent down slightly to take a second and closer look at Red Flame's face.

"A thousand bucks, this Redskin is Red Flame. He must be pretty mean to have a thousand dollars reward and we got him. Alive he's worth a thousand bucks."

At that very second, Shamus, who had not heard a word of what Streaky was saying, withdrew his penis, stood up and as naked as the day he was born started to beat his chest like a gorilla.

"Shit, yeah." He screamed out. It made Red Flame jump.

The sudden outburst caught Streaky unaware too and he turned to see why Shamus was so excited, the sex or the reward. As soon as he looked away Red Flame reached up and punched him in the balls, Streaky bent forward in agony, his mouth dropped open, Red Flame grabbed the rifle from the trader and immediately forced the barrel into the man's mouth and pulled the trigger. The back of Streaky's head flew into the sky. Red Flame stood up shaking with temper, rifle in hand still watching Shamus finishing his gorilla impersonation.

Shamus stopped rigid, swaying slightly and very drunk, not sure what to do next, he was too far from his tent and a rifle to do much in the way of retaliation, he froze. Red Flame walked with Streaky's rifle towards him, bending as he walked he picked up Streaky's hunting knife and continued towards Shamus who knew from Red Flames expression that something gruesome was about to happen to him, his facial expression had completely changed from ecstasy to terror in seconds.

Shamus stood naked before him with his hands in the air, Red Flame, with the huge hunting knife in his right hand swung the blade and cut the traders penis off, it dropped to the ground with what seemed a loud ' plop,' he suddenly thought of something his father had said, 'he who lives by the sword, dies by the sword,' he smiled to himself, in this instance it was a case of 'who lived by the penis, died by the penis', Shamus looked down, his eyes wide in horror, then he slumped down onto his knees, picking up and studying his detached penis there in his hands. Red Flame gave him several seconds to focus on what he was looking at and then swung the knife again slicing Shamus's throat. He then kicked him in the chest so he fell backwards to the ground. He paused, then stamped on Shamus's stomach, just to make sure there was no life left in the body.

He stood looking at the two blood-soaked bodies, blood thirsty it was but bloodthirsty it had to be.

Bastards he thought to himself. He resisted the temptation to kick them both again just to make sure they were well and truly dead. No sympathy, no remorse. Just pure hatred.

He moved over to Martha and cut her bonds so she would be able to sit on the ground, he gently lowered her down, her wrists were white because of the lack of blood, he quickly massaged each wrist to get the feeling and blood back into them and then he went to Libby and did the same thing, both girls looked shocked and dehydrated, he got them both some water.

He then went to Ella, she was still lying face down on the bed of mixed furs, still shaking and crying, he was apprehensive of touching her, perhaps it was too soon, compassion came hard to him, she looked at him, sat up and then threw her arms around his neck, he hugged her tightly. They sat motionless, both with tears running down their faces, wrapped together as one.

He didn't know these men but he hated them, really hated them. Once he had got the three sisters safely out of sight in a tent resting, he would search through the trader's food store and find something sweet and then spread it on the trader's bodies and move them into the trees, there he would leave them for the animals. Waste not, want not. No compassion what so ever.

He quickly got a coffee pot on and gave the girls a mug each and then he left them to sleep. They didn't want to talk anyway.

That night he dismantled the traders camp except for the tent the girls were in and burned what was not wanted on the fire. He tried to remove as many of the bad memories they would have when they got up the next morning.

Early the next morning, he made up the fire and got the coffee pot on again, he had found some edible foodstuffs in the trader's pantry store and had begun preparing it before the girl's appeared. He really wanted them to start moving to a new camp as soon as possible, he felt the sisters needed to get away from the shocking memories that this place provoked for all of them.

He was on his third mug of coffee when Martha emerged from one of the tents, her face was still drawn but she had found some of her old clothes, not quite the immaculate Martha he remembered from just two days ago, but that would come. She smiled at him and walked over to the log he was sitting on and gently stroked his head, just once.

"Once again I have to thank you for saving not only me but my sisters too." She said quietly.

"Well it was the least I could do." They both smiled.

"Thank you, well …. you know what I mean to say."

"There is no need to thank me, I got you into this mess and I'm sorry."

"No, on the contrary, we led you into this."

He just smiled at her again as he poured her a coffee.

"Hey, what about mine," called out Ella as she appeared briskly walking towards them, "hi sis," she said looking at Martha, "how are you?"

"Better after a good night's sleep, and you?"

"I feel better too," she paused momentarily, "Red Flame, I want to thank you for what you did last night or what I can remember of it."

"No need, I have been thanked already. But thanks." He replied. They smiled at each other while he poured her a coffee, neither wanting to say any more in case of what memories might suddenly return.

"It's a beautiful morning, ideal to find a new camp, to get away from here." He said slowly. Suddenly Martha burst into tears, struggling to get her breath. He and Ella jumped up to console her, they both knelt down either side of her, telling her that everything was going to be ok now, they will get out of this place as soon as Libby was up and about. Just then Libby appeared walking toward them, her hair looked dank and she appeared to be about twenty years older than her sisters, she was the elder sister, her mistreatment had certainly taken its toll on her, she stopped dead when she spotted Red Flame sitting with her sisters.

"Oh my God." She yelled. The look she was giving Red Flame was not one of admiration, it was a look of total fear and hatred, panic just spread across her face. She started to scream, stamping her feet and shaking, Martha stopped crying and ran to her closely followed by Ella. He stood up and went over to Laggon and started

132

getting him ready to leave, he needed to get away from them for a few minutes. In the meantime, the two sisters had started to calm Libby down, she had obviously been to hell and back with the three traders, he thought it would take time and a lot of love to make up for what horrors she had endured.

He waited until Ella called him over to the girls who by now were sitting on the log talking, Martha and Ella were explaining to Libby how he had saved them before and he was not as frightening as he appeared, slowly Libby started to laugh at some of the stories they told her about him and her mood lightened and soon she offered to shake his hand and thanked him for what he'd done for her sisters. Quite unexpectedly she stood up and wrapped her arms around him and squeezed him tightly, it was probably the first time for ages that she had been able to touch someone without being abused, he hesitantly put his arms around her, she was ok with that. She smelt awful, these animals that had held her for probably several weeks had not even allowed her to bathe. He wretched when he smelt her hair and body odor but he did not allow her to notice. They stood still in that position while Martha topped up their coffees. He was pleased when she backed away to take her mug and sit down. Libby smiled at him in an apologetic way. He smiled back and nodded to her just to reassure her. They all sat for a few minutes not saying a word but savoring the moment, the wind had dropped and the sun was beginning to heat up the earth, the trees were whispering quietly again and all seemed well. The sisters started talking about their adventures since arriving in America and how different the people and their ways were from their life in England, how everybody here carried guns and how frightening it could be. He let them relax, talking and sometimes laughing for over an hour, he kept their coffee mugs topped up and generally just listened.

"I hate to break up the party but I think we should make a move soon, there is a small lake not far from here and I suggest we find it and set up a camp for the rest of the day and tonight, we can all bathe and have a good meal and tomorrow start our journey to St. Augustine, if that is where you still want to go?" He asked. The girls looked at each other and nodded.

"Yes, I think we are agreed on that. We can then decide where we intend to end up." Said Ella. The other two agreed. He stood looking at them.

"I have to leave you for a few moments, but I won't be long."

"No, no you can't leave." Said Martha dramatically and standing to face him.

"No, you can't just go Red Flame." Reiterated Ella quickly.
Libby didn't seem to mind but he wasn't sure she was catching everything that was being said. He pointed to the hills that towered above the surrounding trees.

"I'm just going to that hill and then I am coming straight back. I promise."

"No, you can't." Said Martha beginning to get visually upset.
He walked back towards her and placed his hands on her shoulders.

"By the time you have got everything together that you need for this journey I will be back," he looked towards Ella for some support, "I will be back in a few minutes. No more than ten."
Ella stood up and put placed a comforting arm around Martha.

"He will be just minutes. Let's get our stuff together so we will be ready to leave when he gets back." Martha slowly nodded.

"Ok. It will be nice to get away from here." Libby said.

"Ten minutes." Ella said looking directly at him. It sounded like a threat.

"Ten minutes, that's all." He said as he strode to Laggon and mounted up.

He sped off in the direction of the hills and disappeared into the trees, within minutes he was visible to the girls and as he looked back he could see them all standing looking up towards him. He waved and continued until he reached the top. Because he had tracked them during the night he had lost his bearings and so as soon as he saw the lake in the distance he turned back towards the camp now knowing what direction to take. The girls were still standing in the same positions as they were when he left them watching and obviously waiting for his return. He waved to them again on the descent before he disappeared behind the trees. Three minutes later he was entering the camp. They were all still standing like statues.

"Have you gathered all your things together?" He asked sarcastically.

"Some," said Ella, "but not all." With a huge grin on her face.

"We won't take a minute." Added Martha. Now looking more like her old bubbly self, he thought.

"Libby, don't let these rascals slow you down." He said playfully. For the first time she grinned.

"They always have." She said. All four of them started to laugh, a laugh that seemed to go on longer than it should have done. They were all relaxed with each other which meant all was well, for the time being anyway.

Each of the girls disappeared into the tent gathering their own things while he built up the fire so it really was blazing, he then took a fur skin off one of the travois and started to send some smoke signals to the Choctaw braves that he knew were somewhere close by to let them know that there were furs and rifles as well as other items that would be useful to them.

He packed up the coffee pot and one cooking pan plus all the coffee he could find plus a few other light utensils they would need on the journey. It was only a matter of minutes before he saw that the Choctaws had received his message and were responding with thanks. The war party would wait for them to leave before they came to the camp.

Martha was the first to appear carrying a small bundle of things, then Libby with a very small bundle, the traders must have robbed her of anything worth having and then Ella with a slightly larger bundle. They all made their way to their respective horses and after securing their things, mounted up and watched him as he pulled down the remaining tent and threw it and everything else that wasn't of any use to the incoming war party on to the fire, that included all of the trader's possessions and anything that he felt Libby would be pleased to see go. He looked at her as he strode to Laggon, she had a slight grin on her face but tears were running down her cheeks.

"That small part of your life is now gone. It's over, it is fading into the sky with the smoke." He said quietly to Libby so only she could hear. He mounted Laggon.

"I would never have thought of it like that," she said, "thank you. You are right."

"What are you two talking about?" Called out Ella.

"Mind your own business." He yelled back. Libby burst out laughing and when her sisters saw that, they all started to laugh again.

"Let's go." He said as he led them out in a single file away from that awful haunting place.

For two hours they slowly wandered through the woods, not much was said except for him turning to each sister in turn periodically to ask if they were alright and did they want to stop for a drink, which was always declined. Each of them he thought were thinking of what had happened to them, and what might have been the outcome. He had been doing the same.

Almost an hour later they rode out from the trees onto a golden sandy beach that surrounded a small lake, huge beech trees all around made it feel very private, it was very picturesque. The girls all took a small intake of breath, he was heartened to see their reactions. He led them a further two hundred yards along the beach and then he stopped.

"Ok. I'm going to pitch camp here, so if you ladies want to go for a dip, now is your opportunity." In fifteen seconds the three were running down the beach towards the water shedding their clothes as they ran. There was a communal scream of delight as they hit the water and disappeared headlong into it.

He gathered up their horses and led them down to the water's edge, he turned back towards the trees and using Streaky's hunting knife started to gather branches and kindling for the fire. The girls were so busy laughing and screaming as they frolicked in the water for some time they didn't notice until they got out of the water that the fire was ablaze and they really didn't have anything to dry themselves with, so the fire was well appreciated as they sat around it completely naked on a couple of logs he'd found. He gave each of them a fur he had found back at the hunter's camp, he had guessed they would come in handy sometime. The coffee pot was on. He gathered up what clothing they had dropped on the beach and went down to the water's edge and quickly washed them. He then walked back to the fire and spread the wet clothes on branches near the fire or where the sun would speed up there drying. Each of the girls sat with just a fur wrapped around their shoulders. He tried not to stare. Just the odd glance as he rattled and sorted all the cooking paraphernalia out. He had managed to grab some of the trader's foodstuffs so he wouldn't need to go hunting for supper.

"How much are you charging us to do our washing?" Yelled Libby laughing.

"Are you going to iron them?" Shouted Martha. The three of them were giggling like kids.

"I didn't bring my Iron." Was his only retort. He remembered what 'Irons' were and what they were used for because his father always insisted on his white shirts being ironed before he left for his daily surgery. Since his murder his mother had never used one again.

"How do you know what an 'Iron' is?" Asked Libby seriously, "have you ever used one?"

"Yes. It's a long story." He replied and carried on getting organized. Immediately Martha and Ella started telling Libby, in whispered voices what they knew about his story. He didn't listen, it would be exaggerated, it always was. Once he got the pots filled and hung over the fire he disappeared into the woods with Streaky's hunting knife sorting out into piles the stronger bowes for building their accommodation and the smaller branches to keep the fire going and the wild animals away while they slept. Even in the woods he could hear the girl's laughter, they were reminiscing about their old school days and which of them had got better report cards, lots of yelling and haughty laughs. It was good that they could relax, he knew the Choctaw war party was close by and they would be watching out for any drifting strangers passing through their lands and would react accordingly.

After an hour or so he had two bivwacs made, one larger for the girls and a small one for himself, both entrances looked out onto the fire. He wished he'd kept a few more of the trader's furs to cover their make shift homes, if it did rain heavily they would all get wet, but none of them seemed worried about it. After all it was 84 degrees, very hot and no rain clouds in sight.

Later in the afternoon after he had prepared some food, he decided to go fishing, this immediately brought shouts of excitement

137

from the girls when they found out, who by now were getting fed up with just sitting around doing nothing. Their energy levels had returned.

"How many fishing rods have you got." Asked Libby.

"None."

"So how will we fish?" She responded.

"Indians don't use fishing rods, they are for you soft white people." He answered teasing her.

"What a cheek, I bet we can catch more than you." She replied laughing.

"Yeah, lots more." Piped up Ella.

"Twice as many." Martha added.

"That's a challenge then? "He said, "but it's not how many you catch it's the total weight of the catch. Agreed?"

"Yeah. Ok." The sisters replied in unison.

"There is some string and other bits over there," pointing to a couple of old saddle bags he had picked up when he left the traders camp, "help yourself and see what you can do." They eagerly ran to where the saddle bags were as if it was a race and started rummaging through them. Meanwhile he lay down on his back and closed his eyes listening to the constant chatter coming from where ever the girls were.

"Can you please be quieter, I'm trying to sleep." He asked good heartedly.

"We thought it was a competition, are you just waiting for us to catch the supper, you lazy thing." Joked Ella.

"Yeah," the other two responded, "you lazy so and so." They were bonding, he was now the common enemy.

"On the contrary, wake me when you have your first fish. Ok?"
After several minutes the girls were running excitedly towards the water, they had all dropped their furs on the beach and were wading in up to their midriffs and throwing bits of string with he didn't know what on the end into the water. He would be very surprised if they caught anything but that was not the point, it was for them to enjoy being together and forgetting the last bad experiences they had been through, particularly Libby. He dozed off listening to the trees swaying and the water slapping the beach.

Next thing he knew he was being soaked by Libby as she threw a bucket of cold water over him.

He rubbed his eyes and focused, the three of them were completely naked and in fits of laughter, they weren't wearing a stitch. It dawned on him that they obviously trusted him and didn't see him as any kind of threat, it was frustrating for him but it was worth it to see their inhibitions had gone for that day, and it probably would be for only that day.

"We can't catch anything." Said Martha disappointedly.

"There are no fish in that Lake," said Libby, "not even little ones."

"Of course, there are," he replied getting to his feet, "there are always fish in water, that is where they live."

"Don't be sarcastic." Said Libby.

"Well, if I catch one in this lake are you three going to cook it and serve it to me like I deserve?"

"Yes, we will, and we are so sure you won't catch any, we will sing and dance for you, we know you Indians like to dance." Now it was Libby that was being sarcastic.

He curled up his nose as though he was not too interested in that. He thought for a few seconds.

"Oh, alright," he purposely sounded bored, "on one condition."

"And what's that?" Asked Ella.

"The three of you do it dressed like that."

"But we are not............, I get it." Said Libby laughing.

"Yes, we will," said Martha, "he's not going to catch any fish anyway."

The three looked at each other and laughed. He suddenly felt uneasy, he should not have said that after what the girls had been through, his male hormones had shown through but luckily the girls had not taken it that way, they had taken it in the way he meant it, in fun.

"Ok, we will do it." Said Ella smugly.

"On one condition," added Libby, "if you don't catch a fish big enough for all of us, then you have to sing and dance for us, naked."

"I can't sing." He said seriously.

"That's alright, you can just dance." She added.

"Yeah, you will have to dance." Said Libby giggling and egging Ella on.

He felt good that Libby was as keen to join in the fun as her sisters after the last few weeks.

"You girls are just rude, you just want to see me naked."

"Yeah." They all shouted and then laughed between themselves hysterically.

"Well, you have had all day to see us in our birthday suits, so now it's our turn." Added Libby.

He shook his head.

"No, it will be the three of you doing the singing and dancing tonight, I'm going to catch a fish." He stood up and walked to Laggon and grabbed his quiver and bow and walked off towards the lake with the girls following and shouting in the background that he was cheating, and that he hadn't mentioned a bow and arrow, he stopped at the water's edge and looked back at them.

"I just said I was going fishing." He turned and walked into the cool water up to his midriff and then he stood absolutely still for maybe five or six minutes, the girls had now joined him waiting at the water's edge, watching patiently they waited silently, then suddenly he fired into the water, a sudden splash, he reached in and pulled out a three feet long flounder, despite losing their bet the sisters all cheered.

"This should feed us all." He said proudly holding the catch in the air.

The girls were jumping up and down clapping their hands, still absolutely naked, and as he turned back towards the beach, they ran into the water to greet him. Ella took the flounder from him, still with the arrow in it, she grabbed his quiver and bow from him while Martha and Libby despite him being wet, wrapped their arms around his waist and hugged him, he reciprocated. They all strolled back towards the fire as though they hadn't a care in the world.

While the girls sat naked by the fire chatting away, he gutted the flounder and prepared things for their supper which would take a couple of hours to cook. Whilst sitting around Libby asked a few questions about his past and although Ella and Martha answered, Libby was insistent that he was the one with the final word. They

140

joked about different things always keeping off the taboo subject which was Libby's incarceration by the Fur Traders, nobody wanted to go there. He marveled at the way the girls seemed to have got over their ordeal so quickly and hoped it wouldn't have any long-term effects on any of them, particularly Libby. The number of weeks she had been held prisoner by those three animals would have stretched anybody to the limit he thought.

Perhaps this new-found freedom they felt, being back together, and being away from the old campsite was why they didn't want to wear their clothes, it was their way of expressing their total freedom, from the dirt and squalor and the darkness of the old camp to the bright sunshine and the cleanliness of the beach here had really lifted their spirits. They obviously trusted him and didn't see him as a threat or sexual predator, which made him feel good.

They all enjoyed the freshly caught fish supper and as darkness descended, talk got around to their future plans, where would they like to live, what they would do to make money and finding someone and getting married. Sometimes he felt as though they were being too honest, saying things that he didn't expect ladies to speak about in front of a man, didn't they consider him a man, or was he now considered more like a brother? Either way it didn't bother him, he was laughing with them rather than at them. He did not like to mention their bet, although he wanted to.

The girls were very tired and soon headed to their tent, he sat on one of the logs after putting more wood on the fire, listening to them talking and giggling for a while, then it went silent.

After an hour he wandered down to the lake and filled a bucket of water and took it to Laggon, he sat down next to his old friend and told him his thoughts, his worries and concerns for the three sisters, and what he hoped their futures would hold for them. He sat thinking. The silence was deafening. He retreated to his small bivwac and lay down with his rifle by his side.

A short while later he heard a branch or twig break, somebody or something had trodden on it, he sat bolt upright and reached for his rifle, slowly and silently he peered out and there sitting on one of the logs was Libby, still naked but crying quietly to herself. The fire offered a warm glow, she was really very beautiful, just like her sisters. As he stepped out of his bivwac, the movement must have startled her, she looked up. The tears were rolling down her face.

"What's wrong Libby?" He asked as he sat down next to her. She paused for a while.

"It's nothing, it's just me," she paused again, "I just …..I can't stop thinking about…… things. The awful things that they did. The way they took turns with me."
He let her continue without saying anything, she had to get it all out. He remained silent.

"They did awful things Red Flame, awful. Sometimes two of them would………., sometimes they made me do things………. they weren't human, they couldn't have been to do such terrible things to another human being." She wiped away the tears with the back of her hands quickly. This was the first time he had heard her mention the traders. He didn't know what to say. He had never been in a position like this. Then he remembered something his ma had said to him when he was young.

"I'll tell you what," he said slowly, "I will buy these evil thoughts from you."

"Buy them?" She said sounding intrigued.

"Yes, it is an old Indian custom. You have to give me all your worries and concerns and I will pay you for them, and for as long as I own them you cannot worry or concern yourself with them ever again."

"Really?" She said looking very amused.

"I don't have money, but, I will give you any of my possessions to take your worries from you. Whatever you want. My most valuable item is my pure white Appaloosa, who I love. I also have several good rifles, a bow and arrows, a spear, a war shield that was especially painted for me, my bravery feathers, a bandolier and that's about it."

"You would give me Laggon? But he's your best friend, you love him."

"I know, but I want your worries and concerns."

"But why?"

"So, you don't have them. What do I need to give you to get them?"

"Nothing."

"Oh yes I do, it won't work if I don't pay you for them. We have to do a short ceremony too."

"Can I decide in the morning?" She asked.

"Of course, you can. Now tell me, when do you want us to leave here?"

"Not yet, not tomorrow," she suddenly was getting upset again, "I don't want to go yet, I love it here. Please don't say we have to leave." He put his hands up as though apologizing.

"No, no, we don't have to leave. We can stay here for as long as you want. Ok?"

She let out a long breath.

"Thank you." She said. A big smile replaced the tears.

She moved closer to him and placed her head on his shoulder, he put his arm around her and held her to him. After a while she fell asleep, and as she slept he carried her into his bivwac and laid her down. He slept outside by the fire.

Early the next morning he decided to have a swim and bathe in the lake before the girls got up, he led Laggon into the water and playfully splashed him. Laggon loved water and was enjoying doing his own thing.

Red Flame took off his breechcloth and washed it and then threw it onto the beach. He then swam for a few minutes parallel to the shore and then back to where Laggon was and began to walk back out onto the beach to gather his breechcloth, it had gone, disappeared. He walked further up the beach, searching, nothing. Where had he left it? He looked towards their encampment, no sign. Then suddenly from out of the trees ran the three sisters still all naked whooping and hollering. Ella was swinging his breechcloth around her head, they were laughing so much they had to stop running and get their breath. He stood absolutely stark naked looking at them as they made funny and rude comments about his manhood and the size of it. Nothing he could do about it, he grinned to himself, he had been watching them for 24 hours, now it was their turn, as they had said the day before. He was a little embarrassed, but that soon passed. It felt so natural, as nature intended, why fight it. He put his nose in the air and walked straight passed them towards the fire, they laughed and ridiculed him but it was all in fun. Libby was really enjoying herself. They ran past him to get to the fire first and one of them had the audacity to smack his bum, he didn't know which one.

He sat down by the fire until the girls eventually calmed down and then they discussed the issue of when to leave the encampment, it was agreed by all that there was no rush and they would just wait until it felt right, he would hunt for more food and do what was necessary to keep the camp working. He got the coffee pot going and started making some breakfast for them all, all without his breechcloth on. The girls were idly discussing somebody they knew from Boston and all seemed well with the world.

Later they all took a walk along the beach picking up odd looking stones and bits of wood that looked as though they had laid there for hundreds of years, having a swim and walking more, it was an idyllic place to relax.

By the time they returned to their encampment they were getting hungry again so Ella and Libby started to made up some soup with some acorns that he had got for them earlier in one of the big pots, while he took his bow and quiver and went off on his own to catch something to add to their soup, or for later, he didn't know what, he would have to wait and see.

An hour later he returned with a small deer, this would last them for several meals. Naturally the girl's ooh'd and aah'd when they saw the young deer but they had to eat something, there could be no sympathy when food was involved. He prepared it ready for a few different meals and the girls took what they wanted for their soup.

The sun was beaming down, it was around 85 degrees and between swimming and drinking coffee and idle chit chat the day flew past, and it wasn't long until supper was being eaten around the fire watching the sun set over the lake. It was a magical time he thought.

Libby had not mentioned his offer of buying her worries and concerns so he had remained silent about it too. He slept well that night.

Most of the next day was much like the day before, except on their walk along the beach Libby approached him quietly and asked if he meant what he had said about buying her worries.

"Of course," he replied, "are you still having a hard time with the bad thoughts?"

"Yes, only at night." She replied thoughtfully.

"So, will you let me buy them from you?"

"Yes," she said abruptly, "if it's still Ok with you."

"Definitely, I wouldn't have suggested it if it wasn't, what do you want for them."

"Your war shield. Because it was especially made for you, you said, and when I look at it, it will always remind me of you."

"Do you really want to be reminded of me?" He asked sounding surprised but smiling.

"Yes, I do."

"Alright, it's a deal. We can do the ceremony when it gets dark, after supper." He was just thankful she hadn't asked for Laggon, that would have been awkward.

"Good," she then turned and ran towards the water, "swim time." She yelled and the other two ran after her and they were soon splashing each other and having a good time. He sat down and watched. It was so hot they didn't need a towel to dry off when they'd had their fun, they just lay on the beach and threw small pebbles at him but when he started throwing some back they all three jumped on him and jokingly wrestled with him and held him down until he playfully surrendered.

They walked slowly back to their encampment, the fire needed yet more wood and coffee was demanded by all. They sat for another hour just chatting about their plans again and it was decided that it felt right to leave the camp and make their way to St. Augustine. It was decided to leave early the next morning.

CHAPTER 10

As the sun rose they were already on the trail all talking to each other, but only a mile from their camp as they were approaching a bend in the trail Libby's eyes suddenly opened wide in horror, he turned and looked ahead to see why, a man was lying on the trail, his horse standing a few feet away from him, it was an Indian pony so he guessed it was a Choctaw brave on the ground.

"Wait here, Ella get you rifle out. Just move into the trees there." He said as he pointed to a small opening, and then he rode towards the fallen brave. He grabbed his rifle from its sheath as he got closer. He stopped twenty feet from the warrior and dismounted, he scoured the surroundings, nothing moved. He moved closer to the body and kneeling down, still looking for any movement in the trees, he felt for the man's pulse. He had been scalped, but no other visible sign of a wound, he rolled the warrior over, he had been shot in the back. He recognized the brave as one of the war party, but why was he out here on his own? He stood up and walked around, there were two sets of horse prints nearby, two men on horseback but only one man had dismounted and done the scalping, and all to earn a 20-dollar bounty he thought, a coward's way. Whoever it was that had murdered the young brave had also taken his rifle and knife.

He carried the body into the trees and covered it with soil and branches, he slapped the horse's rump and it took off, with any luck it would find its way back to the Choctaw.

As he got closer to the girls he could see fear had returned to their eyes, particularly Libby and Martha. They were still staring at where the body had laid, what they were expecting to see he didn't know.

"Can we go back to our beach?" Asked Libby beginning to well up, "I want to go back."

"Yes, can we, just for a few more days?" Said Martha.

He didn't know what to say, how to answer, he wasn't used to making decisions for others, he'd been a loner really since his father's murder. He looked towards Ella for some hint of guidance.

146

She was looking straight at him probably for the same reason. After a few seconds of silence, he shrugged.

"We can I suppose, but this is a wild country, there are many bad men of all colors out here, we could wait another week at the Lake or even six weeks, but this could just as easily happen again. I think we need to carry on, we need to get you to safety as soon as possible, my tribal camp is a good day's ride from here, I suggest we try to keep off the main trail and get there as soon as possible. What do you think? I will go with the majority."

"I agree with Red Flame," said Ella, "the sooner we get to civilization the better."

Martha nodded. They all turned to Libby. She was struggling to agree but after a few seconds of what looked like deep concentration, she finally nodded.

"Ok, let's go."

He turned and headed off at a fairly fast gallop, they all got up to speed and Ella rode up to be alongside him. She mouthed 'Thank you' to him, 'Thank you' he mouthed back. There was no point in talking at the speed they were travelling. For two hours they rode almost flat out, they didn't see anybody else which pleased him until in the distance he saw a man sitting astride his horse across the trail, as though he was intentionally blocking it. As they got closer, he could see the man was dressed like a Fur Trader, identical to the three men that had done so much harm to the three sisters. The man looked filthy, but no signs of furs or anything or anybody else. He scanned the trees around the man, nothing. He slowed down to a walking pace, the girls did exactly the same. The man was about one hundred yards ahead sitting perfectly still, he glanced at Ella, fear written across her face again, he could only imagine what the other two were feeling.

"Libby, Martha its Ok, don't worry. You too Ella, stay close to me but behind me, just you watch the trees on both sides if you can, any movement, and I mean any, you shout, ok?"

"Ok." Said Ella

Slowly he withdrew his rifle from it sheath with his right hand so it lay on his knee pointing towards the ground.

"Howdy," said the stranger, "wow. You don't see many pretty ladies like those out here. Where are you all heading?"

The man had his hand on his revolver on the other side of his body, Red Flame couldn't see whether it was still in its holster or whether the man had it in his hand. He didn't dare take his eyes off the man's eyes, the eyes he believed would always give the game away.

"St. Augustine, and you, where are you headed?" Red Flame enquired.

"Nowhere really, I'm just looking to make a little cash, that's all." The man replied.

"How, bounties?"

"Yeah, I suppose." The man spat a stream of tobacco onto the ground.

"Indian scalps eh?"

"I suppose."

"You get one a couple of hours ago?"

"Yeah. I did matter of fact." The man was very confident in himself.

Red Flame knew straight away there were two of these men, one must be in the woods hiding, but watching them all with his rifle poised.

"Ella, walk behind me, take the reins of the others and go quickly into the trees, do it now." He said it quietly so only Ella heard. She responded immediately.

"So, where's your partner?" He asked the hunter.

"Partner?" The hunter said sounding surprised, "what partner? Hey, where are the Ladies going?" The man asked as the sisters slowly made their way into the trees.

Red Flame ignored the man's last question.

"The one that was with you when you scalped that young Choctaw brave back there."

"I don't have a partner."

"Liar."

"Did you just call me a liar?"

"There's nothing wrong with your hearing then? And yes, I called you a liar."

Suddenly the man's eyes dropped and his right shoulder moved, Red Flames rifle came up as he fired, the bullet hit the man in the chest. Expecting the partner to be hiding nearby, he then dived to the ground as several shots narrowly missed him, another man appeared off to his right running towards him from the tree line. He swung his rifle, aimed and fired, the man dropped to the ground with a hole in his forehead.

"Ella," he yelled," keep the girls in the trees, don't come out yet."

"Are you alright Red Flame?" Yelled Ella sounding concerned.

"Yes, I'm fine," he replied, "but don't come out yet." He got up off the ground and went to the first man and dragged him into the trees and then did the same to the second, he picked up any possessions of the men and hurled them into the trees.
Slowly he walked back to where the sisters had disappeared into the trees, he could see them standing looking out at him.

"Ok ladies, you can come out now." He called out.
First Ella came through the tree line smiling, followed by Martha, there was a pause and just as he was about to move into the trees Libby appeared. She stared at him without saying a word, her eyes didn't move from his. He smiled at her almost nervously.

"Are you alright?" He asked. Libby rode past him stern faced and did not say a word, she stopped when she got to the others. Martha and Ella were looking at him waiting for him to mount up, but Libby was looking into the trees for any sign of the trader that had stopped them.

"We better get going," he said as he turned to lead them off, "it's a couple more hours until we should stop."

"You just killed that man." Libby said abruptly ignoring his comment.

"I did," he replied, "don't you think I should have?"

"No, definitely not."

"But....."

"There is no excuse for killing somebody."
He looked at the other sisters hoping for either one of them to join in the conversation to somehow justify his actions, it didn't happen.

"I killed them, there were two by the way, because if I hadn't they would have probably killed us all." He was annoyed at such an implication.

"Probably you say, but you don't know that do you?" Replied Libby argumentatively.

149

"I do. He was drawing his gun on me when I shot him."

"Where's his gun, I can't see it, it's not on the ground." She was insistent and argumentative.

"I threw their guns into the trees because I didn't want you to see them."

"Well, that was convenient." She replied staring impudently.

He slowly turned and looked at Ella, she was just staring at him, he looked at Martha who had her head bowed.

"Are either of you going to join in with this conversation?" No reply from either.

"Right! Let's go." He took off at a gallop, he knew the others were following. He didn't once look back to see where they were. They rode, fast for over an hour, his blood was boiling, what's wrong with these people he asked himself. Damn do-gooders. Maybe they had witnessed too much killing too soon. Suddenly one of the girls called out his name in a panic, he turned to see which one, Martha was pointing to the right, he spun around to see what it was. There was a group of Indians, maybe a dozen closing in on them rapidly, he could not yet make out which tribe they were from yet. They were approaching from an angle of about 45 degrees, it was no good trying to outrun them, they had the momentum, they would catch up in minutes and likewise if they tried to disappear into the tree. He had no option but to stop and face them.

"Stand still," he yelled out to the girls, "do not touch your rifles, I repeat, do not touch your rifles and say nothing," the war party was now just sixty yards away, they were not looking as if they were going to attack in fact none of them had weapons of any sort in their hands.

"Red Flame do something." Yelled Libby.

"Keep calm Libby, stay still." He replied.

"Oh my God, oh my God." She started crying hysterically.

"It's ok Libby, its ok. Stay calm everybody."

He looked towards the advancing Indians as they were slowing down to engage.

"Red Flame." The War chief asked.

"Yes." He replied.

"I am Two Birds, you know my brother Yellow Hawk."

"You are Two Birds? The last time I saw you, you were this high." He held his hand out and gestured about three feet off the ground. The whole war party laughed. Two Birds moved closer to him and they hugged.

"You have grown a little since then Two Birds," he added sarcastically, "not much, but a little." The warriors laughed again.

"We all know what you have done for us in the Indian nations and I would like to welcome you to our lands but more importantly I want to thank you for what you did for our warrior, those traders you killed were the ones that scalped him and we thank you for avenging him."

"How do you know they were the ones that scalped him." He asked.

"Because after you moved their bodies into the trees we checked their horses and in one of their saddle bags we found his scalp."
Red Flame shook his head.

"This can't go on Two Birds, to many of us are dying. There will be no Indian nations left in ten years at this rate. I don't know the answer, do you?"

"We are all joining Sitting Bull. All the young warriors are anyway. The Big white chief has sent yellow hair to wipe out all Indians, to hang all the warriors and imprison all the women and children."

"When did you hear this?" He asked sounding concerned, "has Custer left Washington yet?"

"We heard Seven moons ago, and yes, Custer is on his way. Will you join us Red Flame?"

"I will, as soon as I get these ladies to St. Augustine and one small thing I have to take care of in Tallahassee. I will catch up with you in Montana at the Sioux camp."

"Good," said Two Birds, "more braves will join us if they know you will be there too."
They both moved forward to each other, they hugged again and then Two Birds led his warriors back the same way they had come.

Red Flame did not say a word to the sisters, he just sped off at a gallop. They followed but not a word was heard from any of them. As he rode it ran through his mind that why was he so anxious about three white girls when his whole nation was at deaths door. His priorities had to be put in order.

They rode until sunset, nobody said anything until they entered a small clearing some two hundred yards from the trail.

"I'll get the fire started if you get the food out from your bags." He said angrily as he walked off into the woods to get some fire wood as he didn't really want to talk to any of them, he felt they had let him down. Just get them to St. Augustine as quickly as possible. Their recent intimacy seemed years ago. He struggled to look at them, what he thought were his good friends, now seemed like strangers and he wasn't sure why.

He returned minutes later with armfuls of branches, twigs and kindling, he dropped them to the ground and started to arrange them when in his peripheral vision he saw a pair of lady's legs, he looked up and Ella was standing looking down at him.

"Red Flame we need to talk."

"What about?" The anger was still in his voice.

"Us," she said, "all of us."

"Us. What about us?"

"Please don't sound so angry."

"Why not, I thought we were…….."

" We are, we are more than just friends, but….."

"In my world friends stick up for their friends."

"I agree, but are you so naive, don't you understand, we love you, each of us does in our own way, but…. but two of us are having a hard time just now….., the shootings…, the blood…., it affects us all in different ways."

"I know that," he said, but he didn't really, "but you didn't say anything."

"I love you Red Flame, Martha loves you, Libby loves you, do you think any of us could be with a man we didn't love and behave like we did for the last few days?"

He paused momentarily. He suddenly felt stupid.

"You love Me? After all the killings I've done….. your words not mine."

"Of course, it's just the anger coming out. Libby is finding it terribly hard to come to terms with. But…….."

"It's what she has been through," he added, "it's a terrible thing she went through." He was now defending her. He thought again about what he had just said. He wished he was more intelligent.

"Exactly. Please forgive us, we don't know how to handle this sort of thing. Nobody does. The last thing we want to do is upset the man we love and the man we owe our lives too, many times over." She smiled at him sympathetically. He stood up and put his arms around her.

"I'm sorry Ella, I'm a black and white sort of man, I don't know about these things and I'm not intelligent enough to understand what these feelings mean, when somebody says something to me, I believe them and take them at their word, I just don't get it otherwise."

She pulled him in closer, looked up at him and kissed him on the lips for several seconds. He noticed that she kept her eyes closed all the time they kissed. What did that mean he wondered?

"Oh, Red Flame what are we to do?" She asked.

" Let's get some food." He replied trying to lighten the mood.

" Yes lets. And coffee." She said grinning at him.

Twenty minutes later the four of them were sitting around a roaring fire eating deer meet, slowly they had got back to chatting as they had done at the lakeside encampment, whether Ella had spoken to the other two he wasn't sure, but all seemed to be well among them again, just as it had been, except that in his mind he felt that his and the others relationship would never be the same after Libby's outburst.

As they sat chatting it was Libby that suddenly stood up.

"What are we doing tomorrow?" She asked.

"What do you want to do Libby?" Asked Ella.

"Can we go back to our old camp by the lake?"

Libby looked to Red Flame, her eyes asking the question again.

"Not really Libby." He replied after several seconds.

"Why not?" Asked Libby angrily.

"We need to get to St. Augustine Libby, we have discussed this." Replied Ella a little abruptly.

"I know but every time I see a bend in the road, I'm terrified. Who will we meet, will they kill me or worse, will they rape me again. I don't think I can stand it anymore." Said Libby getting agitated and burying her head into her hands.

"Well we need to……." Ella said sounding annoyed.

"Ladies, can I make a suggestion?" Interrupted Red Flame.

"Of course." Said Ella sounding relieved by the interruption.

"We don't need to go to my ma's camp, that was just a suggestion. I have a little hideaway, in fact it's a small cave on a cliff face, very primitive, but it's very secluded like our place was by the lake, it's a good day's ride from here but if you want to stop there for a day or two that's Ok, it's up to you. It's on our way to St. Augustine."

"That great, that sounds perfect," said Libby excitedly, "when can we leave?" She asked looking directly at him impatiently.

"Well," he looked at the other two for some guidance, he shrugged, "we can leave in the morning and we will stay off the main trail. Ok? That will take a little longer though."

Ella nodded at him, it seemed as though she had just understood that Libby was going through more mental turmoil than any of them had realized.

"That's great, thank you. I really appreciate that." Libby looked at each of them in turn and smiled, the relief on her face was obvious to them all.

They all sat for another hour joking and relaxing, several coffees and more joking, it was heartening to them that Libby was more like her old self again.

They all went to their own beds and slept well.

The next morning, they left for his cave, his own sanctuary. They rode all day just stopping for water, never even crossing the main trail, always hidden by trees and undergrowth. Several travelers passed them going west but didn't see them. He couldn't remember being so hesitant or nervous before about a simple journey. It was mainly concern for the girls causing it.

They rode well into the night, talking advantage of the cooler temperatures. Most other travelers taking this route would be snuggled up in their beds by the time they arrived at the cave.

They arrived just as the sun was rising so he was able to lead the girls up near to the grassy open area just in front of the cave entrance and they walked the last thirty yards leading their own individual horses. Again, he went cautiously into the cave just to make sure no animals had decided to take up residence. It was all clear.

As the girls unloaded their belongings into the cave he set about building a fire and getting some fresh water. Ella made some coffee for them all and they sat around not saying much as they were all very tired. Gradually they all dozed off and slept for several hours.

He was up first about lunch time and went hunting for any type of food, he also replenished their water supply and found unexpectedly a deep fresh water pool just above the cave entrance, this he thought they could use to keep cool in the midday sun and bathe.

Three days went very quickly, all they seemed to want to do was eat, sleep, relax in the pool and talk.

They didn't ride anywhere.

Libby was definitely on the mend, she was confidently joining in conversations with her sisters more and more and enjoying herself, in fact her sense of humor had definitely returned.

On the third day he decided that the next day should be the day to make the short journey to St. Augustine. He told the girls as they sat around the fire eating their supper of his idea, and although disappointed they thankfully all agreed the time was right.

CHAPTER 11

They were only about two miles from St. Augustine when in the distance the trail suddenly widened, his first thought was that maybe it had been done that way so that wagons could pass as they arrived or left the bustling town. About one hundred yards ahead was a large white magnolia bush blocking the right-hand side of the trail, he didn't think too much about it until he saw a man astride a large black horse which was standing perfectly still as though he was waiting for them. Red Flame had got so involved with the girl's conversation that his natural sense of survival had deserted him, his rifle was still in its sheath, they were all at the man's mercy. He was smartly dressed in blue jeans, a light cowhide jacket, black shirt and very highly polished boots. His white hat was cocked to a slight angle. His clean-shaven rugged face gave his age at about thirty.

"Good morning ladies," he smiled and nodded towards them, "Red Flame." He nodded again towards him. Not smiling, more a suspicious glare.

How did he know my name Red Flame thought? The man had his right hand on the handle of his revolver, meaning he could shoot all four of them before he even got his rifle out of its sheath.

"Good morning." The ladies replied with suspicion in their voices.

"Good morning." Replied Red Flame looking the man straight in the eyes.

The stranger was very calm, he had no reason not to be, he had them at his mercy and he knew it.

"I'm David Wilson, Sherriff David Wilson of St. Augustine. I have come to escort the ladies into town."

"We don't need an escort but thank you anyway." Replied Ella indignantly.

"That wasn't my only reason to come here to be honest, I wanted to meet Red Flame too."

"You wanted to meet me?" Asked a surprised Red Flame.

156

"Yes. My friend Pete Davidson, sheriff of Lancaster told me how you saved his and young Williams life. I have read all the newspaper articles about you, but I wanted to meet you and thank you personally. He's a good friend, they both are. Also, I didn't want you coming into my town, there are at least a dozen bounty hunters waiting for you in the bars to show up."

"Really?" said Red Flame.

"Yes. It is common knowledge that you had gone looking for the girls missing sister, and also obvious that if you found her then St. Augustine was the place to bring her for her own safety. They are waiting for you. They all want the $1000 reward."

"Don't you want it?" Asked Martha abruptly, testing the sheriff.

"No," he replied bluntly, noticeably offended, "I understand why he's doing what he's doing and I don't blame him, I'd do the same if I had the courage, but I don't. I just don't want some mountain man to shoot him in the back for the bounty, I think he has more to offer all of us than that, as a peace maker as well maybe."

"We agree with you." Said Ella. She smiled at Red Flame.

"Right," said the sheriff, "I think you need to get going Red Flame, this is quite a busy stretch of road, and the word is that you will travel this trail back to the Indian lands, so either travel fast or take a different route."

Red Flame nodded as he thought what to say and do.

"Thank you for the advice Sheriff. I have a small job I need to do before I head home, I will travel south first to Tallahassee and then back to the Indian lands."

"Good, well get going." Said the sheriff dismounting, smiling and offering his hand to him.

Red Flame clearly for the first time saw the sheriffs star, it was pinned to his shirt but hidden by his jacket. He also dismounted.

They shook hands slowly but eagerly, then the sheriff pulled him forward and hugged him.

"Thank you again, for everything," added the sheriff, "I will make sure the ladies are safe from here."

"I hope we meet again," said Red Flame genuinely, "and thanks for this. I know you will look after them Sheriff. He walked over to the girls, one at a time they dismounted, hugged him in turn, Ella and Libby were in tears. Martha just stared at him, no sign of emotion.

Then she kissed him. Not a word was spoken. He remounted Laggon, waved as he turned and galloped off quickly in a southerly direction. He didn't look back, either physically or mentally, he just rode on. His job was finished.

Six hours later he arrived on the outskirts of Tallahassee, the town where he spent his child hood growing up and where his father had been murdered. He slowly gathered his bearings, he stopped and looked into the small house on the edge of town that his mother and father had been so happy in and where he had been born, everything looked the same except the neat lawns and flower gardens had gone, long overgrown but after a glance through the windows he realized that nothing had been disturbed within the house. His mother, after finding out about his father's murder must have literally locked the door and headed back to her family on the Indian lands taking Red Flame with her. He walked slowly around the little house, stopping to check in each window. The pictures were still hanging, the cushions were on the couch, the chairs were still plumped up and it was completely habitable, which surprised him with all the new settlers flooding into the area, he expected someone to have taken it over and be living happily there as he used too. He didn't go in.

He rode a further two hundred yards until he came to his old school girlfriend's house, Ally had been his best friend at school, from day one they had walked together to and from school every day, confiding in each other, sharing tea at each other's house, knowing each other's parents and also being ribbed that one day they would marry. She was shattered when his father was killed and because they had moved away, they had long lost touch. Was she married now, he had no idea. Should he stop by her place to see her, would she remember him, it was six years ago since he last saw her, it was the day after his father's body was found by the road side.

He slowly rode down the road getting closer to Ally's house, his stomach was churning, she might be married with five children, how would she react? He dismounted and led Laggon the last few yards to the house, it looked just the same as he remembered, maybe a little run down but it showed signs of occupancy and suddenly he really

158

wanted to see her, excitement overtook him and he ran the last ten yards with Laggon trotting along beside him. He pushed open the white gate and leapt the steps on to the porch.

He banged loudly on the door and waited, nothing, he thumped the door again.

"Who is it?" Asked a Ladies voice," what do you want?"

"Ally, is that you?"

"Yes."

"It's me Red flame."

"Red Flame?" The sound of several bolts being feverishly opened followed.

The door opened and she stood looking at him, her eyes wide in astonishment.

"Why are you here, they are looking for you."

They stood and looked at each other, each wanting to ask the other many questions, but they didn't.

Ally stepped out and hugged him, he wrapped his arms around her, they stood for what seemed minutes.

"Quickly, come in," she pulled him in, quickly glancing up and then down the road several times, "what are you doing here? Bounty hunters have been here several times to your old house and mine looking for you. What do you want?"

"I wanted to talk to you about my father but I also wanted to see you and your family, your mother and father, they were always so good to me." They were both still standing just inside the front door.

"Quickly, move your horse around the back, out of sight, do it now Red Flame please. I will open the back door for you. We will talk later." She almost pushed him back out the door.

He looked left and right, nobody in sight. He walked to Lagoon and led him to the rear of the small house, tied him up and scooted in through the open back door that Ally was holding wide open. As he went in she slammed the door and locked it. She turned to him and hugged him again.

"It's so good to see you again," she said bursting into tears, "I can't believe you're here, I thought you were dead."

"Nearly, several times, but they always missed me." He replied laughing.

"It's not funny, it's just not funny." Tears flooding down her face. She looked away.

"I'm sorry Ally. I hadn't realized how concerned you were." He placed his hand on her shoulder.

"Well I have been," she said bluntly, she turned and hit him on the chest with both fists. She looked him in the eyes, and paused, "I have been worried sick about you, every night since I last saw you."

"Why, what do you mean"?

"Because I thought they would kill you as well."

"Who? Who did you think would kill me?"

Ally looked down at the floor and didn't want to answer.

"Ally. Who do you think?" He asked again.

She thought for several seconds.

"The Murphy's."

"The Murphy's? But why would they?"

"I think it was Donald and those two friends of his, Peter something and David, the two that always followed him around at school. You know, he treated them as his bodyguards, he still does, do you remember?"

"I do yes, Peter was a skinny kid but David was bigger, even bigger than Donald."

"That's right, but because Donald's father ran the town, they were both scared of him."

"Yes, I remember, but what makes you think it was them?"

"Two things. One, years ago Donald bragged several times when he was drunk about how he had killed a local man but the others always shut him up. Secondly, old Harold, the blacksmith, you remember him, he told me two years ago that one night in the saloon, Donald ran out of money in a card game but he placed an old pocket watch on the table instead, and Harold swears it was your fathers old watch. He said it was definitely the Doc's watch."

Red Flame turned thoughtfully and stared out of the window.

"I'm sorry Red Flame, where are my manners, please sit down while I make us some coffee."

"Don't worry, but a coffee would be nice, thanks," he replied still taking in what Ally had just said, "I'd forgotten how beautiful it is around here. It's hard to believe we used to walk down this road every day, how the trees have grown."

"I haven't noticed, well, you don't when you see something every day do you?" Said Ally as she disappeared into the small kitchen. Red Flame stood at the window thinking about his father and how many times Ally's parents had invited them around for supper or a drink on the porch to watch the sun go down. Happy days he remembered.

"Come and sit down for your coffee." Ally said making him jump.

"Oh right, I was just thinking about the evenings we used to spend on your porch. I forgot to ask you about your parents, are they away?"

"No, they are both dead."

"Dead? No. I'm so sorry Ally, I didn't know."

"Mammy died four years ago and Papa died last year."

"What? I'm so sorry. How did they die?"

"Mammy died of cancer and Papa died of a heart attack, or so they said, but I think it was a broken heart really, I'm not sure though."

He reached out and pulled her to him. They embraced for several seconds.

"If only I'd known."

"You're here now and that's all that matters." She smiled as she said it.

For the next three hours they talked about growing up, the things they used to do, the fun they had and apart from the odd cup of coffee they both sat on the couch enjoying each other's company. It wasn't until Ally asked why he had come back to the town that the conversation turned to his father's death again.

"I have long thought about pa's death, or murder should I say, but it was the last time I saw ma and spoke to someone else about it that I realized I needed to find out the truth, but, and it sounds awful but the timing just hasn't been right."

"I know, I have been following your exploits in the paper, you have done some very brave things and that's why these horrible men have been sniffing around looking for you. But, how are you going to find out who actually did murder your father?"

"Well, after what you have told me today I think I should start with Donald and his men, don't you?"

161

"Well, it's only one man now, David disappeared last year, nobody knows what happened to him, but the rumor is that he fell out with Donald and Donald had him killed."

"Really?"

"So, the rumor mill goes." She said shrugging her shoulders.

"I suppose I had better see Donald and ask him. See what he says."

"Red Flame, he is dangerous. Since his father died a couple of years ago he has taken to running the town the way he wants, and he doesn't care who gets hurt. I think his friend Peter is good with a gun and is not worried about using it, so watch him. Donald has taken over all his father's businesses, he now runs the Bank, the trading post and of course the saloon. It seems he really mistreats the ladies that work for him at the saloon as well."

"Right, well I better go and see him then."

"When?" Ally asked sounding concerned.

"There is no time like the present as pa used to say."

"Now? But it's dark." Said Ally sounding alarmed.

"Yes, I know, but let's get it over with, it will be easier for me to move around the town too. I won't be long. It will be a short chat, that's all."

"Oh no, please be careful."

He smiled reassuringly.

"Of course, I will. See you soon." He turned and walked through the kitchen and out the back door to where he had left Laggon. He mounted up and slowly and quietly they made their way down the track passing several small houses that he remembered from his school days, and then left towards the Murphy's old ranch house. The house sat on many hundreds of acres but was built very near the approach road, set back only about thirty yards. It was very well lit with lights everywhere; all the drapes were open and so easy for him to see into most of the rooms. He could also see how many horses were tied up outside the house. There were two. Donald's and Peter's, he assumed, although he remembered there were stables at the rear of the house. But Donald was always lazy and didn't like to walk far. He left Laggon on the road and walked up the driveway and around the perimeter of the house glancing in all the windows as he went. It was very grand. Chandeliers and porcelain figurines from

162

Europe stood out. In the lounge sat Donald on a green and gold sofa, he was talking to a young squaw or rather he was yelling at her, while Peter sat on a chair reading a paper next to a large ornamental fireplace with a huge burning fire, they both looked a lot older than he remembered. He didn't see any others in the house. He walked up to the front door and knocked loudly. The door was solid mahogany with a small glass window at head height, he waited until he saw Peter look out at him, he waved, Peter acknowledged him with a nod. Red Flame was only armed with a knife.

"Hi Peter, how are you?" He asked as the door opened. Peter was dressed completely in black, including black boots and gun holster with a shining smith and Wesson revolver. Expensive, Red Flame thought. Peter's hair was longer than he remembered with a long moustache, very much like a gunslinger. A skinny gunslinger.

"What do you want?"

"I'd like to see Donald please, just a short chat."

Peter just stared, then he threw his head back as if beckoning him into the large hallway and closed the door.

"Wait here." Peter said, still watching him suspiciously. Peter strode to the lounge and stood at the door between the hall and the lounge keeping one eye on Red Flame.

"There's someone to see you, and you won't guess who it is."

"Who is it?" A voice replied. Red Flame assumed it was Donald.

"Its Red Flame." Replied Peter.

"Red Flame, what the hell does he want?"

"I don't know, but he's here."

"Ok."

Peter beckoned him to the lounge door.

"Come in."

As he walked into the lounge, he got a good view of the young squaw, she was sitting on the floor with her legs crossed wearing only a wrap, she had been very pretty, but her face was badly bruised and cut as if somebody had beaten her up very recently, she looked petrified and looked away in embarrassment when she saw him.

"Get out." Donald shouted at her. She jumped up and disappeared into the kitchen. Her wrap was way too small.

"What do you want Redskin?" Asked Donald sarcastically.

"Nothing, this is purely a friendly visit to see a couple of old school friends, that's all."

"Well you have seen us, now clear off out."

Peter had walked around the back of the sofa, behind and to the right of Donald. His gun and holster were hidden behind the high back of the sofa and Red Flame could not see his hands.

"Ok. I just wondered if I could see your pocket watch, somebody told me it was a nice one." Donald was taken aback, not what he was expecting.

"Yeah, ok. It is an excellent piece." He stuck his fat fingers into his breast pocket and pulled it out. Donald tried to show it off to its best but without undoing the chain it would be impossible for Red Flame to see it clearly. Red Flame knew at first sight it was his father's old Cartier.

He was showing so much interest that it was natural for him to want to get a closer look, he went behind the sofa so he was looking over Donald's shoulder, he was now standing next to Peter and could see his hands were not on his gun, but surprisingly Peter's mind was also on the old watch. They were all looking at it admiringly. He slowly pulled out his knife and while Peter was still engrossed in the old Cartier he turned and wrapped his hand around Peters mouth and thrust the knife up under his rib cage. Red Flame slowly let Peters body silently drop on to the thick carpet, no sound. He wiped the blood off the blade on Peter's nice clean black shirt. Donald, oblivious as to what had just happened right behind him was still yapping on about how much it was worth and where his father had bought it in Boston.

Red Flame moved from behind the couch and stood back in front of him, seething with anger but smiling.

"That's it. Now clear off before I get annoyed. The shows over." Snarled Donald.

"I don't feel like leaving until you answer some questions for me."

"What did you say? You leave when I tell you, and I'm telling you."

"You were always a bully Donald, a loud-mouthed fat bully."

Donald stared at him and then grinned menacingly.

164

"Pete, kill him," there was a long silence, "Pete, kill him." Donald yelled.

"Peter's not here, he's gone."

Donald, still sitting, spun around but couldn't see Peter on the floor hidden behind the sofa.

"Why did you kill my father?" Red Flame asked quite calmly.

"Clear off out you......."

Red Flame stepped forward, pulled his knife from its sheath and stuck it into Donald's right thigh, Donald screamed and grabbed the wound. Blood was seeping through his fingers and pants and dripping on to the sofa. Donald's eyes were wide open in pain and disbelief.

"One more time. Why did you kill my father?"

"I didn't."

"Who did then."

"I don't know. You're mad you are."

Red Flame moved forward again and plunged the knife into Donald's left thigh, this time it hit the bone. Donald again yelled in agony.

"No stop, stop. Your mad, mad." Tears streaming down his face.

"Once more, why did you kill my father?"

"I didn't, it was Pete."

Red Flame lent forward again and sliced the pocket on Donald's waist coat and took out his father's watch and chain, he stared at it momentarily, then he cut Donald's throat with one stroke of his knife.

He walked to the kitchen where the young squaw was cowering under the table.

"Get your things and anything else you want, take a pony from the stables and get back to your own people. You haven't seen anything. Ok?"

The squaw nodded, smiled awkwardly and ran out of the room. A minute later the back door slammed, he watched from the kitchen window as the squaw ran into the stables and seconds later rode off on one pony and leading another. Payment for services rendered he assumed. Well, why not he thought to himself, Donald won't need them anymore.

He waited for the young squaw to disappear down the road. He then strolled into the lounge where the open fire was blazing, he snatched a cut-glass whiskey decanter off its silver tray and poured it over the sofa and Donald. He then opened what he thought was a drinks cabinet, it was, it contained only bottles of scotch, how ironic, his father would be laughing at that. He took out four of the bottles and then unceremoniously dumped one over Peter's body. He threw another bottle onto the kitchen floor smashing it and one into the hallway, also smashing it. He held onto the last one.

He used the fire shovel to throw some burning embers from the fire into the kitchen, it immediately ignited and burst into flames, he turned and did the same thing throwing embers into the hallway, again the whole floor ignited. That left just the sitting room, he looked down at Donald's massive body and then threw more embers on to the sofa and Donald and then threw the last bottle on the floor under the sofa. 'Whoosh," the flames erupted and completely engulfed Donald's body, he paused for a second just to make sure Donald wasn't coming back. He felt the extreme heat on his face and body and so he then ran to the back door, leaving it open so the air would feed the flames. He sprinted around the house to the front and called for Laggon who appeared immediately. He needed now to get away from the burning house in case anybody from the town spotted the flames and came to investigate. He didn't want to be recognized, it wasn't something that would go down well with people who didn't know the reason behind his actions. They set off at quite a gallop considering it was so dark. After ten minutes he was back tying Laggon up at the rear of Ally's place, she was waiting at the back door and had sensibly turned the lights off until he was inside and all the drapes were closed.

"Well?" She asked impatiently.

"What," he said, "what do you want to know?"

"Did you speak to Donald?"

"Yes, I did," he paused momentarily, "can we have some coffee. I'm really dry."

"Red Flame," she hit him on the arm getting slightly exasperated, "what did he say?"

"He killed my father! He blamed Peter, but he did it."

"He admitted it?"

"Yes. He even flaunted the fact that he had my father's pocket watch."

"No. Really? what did you do?"

"If you look out of your bedroom window you will see."

Ally disappeared into her room and pulled open her drapes.

"Oh my God." She called out. She ran back into the kitchen. Eyes wide open. He was nonchalantly waiting for the water to boil to add to the coffee as she entered. A look of fear on her face. There was silence as she looked at him waiting for an explanation. None came.

"Red Flame. Where is Donald now?" She asked slowly.

As he poured the boiling water into the two cups, he raised his index finger skywards.

"What does that mean." She asked angrily.

"He's with his maker."

Silence again while Ally thought what Red Flame meant.

"You killed him?"

"I did. Peter too. They were going to kill me. So, I had to." He shrugged. He opened the pouch on his belt and withdrew his father's watch and laid it on the table. They both stared at it without saying a word for a couple of seconds.

"Are you ok?" She finally asked.

"Yes of course."

"Really? Are you sure?"

He smiled at her.

"I'm sure. Pa can rest easier now.....vengeance has been done."

"How did you kill them?"

"You don't want to know."

She wandered back to the bedroom and looked at the fire still burning nearly three miles away, the flames were still shooting way into the air. Burning embers drifted into the sky, the fire must have been visible for miles around. He waited in the kitchen for her to return expecting more questions. He heard the drapes being drawn closed in the bedroom. She appeared at the kitchen door.

"What do you want to eat tonight." She suddenly asked.

"Err, whatever you do." He was so taken aback he couldn't think straight.

"I have some steak, will that do?" She asked with a warm smile.

He smiled back at her. He hoped she wouldn't ask more questions.

"Of course it will, unless you're going to poison me."

She held his gaze momentarily. Her big blue eyes focused on his. She smiled again realizing he wasn't going to tell her anymore.

"I hadn't thought of that, but it's a good idea though. Think of the bounty I would get."

They both laughed out aloud, his was with relief. After the last incident with the sisters he hadn't been sure how Ally would react to having a killer in her house, so he was pleased to see her positive reaction. He was also glad today was finally over with. Whatever happened in the future he could now rest easy, he had finally repaid the debt he felt he had long owed his father. He couldn't wait to tell his mother, she would be delighted that finally vengeance had been achieved. While Ally and he sat at the table drinking coffee, they talked again about old times, their parents, the other people they knew from school and how the war between the Indian nations and the Army was affecting everybody and how it could devastate the country.

It was after they had finished and Ally had cleaned up, that she suddenly asked what his future plans were.

"I'm not really sure. I had intended to go back to the tribe but I believe there are bounty hunters on the trail looking for me, that's what the sheriff of St Augustine told me anyway. So, I'm not really sure. I know that many warriors from different tribes are heading north to join Sitting Bull who is building a huge army to fight the bluecoats, the intention being of pushing them back to the east coast. but that might take years. But, I don't think that's possible, I think we could win the battle but not the war. The cavalry are too many, they will just send more men, but I can't think what else to do."

"Do you know what I think you should do?" Asked Ally very seriously.

"What should I do?" He smiled at her, "tell me."

"I think you should stay here, with me"

"But I....."

"Hear me out, please." Again, she was very serious.

"Ok."

"If you leave here there's a good chance you won't even get back to your tribe, there are too many bounty hunters out there searching for you, the whole of America is looking for you at the moment, but even if you did get back and with luck on your side you could, and you could go and fight with Sitting Bull, he might win, he might lose. Then what? The whole cavalry will be out looking for you all over again."

He sat, expressionless, staring at her. He nodded slowly.

"Do you agree?" She asked.

"Yes. The way you explain it. I do. I have always said it would be a no-win situation and you have convinced me of that even more. It's what I do instead that is concerning me."

"As I said, stay here. With your knowledge of languages, you could do more for your nation by talking, than ever you would do fighting, by bringing both sides together peacefully."

"But that won't stop the bounty hunters will it?"

"No, but just listen for a minute. What if, and I think this is necessary, you change your identity. If you cut your hair and wore white men's clothes nobody would even know you were an Indian. Your features are European, it's just your hair and the way you dress that tells the world you are an Apalachee."

"I can't imagine dressing like a white man." He remembered what Ewan had said, but didn't want to tell Ally.

"You did when we were at school, you only changed after your father was killed and your mother went back to the tribes. Before that you used to wear short trousers and shoes," she roared with laughter at the thought of him," now look at you!" He laughed with her.

"Let me think about it."

"Don't rule it out Red Flame, give it some thought. You can stay here for as long as you need. Ok?"

"Stay here?" He laughed again, "what would our parents say? They would be disgusted."

"They sure would, but under the circumstances they would understand. I believe they would like it."

"I'm sure they would. Thank you Ally." They smiled at each other.

"Well I'm going to start on the supper, do you want to help?"

"Of course." He replied.

For the next hour they both stood in the kitchen preparing a feast, or at least he thought it was a feast and then they sat opposite each other on either side of the kitchen table eating and talking about how things could work if he stayed with her. He really did enjoy her company, he had forgotten how well they had always got on. They had always had a special relationship. After a while he reached out across the table and cupped her hand in his, they looked at each other and smiled knowingly. That night they made love.

CHAPTER 12

That night he didn't sleep much, not only was he excited about his new-found feelings for Ally but her suggestion about becoming a 'white man'. He had never considered that after what his old friend Donald had said, maybe it is worth considering. He had always known that if he did not dress as he did, an Indian, he could pass as of European descent, for how long though was the question. The Army and the bounty hunters wouldn't just stop looking for him, as long as his scalp was not presented to an Indian agent or to a sheriff's office, he would be presumed alive, so the hunt would continue. He thought about his mother, what would she think about this sudden change, she had always said how proud she was of him, but that had been when he was Red Flame, but now as Mr. Mackintosh, if he was to use his father's name, would she feel the same or would she think he had betrayed her and the Apalachee way of life. Even more worrying to him was the fact that he didn't know if he could accept the way of the white man, living in a house in one place, getting some sort of job to pay for things he didn't even know he needed, wearing white man's clothes, white men always seemed to him to be sweating all the time, was it any surprise with all the clothes they wore, would he get used to these things, he felt a shiver travel down his back.

Just then Ally made him jump.

"What time is it?" She yawned as she spoke.

"The suns just coming up."

"So what time is that?"

"The sun is just coming up." He repeated. It suddenly dawned on him that this is something he would need to master if he was to become a white man, albeit it very few carried time pieces, only well-off ones, Indians don't carry time pieces, you just get up when the sun comes up. All Indians do, always have.

"There is a clock on the dressing table, see it?"

His eyes strained through the darkness, luckily his father had taught him to read the time on his old pocket watch but it still took him several seconds to work it out.

"Six err…. twenty."

"Too early to get up, go back to sleep." Ally muttered and immediately started snoring gently again.

He lay with his hands behind his head thinking how he as an individual could affect the outcome of the war, would he be able to convince the white hierarchy that just killing Indians was not only wrong but quite futile as it would take years, with many deaths on both sides before one could call themselves the outright victor.

He needed to tell his mother first of Ally's idea, this would be dangerous, three hundred miles he would need to travel to the encampment, countless bounty hunters, cavalry troops and gun happy scalp hunters, all out there looking for him. Money and fame were waiting for the white man that could kill the infamous Red Flame, but he was used to that, so far, he'd been lucky and he could see no reason why that should change. He would he decided, discuss this with Ally as soon as they were properly awake. Ten minutes later he got up and made them both a coffee, Ally lazily opened her eyes and asked what he was doing up at this ungodly hour.

"Making us some coffee," he replied from the kitchen, "we need to talk, urgently."

"Oh. I thought so, you have been restless all night. You kept me awake."

"Sorry," he said as he walked into the bedroom with a cup of coffee in each hand, "I didn't mean to disturb you."

"I know." She reached out and touched his arm as he placed the cup on her bedside table.

"I have decided that I think your idea is good but, I need to discuss this with my mother and tell her why I'm doing it. I'm not sure she will understand. I still need to think it out."

"I think she will," said Ally thoughtfully, "after all, she wants you to stay alive."

"This is one of the things that is different with our cultures. The white man's way would be to give in if the only other option is death, the Indians way would be to die with honor than to look like a coward. So again, it would provoke a different answer from both my parents, I mean if my father was still alive."

"Hmmm, I see your dilemma. Would you like me to make the journey with you? Talk to your mother?"

"No, definitely not. It's far too dangerous." He took a swig of coffee.

"It's not because you are afraid of what your mother will think of us being together?"

"No. My mother has always loved you like a daughter. She always wanted us to get together, remember, right up until my father's death when we left Tallahassee. She will be excited about that part, it's the part of me dressing as a white man basically to hide she won't like."

"But you're not hiding, just changing your name." She sipped more of her coffee.

"No Ally, be honest, I'm changing my looks, my name and living with you. I will become a white man until I am recognized. I'm going into hiding from all those who wish me dead."

"You are an intelligent man, you will do more to help the Indian Nations with your brain than you could possibly achieve with your rifle. Now, can I have another coffee please?" She grinned sexily at him.

"I suppose. No peace for the wicked." He grinned back at her. He stood and got back out of bed and walked naked back into the kitchen with the two cups.

"Nice buttocks."

"Don't be rude." A few minutes later he returned with the drinks.

"When will you leave for the reservation?" She asked immediately sounding suddenly worried.

"I need to see if I can carry off looking like a white man first."

"Well I still have some of Papa's clothes here, you could try some of them on and see how they feel."

"Good idea, we can do that later." He rolled over and kissed her. They soon forgot about their coffee's getting cold.

That afternoon they went through some of Ally's father's clothes, in fact he had to admit that some looked pretty good on him, he hadn't realized before that Ally's father had been so tall, the pants he had selected from the wardrobe were maybe a fraction small but with boots on that wouldn't be noticed. The jackets and waistcoats of which only two of each fit him were good enough to pass any scrutiny so he was pleased. An hour passed with him offering Ally a fashion show that ended in raucous laughter from them both. It had been a nice uneventful day and he was getting to enjoy these last two days more.

They both sat out on the front decking enjoying a cold drink in the late afternoon sun, him wearing a pair of his new-found pants and a clean white shirt that he didn't think Ally's father had ever worn.

Ally tied his hair back in a ponytail, at first it was uncomfortable but he soon got used to it. She said he looked very handsome. He scoffed but inwardly he was pleased.

Ally thought that by them being seen outside should anyone pass by, they would see she had a 'new man' and so they wouldn't be so inquisitive when they saw them out and about town. Gently - gently she had said.

Several of the locals enjoying their sunny afternoon outings did pass by in their carriages or on horseback but only waved, they did not seem to realize that he was sitting on the same swing chair beside her until they had almost passed the house and then it would have looked very nosey indeed to stop and back up to make any enquiries as to who her new beau was. But they all noticed him, that was obvious the way they whispered to each other and glanced back as they disappeared down the lane.

"Look at them," she laughed and pointed at the last couple just disappearing into the distance in their carriage, "nosey things. See, you're already a celebrity. Your description will be all around the town by tomorrow, you watch, this lane won't have seen so many goings on, such backwards and forwards as it will see in the next couple of days." She tutted. He roared with laughter, he was a celebrity already she had said, if only they knew who he was they wouldn't rest so easy in their beds at night he thought. He laughed out loud.

"What?" She asked.

"Oh nothing."

They sat and chatted again about his planned visit to his mothers, which they agreed should be as soon as possible. They decided on the day after the next and rehearsed how he would handle her many questions. They relaxed outside on the decking until the lazy beautiful red and purple clouds of the sunset had finally rolled over the horizon.

"Supper I think, what do you say?" She asked.

"Sounds great." They both stood up, kissed and went into the house.

The following morning after their usual three cups of coffee in bed, they dressed up, him in his new pants and shirt and Ally in a fashionable floral dress. He hitched up her little two-person carriage that had belonged to her parents to her horse, and off they went to town to pick up some supplies, but really it was to make the townsfolk aware of his existence, that he and Ally were an item, he just hoped that nobody would recognize him, including any old school friends that had stayed in town, there had to be some. He drove the small old rickety carriage down the narrow lane for about a mile before it joined a wider main trail that ran right through the town of about one hundred residents, most others lived like Ally on smallholdings a short distance from the town. The place hadn't changed much since he had left, the school looked exactly the same as it had some six years ago, the Ladies fashion shop had a new lick of paint as had the Bank, the Saloon was the only premises that had been really upgraded. Painted grey and burgundy with lights everywhere it stood out, at night it must have looked like a circus, obviously business was flourishing, but it was a place he knew he needed to stay away from, all the scalp hunters, fur hunters and bandits along with the locals would congregate there every night of the week, some to seek solace in the bottom of a bottle, some to try and win some money and others were there to enjoy the company of a lady or two, if they already had the money. He thought he would be recognized if he took a step inside within two minutes.

As they rode together Ally acknowledged some of the townsfolk as they walked along the boarded sidewalk, he pulled the cart up outside Greens grocery, he had always been amused by Mr. Green the owner, ever since his father had commented that Green was a great name for a green grocer. Red Flame stayed on the cart while Ally went in to buy a few items, Mr. Green who still ran the store probably would recognize him, he used to pick up groceries for his mother on the walk home from school. He sat motionless on the carriage seat watching the old man through the window, marching from item to item, filling bags and handing them to ladies and taking their money just as he always had. Several people looked at him, some suspiciously while others nodded to him or said good morning. He noticed the men all lifted their hats to her, she would be a good catch for any of the town's single men, but now they knew she was taken, that's why some of the men gave him the look they did. He smiled to everybody.

Ally emerged from the store laden with various grocery items, he jumped down from the carriage and took them from her and placed them in the rear of the carriage and then joined her on the seat.

"All ok?" She asked.

"No problems," he smiled at her, "where to next, home?"

"No, I'm going to Mrs. Jameson's store for some darning wool, she is also the towns gossip monger so I will find out what people are saying about us. I think you should go to the saloon and have a beer, it will be quiet at this time of day so it would be good to see if anybody recognizes you and you can make some new friends." He looked at her as though she was mad.

"Do you think that's wise?"

"Well, it's better to know now, at least you will have time to get away."

"Your very clever. You have thought this through, haven't you?"

"I try. It seems there was a big fire near here a couple of nights ago, seems a couple of men died." They both smiled to each other. She opened her purse and gave him a dollar.

"So, this is what a dollar looks like eh? My scalp is worth twenty of these," he held it up to the sky scrutinizing it, "or 1000 if they can prove its mine." He shrugged his shoulders.

"Don't tempt me," she laughed, "I'd be a very rich young lady."

"A beautiful rich young lady."

She smiled, lent forward and kissed him on the cheek. She carefully got down from the carriage and walked up the street. She stopped and looked back.

"See you back here in half an hour." He waved to her acknowledging he had heard her.

I don't have a watch; how do I know when half an hour has gone he thought to himself. The Saloon will have a clock, get in there quick and check the time. Suddenly as he approached the doors he felt very nervous even a little scared, perspiration was running down his back, he knew that would show up on his new white shirt. Confidence he uttered to himself, walk straight in and up to the bar. He pushed the doors open, ten people inside, he made a mental note of their positions, old habits he thought, four playing cards at a table to his left, two just chatting at a smaller table on his right and four sitting at the bar with their backs to him, that was until he let go of the doors. As they closed they let out an almighty prolonged squeak, everyone inside turned to see who had just interrupted their game, conversation or what have you, seeing just an unarmed single white man they all turned back to what they were doing. He glanced at the clock behind the bar, 11.50. Ten to twelve, got to be back at the carriage by 12.20. The barman kept watching him as he approached.

"Hi there, what would you like." The barman asked in a friendly southern drawl.

"Hi there, a beer please." Placing his dollar bill on the bar.

"New to town or passing through?"

He was concerned at the question but then realized the man was just being sociable, as good barman are supposed to be.

"I'm new here, just thought I'd check you out. I'm told your beer is good." He lied.

"Best for miles around." The barman replied placing the beer on the bar in front of him and then placing his sixty cents change next to the glass.

Of the four men standing at the bar, two were deep in conversation while the other two seemed to be listening in on what he was saying to the barman. Red Flame looked at one of them who was staring at him. He turned away. He had no weapons on him.

177

"I know you from somewhere don't I?" The man asked bruskly from behind him. He was a large man, no gun, bearded with a friendly reddish face. He turned to face the man.

"I don't think so, I'm new here."

"I know I recognize you. Where are you from?"

He was beginning to sweat again as he realized he did know this man. It was Billy Webster. Shit, he thought to himself. They had been at school together although they hadn't been particularly good friends, in fact, they had over the years got into several fights. Billy was three or four years older and had been bullied by Donald and his mates throughout his schooling and had suffered for it. People had always said that Billy wouldn't amount to anything because all the confidence had been knocked out of him by Donald. Now he looked like the town drunk, wearing dirty old clothes, a real ruddy complexion from the alcohol and looking as though he hadn't bathed for days. Not at all aggressive. But loud.

He wanted to say it's me Billy, you know we were at school together, but he didn't. He needed to think quickly.

"I'm from St. Augustine originally."

"What do you do there?"

He paused by taking a drink of his beer to give himself time to think of a response.

"I'm in politics."

"Ah, that's it. I've seen your picture in the paper."

Suddenly the other men who had overheard Billy's question's all turned and looked at him again, studying him.

"Yes," said one, "you've been in the paper."

"Yes," said another excitedly, "I knew I recognized you too." The three looked at each other smiling and started nodding in agreement. They seemed very pleased with themselves.

"Of course, I have seen your picture too," said the fourth man joining in, "what's your position in Politics?" The man asked suspiciously.

"Um, I'm an Indian Agent." He looked at the clock. 12.05 pm.

"Of course, I remember now." The man replied nodding his head.

"Well it's been nice talking to you all but I have to get back to my Lady. She doesn't like it when I'm late. He still had fifteen minutes yet but this inquisition was making him feel uncomfortable.

"No, they don't like that." Billy said. Red Flame wondered how he would know that as he didn't look like the marrying kind or even the type to have any luck with women.

"No, don't be late," said another, "otherwise you will be in trouble." The men laughed.

"I will see you all again soon. Great beer." He smiled to the bartender and then made his way to the doors, he turned and waved to the four who had all swiveled on their stools to bid him farewell.
As he opened the bar room doors he could see Ally approaching their carriage, she was early. He ran to intercept her.

"I'm an Indian Agent from St. Augustine if anybody asks. Ok?" He said quickly.

"Of course, you are. Where did that come from?" She replied somewhat startled.

"Billy Webster was in the saloon and thought he recognized me."

"Oh no," said Ally aghast climbing on to the carriage. He followed her onto the seat.

"He said he'd seen me before, and of course he had, then another fellow said he'd seen my picture in the paper and what did I do as a job. I said a Politician, an Indian Agent and they all agreed that's where they had seen my picture. I had a beer with them. I'm actually half drunk, I can't take beer, only scotch. It's the Indian side of me. I wanted to tell Billy who I was and ask how he's done since leaving school." Ally raised her hand and covered her mouth laughing. He snapped the reigns and the carriage jerked forward.

"No. Oh my God. You can't do that." She said.

"I know. I need to sleep."

"You need to sleep after one beer?" She said between laughing raucously.

"Yes, I do."
Twenty minutes later they were home. Immediately they were in the house he lay on the couch and passed out.

The next morning as the sun was rising he kissed her on the forehead, she opened her eyes somewhat startled.

"I will see you in three days, take care." He whispered. He was already dressed as an Indian with all his weapons. His ponytail had gone, two feathers had taken its place.

"You are leaving?"

"Yes, we agreed."

"Yes, I know, I'm sorry."

"Don't be sorry. Three days, that's all." He leant forward and kissed her again.

"Be careful."

"Of course. You too."

He turned away and closed the bedroom door behind him. Four minutes later she heard Laggon galloping northwards up the lane.

It was good to get an early start he thought, there would not be too many travelers on the trail this early so he would be able to make good progress. He kept as usual to the north of any tree lines so he was basically hidden from any other trail users heading east to west or west to east. About midday he stopped for some bread and water he had taken from Ally's earlier in the morning, and after stopping at a small stream for Laggon to get water and rest for a while they were back on their way.

He was just thinking how lucky he had been in his life and how the future looked exciting, starting a new life with Ally when there was sudden crack of a rifle and a bullet passed two feet over his head. He turned in the direction of fire and saw two white men galloping towards him, he immediately swung Laggon in a more northerly direction away from the advancing men, he knew Laggon could outrun the other horses and although one of the men continued firing it wasn't long before Red Flame knew he was out of range, he then swung south into the trees, galloping at such speed the branches cut and grazed his face, arms and legs. He felt for Laggon, and as soon as they were out of sight he pulled up and dismounted, he took hold of Laggon's face and gently checked for any wounds he had, he had taken the brunt of the trees and bushes. After extracting several thorns from close to his eyes he checked Laggon's front legs, they seemed fine.

He grabbed his rifle from its sheath and stooping he moved to the edge of the tree line. The two men had by now slowed down to a walking pace to see where he and Laggon had entered the trees, only one man had his rifle out. He was the shooter, why had he opened fire without knowing who he was shooting at, perhaps he just wanted the $20 reward for any Indian scalp. He wasn't going to get it today or any other day come to that. He waited until the men were about sixty yards away, he aimed at the one still holding the rifle, the man was wearing a bright red shirt with a buckskin waist coat and a large tan hat, very smartly dressed, he wasn't wearing a badge of any type so he wasn't a lawman. Aiming for the chest he fired, Crack, the man fell to the ground with a wound in his left shoulder. The second man froze, he must have had a lot of confidence in the red shirted man not to have even got his own rifle ready, he looked down at his partner lying on the ground still moaning and clutching his upper arm, then scouring the tree line to see something, the Indian or his horse, anything but there was nothing to see and still he didn't go for his rifle. He just sat on his horse, his eyes fixed on the trees, waiting, maybe expecting the next shot would be for him.

Red Flame stepped out from the trees, his rifle down at his side but still aimed at the man. They were about thirty yards apart, the man's head jerked towards him as he saw him emerge from the trees.

Red Flame walked briskly towards the man who still hadn't made a move for his revolver or rifle, perhaps he was so lightning fast on the draw that he wasn't worried about some Indian with a rifle.

They were now ten yards apart, Red Flame could smell the man, it was a soap smell so the man wasn't even sweating. The man had not long ago bathed. Was he a Lawman? He looked like one just like his partner, usually Lawmen were smartly dressed and had an air of confidence about them. This man had the same air. A US Marshall maybe or a local Sheriff. No visible badge though.

"Who are you?" Red Flame asked," and what do you want?" Were these two the Bank robbers that Sherriff Davidson and William had been after? He wondered.

"We were just out hunting."

"You were out hunting what, Indians?"

"No, no, we wouldn't hunt Indians." The man replied calmly.

"So why did you shoot at me? Are you Lawmen?"

"No, we're not lawmen." Said the man now laughing at that thought.

The man's hand was very slowly moving from on the top of his leg to the handle of his revolver.

Red Flame was hooking his finger around his trigger slowly increasing the pressure. The man said nothing, no sign of fear yet.

"So why shoot at me? I will only ask once more."

"Huh," the man sneered as his hand went for his revolver.

'Crack,' 'crack' almost together. Nothing between the two shots. For a split second he couldn't figure who had fired first. Was he hit, was he bleeding. He didn't think so. The man did have a fast draw, very fast. He'd got his shot away before Red Flame had reacted. They were both motionless for what seemed ages, looking at each other, eye ball to eye ball, neither moved. Slowly blood began to seep through the man's shirt just above his heart, his eyes were open but then slowly closed and he fell backwards from his saddle awkwardly almost in slow motion, and as he hit the ground there was a horrible noise as his neck broke.

Red Flame turned and walked to the other man who was still moaning and clutching his shoulder, he picked up the man's rifle and snatched the revolver from his holster, he wasn't about to get caught a second time in one day. He prodded the man with his rifle.

"Who are you?"

Silence, the man just groaned. Red Flame prodded again but this time at the man's wound.

The man yelled in pain. It was genuine pain.

"Who are you?" He repeated. He took two steps back and was standing six feet away.

No response. The man just laid there groaning. Red Flame took another step back, now he was eight or nine feet away, he looked at the man, studying him from head to the bottom of his newly polished boots, something was not right. The man's groaning intensified. He was acting.

I have his rifle and his revolver, what else could he hurt me with, he thought to himself. Some Lawmen carry a derringer in their boot, this man's boots were too tight though. No, definitely no derringer.

182

Maybe a knife, just don't get too close to him. The man could have a sheath behind him on his belt or down his boot. His boots could hold a knife easily, he needed the man to stand up.

"Stand up."

The man just continued to moan loudly. He was still acting.

His left arm was injured, not too badly to use a knife though, was he lying on top of a knife just waiting to use it if Red Flame got too close.?

"Stand up now." He repeated. No response. What most men would do now would be to help the man up, and he felt this man knew it. He wasn't going to oblige. He raised his rifle and shot the man in the right shoulder. 'Crack.' The man screamed in pain and started to roll from one side to the other, as he did so Red Flame using his rifle butt pushed the man on to his stomach, there lying on the grass underneath where he had lain was a hunting knife.

"Playing possum eh? Who are you?"

Silence again apart from the exaggerated moans.

"Last time, who are you?"

Again, silence. He waited five seconds and then he raised his rifle and fired into the fleshy part of the man's thigh. The man screamed again.

"Oh, I missed. I was aiming for your knee."

"Stop, stop. I will tell you."

"Speak."

"My name's Billy McCain, that's my brother Jimmy. I suppose you're going to hand us over to the law now?"

"Why would I?" These must be the Bank robbers he thought again.

"Because there is a bounty on us. We are famous. We are worth $500, that's what you'll get for us. We rob banks. So………you're going to hand us in now? Right?"

"No, I don't think so."

"No? They say you Indians are dumb, now I believe it."

"Really? You tried to kill me for my scalp. What's that worth…..$20?"

"Yes, but we are worth more now because of the things we have done, the number of killings, we are famous."

"So, if somebody has a bigger reward than you, does that make them more famous?"

"For sure. There are only two or three people worth more than us at the moment. One of those is an Indian."

"Really? A lowly Indian?" He asked.

"Yes. He's killed thousands of white folks. Yeah, he's a real bastard."

"But he's not as dumb as you two."

"Why?"

"You were going to scalp him for $20. Take his body, dead or alive and you would have got $1000. So, who is the dumb one now?"

"Your him, um Red ...." Suddenly the man showed fear.

"Red Flame, yep, that's me."

Billy's jaw dropped. He started to get up but winced in pain and dropped back to the ground.

"So, are you going to take us to the nearest Marshalls office and get your money?"

"No, I'm not like you, I don't kill for pleasure or money. I only kill people that deserve to be killed."

"So, what are you going to do with us?"

"Not us, it's just you. Your brother's dead."

"Is he? Oh well, that's more money for me then." Billy said coldly.

"So, you were close then?" He asked sarcastically.

"No, he was always stupid. Since he was a kid."

"He was very clean though. Why was that?"

"We were on our way to town to meet some ladies until we spotted you. I won't go like this now, all this blood. That will put them off. I'll need to get cleaned up first, but I'll show them the wounds, they like that." A very confident bank robber this one he thought.

He looked at the man in astonishment, was this man an idiot? Did he really think that he was going to let him walk away after trying to kill him? How many other Indians had this man shot from a distance to claim the $20?

"I have some bad news for you." Said Red Flame apologetically.

"Oh yeah, what's that?"

184

"You're not meeting any ladies tonight."

"Oh, why's that?"

"You're not meeting any more ladies, ever."

Billy's face changed, it suddenly dawned on him what Red Flame was implying.

"You mean, you're going to kill me anyway?"

"Yes. Just like you'd kill me if I turned away."

The man nodded and shrugged. Obviously, death didn't scare him.

"I suppose so." Billy added.

'Crack.' Red Flame shot him between the eyes. He turned and picked up the two rifles but left the bodies where they were for somebody else to claim the $500.

The next morning, he arrived at his mother's encampment. There were lots of children and dogs running around and they ran towards him as soon as he was spotted, the extra noise drew others from their tepees to see what all the excitement was about. He saw his mother standing outside waving to him with a big grin on her face. He dismounted and led Laggon towards her, instinctively they both ran towards each other and embraced. They hugged for what seemed like minutes, she looked frailer than he remembered.

"Are you alright ma?"

"Of course, I am. Now you're here."

"Good. I am sorry I couldn't get to see you sooner, I have no excuses."

"Don't worry about me, you are doing important work."

"Not as important as you though." They clasped hands and walked back to her tepee.

Some of the kids were still petting Laggon and feeding him water and fresh grass.

Once inside his mother started to make some coffee.

"Did you get to see Ally? Did you manage to find out who had killed pa?"

"Yes ma, I did."

"You did? Well done. Did you tell the sheriff?"

"No, I can't really go to a sheriff's office ma, they would lock me up", he laughed, "as soon as look at me I'd be in the cell."

"So, what will you do?"

"The two men concerned are both dead and," he smiled, "I have pa's watch back."

"That's wonderful news. Who were the men?" She asked excitedly.

"Donald Murphy and Peter………. whatever his name was."

"That Donald Murphy was always evil, just like his pa. Is his pa still alive?"

"No, he died several years ago," he shrugged, "I'm not sure how."

"Good, I'm surprised the spirits let him live so long. He did a lot of bad things."

"Well there is nobody now to carry on the blood line as far as I know."

"Good." She said handing him his coffee laughing.

"I need to tell you about Ally's idea though. She has suggested that…"

"She is a lovely girl, isn't she? You know your pa and I and Ally's folks thought you would end up together. You both got on so well from when you first started school."

"She is still lovely and very intelligent ma, but I have to tell you her suggestion, I need to know what you think. It's important to me." He was trying to remember the order he and Ally had practiced his speech to her.

"Oh, ok," she said realizing she had interrupted him, "I'm sorry."

"Don't be sorry ma, it's just it might come as a shock…."
Just then Little Bear burst in immediately grabbing him and bear hugging him.

"Red Flame! It's so good to see you."

"It's good to see you Little Bear." Returning the bear hug. He lied, he really wanted time to explain his and Ally's plan to his mother without interruption.

For the next hour his old friend sat and told him about the tribes hunting exploits, how the fighting with the army had intensified and who had been killed in the latest action. It was only when asked if he was back to stay that he was able to explain that his mother and he were in deep conversation about his future plans when he had arrived.

186

"I can't tell you how long I intend to stay, it all depends on what ma and I decide. As soon as we know I will tell you."

"I'm sorry to have interrupted you, I just didn't think." Said Little Bear apologetically.

"Don't be silly, you are always welcome here." Said ma looking daggers at her son.

"I will come and see you later." Red Flame said.

Little Bear turned, nodded to ma and left the tepee. Silence.

"You were very abrupt with him, he's your best friend after all."

"I know ma, but he should give us time together before barging in."

"He doesn't know we have things to discuss. Be patient."

"Yes ma. Sorry." He knew he wasn't going to win this argument, so he decided silence was the best thing.

"Now, what were you saying about Ally?"

"Firstly, I went to Ally about pa's murder. She was able to give me some information about Donald and how he had been seen using pa's watch in the bar and also some rumors she had heard. I went to Donald's house and Peter was there too. Remember him? It seems he is Donald's bodyguard now, or was. I asked some questions which they didn't like and so Donald told Peter to kill me. He was that brazen. I killed Peter first and then Donald.

That was the first thing. Next, Ally asked me to stay the night at her house as there were too many bounty hunters in the area looking for me."

"No," said ma, "you didn't?" Looking deeply shocked.

"I did ma. Ally was thinking of only my safety, nothing else. Anyway, she made me supper and we sat for hours discussing my infamy, the stories and lies that were being told, and so on. She slept in the bedroom, me on the parlor floor. She is a very smart lady and the next morning when I was about to leave she said she had an idea and would I listen to it. Of course, I said yes."

She pointed out that by the time I got back here to you today I probably would be killed by a bounty hunter or whoever. She told how the army had increased the number of men looking for me and there was now a big reward for my capture, dead or alive. She asked me how long I could go on killing soldiers before they caught me and hanged me, if I was still alive by then.

"Can I have a coffee ma? All this talking is making me dry." Nervous as well but he didn't say that.

"Of course, I should have got one for you earlier." She stood up and went straight to the coffee pot on the open fire, poured one for each of them and sat down again. He didn't say a word while she was up and neither did she. He was coming to the part he felt she would not understand and he needed to concentrate on how to say it.

"Ally said that as good as I am at fighting I would be better at talking to both sides and to get them to make a proper peace agreement that both sides could honor and maintain, almost like a politician. I said that as soon as a soldier saw me, I would be killed. She said, not if I was a white man."

Ma's jaw dropped yet again, but she stayed silent. Perhaps she was biting her tongue.

"When Ally suggested it, I laughed, but she said that was because for the last few years or so I have been an Indian, but she pointed out that my features are European like pa's and if I put my hair in a ponytail and dressed in white man's clothes nobody would know any different."

Ma still sat silently. Her facial expression had not changed. Maybe she was just visualizing him as a white man.

"Ally was so confident that she dressed me in some of her pa's old clothes and we went into town. Nobody took any notice of me even when she sent me into the saloon to buy a beer, I spoke to a few men including Billy Webster from school, do you remember him? He didn't recognize me. Well, he did but not from school."

Ma's jaw dropped again, she covered her mouth with her hand and laughed loudly.

"Good for Ally," she said amid fits of laughter, "I'm so looking forward to seeing her again."

"You are?"

"Yes," she nodded, "of course I am. We always knew she was right for you, pa and I."

"But ma, me being a white man?" He decided not to mention Ewan and his thoughts on the subject.

"I'd rather you be a white man than a dead man. At least I would see you sometimes. And Ally? I suppose you were going to tell me that part of the story later?" She grinned.

He was so relieved, nothing like what he had expected from her, that a tear ran down his cheek.

"My son, was it such a worry to you, I mean my reaction? I haven't seen you shed a tear since you were five years old. I began to think you didn't know how to cry. My poor Red Flame, I can't believe my approval would mean so much to you."

She placed her hands either side of his face and standing on her toes reached up and kissed his forehead. He couldn't say a word otherwise the tears would just gush.

"You have not answered the bit about Ally. What are those plans? Will I be a grandma?" She asked with a glint in her eye.

"I don't know that yet ma, we are close, there is no doubt about it, and I like the idea, but I think it probably depends on what happens with this white man thing, after all if it doesn't I could be dead in no time, and that wouldn't be fair to her."

"Don't say that."

"But it's true ma. I nearly didn't make it here today. Some stupid bank robber took a shot at me, luckily he wasn't a good shot."

"Really?"

"There are lots of Bounty Hunters looking for me at the moment, I'm worth a lot of money ma, dead or alive. In fact, if you shot me now the government would give you a $1000."

"$1000? Let me find my gun." They both roared with laughter again, it was good to see her laugh.

"If it's alright with you I will run to Little Bear and apologize for earlier, not for long, and then we can carry on with this conversation."

"That's good. You will make a good politician. I will make some food for when you get back."

"Thanks ma. I will be back soon." He turned and left the tepee and walked to Little Bear's tepee who was sitting outside with his new lady friend, they both stood up and greeted him. He apologized for his earlier rudeness.

He did not mention Ally and what their plans may be, he stuck to Indian problems and how the tribe could solve them.

After an hour he was back at his mother's tepee enjoying a nice bison meal. After which they sat outside enjoying the sunset and just talking about their futures.

"I suppose your leaving tomorrow."

"No. You suppose wrongly. I am staying here with you tomorrow. Is there anything you would like to do? Anywhere you would like to go?" He smiled as he said it.

"Oh, well yes, there is actually. I would like to take a ride to the Black Warrior river where pa and I used to fish, not to fish but just ride along the banks. Can we do that?"

"Of course, we can. Is it still safe for us there?"

"No white men have been sighted there, not recently. So, I think it's safe."

"Good, then we have a date." He said cheekily.

"We do have a date." She was beaming with delight.

That night ma slept in the tepee and he slept outside under the stars, it had been a good day and now he could sleep thinking of Ally and their future.

The next morning, he woke with the sun rising, ma was already up and making a snack for their journey, he could tell she was eager to get going. In no time they were on their way, he could relax as there was no chance of running into any bounty hunters or cavalry, they were off the beaten track and as ma had said no white men had been seen in the area. For nearly two hours they plodded on until the river came into view. Ma knew exactly where she was heading, she was excited, it was the place where she had first met pa. A small clearing surrounded by trees on three sides and the river on the other. She dismounted and pointed to the river bank.

"It was just here that I was standing fishing, when I heard a man's voice say it's a lovely day for fishing wouldn't you say? Of course, I didn't know that was what he said at the time, I didn't understand English then. But he was very handsome like you, and he had a kind gentle nature," she led him to a fallen tree and sat on it. She patted the trunk for him to sit too, "we sat there together," she pointed to an area next to the river, "and we fished for the rest of the day," she laughed, "he got so annoyed because I caught more fish than him with his fancy rod and fly's. He was used to salmon fishing in Scotland, I had a wooden pole and an old fish bone as a hook," she stopped talking as though reliving the moment, "wonderful times. Wonderful man," she muttered, "he taught me so much."

Red Flame inhaled and turned slowly to his right.
"You did say no white men have been seen here recently didn't you ma?"
"Yes, why?"
"I can smell one. Very near."
"Really?"
He raised his finger to his lips and listened. Nothing. He waited several seconds. Suddenly two riders broke through the trees, after all the silence of the last few minutes it sounded deafening.

He realized immediately they were bounty hunters. He stood up. He wasn't armed except for his hunting knife. One had his rifle across his legs the way he himself preferred to ride, the other had nothing in his hands except his reins.
"Well what have we here?" Asked the armed man.
"We got $40 dollars that's what we got." The second man said. They both laughed.
He knew they were referring to the $20-dollar bounty for each Indian scalp taken.
"What do you want?" He asked.
"I'll take that horse," the second man said as he dismounted and walked towards Laggon, "they sure are unusual markings."
"You can have the horse, I'll have his rifle." The armed one said matter of factly.
"You can't just take a man's horse." Said Ma sounding extremely angry.
"Ah, did we interrupt a little romance going on here?" The armed man said.
"Romance? He's my son." Ma replied.
The second man was only interested in Laggon.
"What a horse, I bet he can fly when he wants to."
Red Flame was now between the man with Laggon and the armed man who was now studying him carefully.

191

"Hey, get over here and check those wanted posters we got," insisted the armed man to the other, "how many Redskins do you know that speak English that good?" The man nodded towards Red Flame.

"Just a minute." The second man replied trying to mount Laggon. He wasn't used to not having any stirrups to climb up into the saddle and as the man tried, Laggon kept moving in a circle, seemingly making it more difficult for the man to mount. All eyes were on the man, would he or wouldn't he get up. Even ma was smiling as the fiasco continued, Red Flame though was watching the eyes of the armed man who was highly amused by his partners antics, Red Flame realized that the man's focus was now not on him. As the man finally got on to Laggon, Red Flame let out a high pitched whistle, which he knew Laggon would know meant danger, and reared up, the bounty hunter started to fall backwards to the ground, but more importantly to Red Flame the first man's horse panicked and reacted by spinning around, taking the man's aim away from him, he took two strides forward while pulling his knife from its sheath and jumping up he embedded the huge knife into the man's kidneys, who now was trying to control his own horse and had his back to him. The horse's rump then swung around, still in a state of panic and hit him sending Red Flame flying to the ground, the man unable to keep control of the horse dropped his rifle then fell to the ground yelling in pain, blood pouring from his kidney area. Red Flame hauled himself up, in pain, his back had taken the brunt of the horse's rear end. He saw the rifle on the grass and hobbled painfully to it just as the second man was getting up. Seeing Red Flame move to the rifle he started to draw his revolver, the man was definitely stunned, he slumped onto his knees which gave Red Flame the vital second he needed to aim and fire. 'Crack.' The man fell back and then to one side, the bullet had hit him in the chest. He looked over to see where ma was, she was still exactly where she had been when the Bounty Hunters had arrived, she was pointing madly to the first man who was trying to stand up to pull the knife out of his side, Red Flame paused a second to see if the man was going to go for his revolver, the man looked over at him and did exactly that. 'Crack.' The man dropped to the ground. Red Flame was surprised how tough this man must have been to be thinking of him, with a 14-inch blade stuck in him. Both bounty hunters were dead. Ma ran over to him and wrapped her arms around him. He could feel her shaking.

"Thank the spirits you are ok. I thought they were going to kill us both.......for $40."

"I think the first one had figured that we were worth more than that when we both spoke English, luckily he didn't get to see the wanted poster."

"I hadn't realized what you have been going through all this time. These men, bad men will just kill for a few dollars. You have to get away, back to Ally as soon as possible otherwise they will get you, you know that don't you?"

"Yes ma."

He patted Laggon several times in thanks as he always did, then rounded up ma's horse which he led to her, she mounted and they cantered back to the safety of the camp. They did not stop to admire the scenery or to reminisce. Not a word was spoken between them.

When they got back to their tepee ma dismounted and ran inside. He thought all the bloodshed she had just seen was too much for her, he couldn't remember if she had seen such violence since the camp was attacked by the cavalry, that was real blood lust, and she had seen that so why was she so annoyed at him?

He went inside and she was sitting on the mat crying.

"I'm so sorry ma, I didn't want you to see that but…"

"It's not you son, it's not you. I just find it so hard to believe that there are men out there that can be so hostile, so full of hatred towards us, wanting to kill us for no reason, I can't believe it, that's all."

"We live in troubled times ma, and I can't see it getting any better, only worse. The white man is not going to rest until we are all defeated and long gone. They want the land, the buffalo and any memory of the tribes destroyed, as if we never existed. We just can't let it happen without a fight ma, they will win of course, there are just too many of them, they will just keep coming, especially with Fort Dade so close."

"I know son, I know." She stood up and they embraced.

193

Later that evening a celebration started around the main fire, the whole tribe came together as one, playing music and dancing and of course eating, they partied till dawn or passed out. Then they slept.

Ma woke him quite early, early considering they had only had a few hours' sleep.

"Do you think you ought to get away soon, the sooner you leave the sooner you get to Ally's, and I'm more worried about you than ever after yesterday. I have prepared you some food and drink and although I want you to stay longer, you can't."

"Yes ma, you are right. I ought to get going. It makes sense." He stood up and stretched, his back was still a little sore from when the hunters horse had side swiped him the day before. He would get over it. He rolled up his blanket as his ma watched him proudly, he assembled his weapons and taking the bag of supplies from her he secured them to Laggon. He kissed her on the cheek, mounted and slowly rode off. After one hundred yards he pulled up and turned to face her, he paused just looking at her, they both waved, longer than he normally did, why, he didn't know.

Then he rode off into the distance gathering speed, with a cloud of red dust following him.

Ma watched until it had disappeared.

CHAPTER 13

He arrived back at Ally's just before midnight, it was warm and humid and he was covered in dust from the long ride, walking Laggon down the narrow lane towards her house he could see through a crack in the drapes that only one light was on, it was probably her bedroom light. He led Laggon around the back so that he wouldn't be seen by any passersby and then knocked softly on the back door using his knuckles. It was heavy wood and so would vibrate around the inside of the house. Silence. He waited. He knocked again, this time slightly louder.

"Who's there?"

"It's me Red Flame."

"Oh my God." He heard her say.

Several bolts clanked as Ally made her way down the door unbolting as she went. The door flew open and she immediately wrapped her arms around him, she was crying and shaking.

"What's wrong Ally?"

"Come in, get in quickly," she grabbed his arm and almost pulled him in to the kitchen, "I'm so pleased your back. I was worried sick something had happened to you."

"Why? What is wrong." Then he saw her lip was swollen and badly cut.

"Well it was after, he came, he came here and ......
sex.......and....."

"Ally, you are not making sense. Sit down in the parlor, relax and I will get us some coffee."

"Oh....... yes, ok." She was all over the place, definitely not thinking straight. She sat on the sofa looking at her hands shaking. She seemed distressed and miles away.

He made the coffees and took them into the parlor, he placed one next to her on the small table and carried his to the other chair and sat.

"Now what's gone on?"

She took a deep breath and gathered her thoughts.

"You know before you left to see your ma, you had said that when you were in the saloon you had met Billy Webster, right? But he hadn't recognized you?"

"Right."

"He had."

"What do you mean he had?"

"He did remember you and where from after you left the saloon. He also watched as we left town together that day. Do you remember?"

"Of course."

"Well he showed up here, the day after you had left. He was drunk."

"Why? What did he want?"

"Sex. He said if I did not have sex with him he was going to the Sheriff and tell him that I was hiding you."

"What?" He said jumping to his feet.

"I told him to go away. He could tell the Sheriff whatever he liked," she said looking up at him, "the next thing I remember was him punching me here," she raised her hand and pointed to her cut lip, "and then when I came to he had stripped me of all my clothes. They were all over the room and he was trying to rape me." She stood up and wrapped her arms around him. Tears flooding down her face. He held her tight.

"It's ok now, its ok."

"He tried to…., he tried several times but he couldn't. He……."

"It's alright Ally, he won't come near you again, I promise." He clasped her hand and gently eased her back on to the sofa.

"But you don't understand," she said gathering her thoughts," he came back with the Sheriff and three deputies looking for you the next day."

"What did the Sheriff say?"

"He said that Billy had told him that I was harboring a fugitive, which was a serious offence and I could go to jail if it was proved. I told them what he had tried to do, he was trying to blackmail me but they didn't listen. They left here but have returned every day since looking for you."

"What time do they come?"

"About ten or eleven, never before."

196

"Does Billy come with them?"

"No, never. But I have seen him slowly riding past and looking in the back to see if there is another horse tied up. He would soon get the Sheriff then."

He stood thinking to himself, his mind was racing.

"First things first. I'm going to move Laggon over into the wood's opposite, just in case the Sheriff or Billy show up earlier. Does the Sheriff come into the house when checking?"

"No. He just stands out front looking in. Sometimes a deputy walks around back to look, but that's it. I'm usually in the kitchen when they arrive."

"Right, I will walk Laggon over the road to the woods and when I get back I will make some fresh coffee. Ok?" He didn't wait for an answer. He turned and went out the back door. Outside into the pitch black.

Quietly he closed the door behind him, he stood absolutely still for several seconds and only when he was sure nobody was around or watching him he moved towards Laggon and petted him. He picked up a bucket of water that Ally used for her own horse, and slowly led Laggon out of Ally's front gate and across the narrow trail into the woods. They meandered through the trees for about one hundred yards until they came to a slight clearing, his eyes were now adjusting to the darkness, here he loosely tied Laggon to a stout tree stump and placed the full bucket down beside it. He looked towards Ally's place but could see no sign of it, the woods were so dense not even the porch light could be seen.

Four minutes later he was back in the house refilling both their coffee cups.

"Right, where were we?" He asked.

"You asked about Billy?"

"Yes. He comes here on his own to see if I'm here, or is it he just wants to see you? Maybe he just has a 'thing' for you."

"No, he hit me, and then he stripped me, and then he tried to rape me. That's definitely not 'a thing'." Ally was getting a little upset and annoyed with him, understandably.

"Sorry Ally. I am not trying to upset you, I just want to try and understand this whole situation."

She took a gulp of coffee. Then looked to the floor.

"This change's everything Red Flame. All our plans. Gone."

"In what way?"

"Well, there is no way you could live here as a white man is there? They would know it was you. This Billy Webster man has really frightened me, he's not going to leave me alone. I can't sleep at night, I keep waking up thinking he's in here."

He leaned forward and clasped her hand.

"He will not bother you again, you have my word."

"It doesn't matter Red Flame. The Sheriff suspects me. They will keep watching me for a long time or until they know you have been caught or are dead." Tears rolled down her face. Her eyes were still full of fear.

They sat looking at each other. Staring into each other's eyes neither saying a word. Neither sure how to continue the conversation. A minute later he finally gulped his coffee down.

"I think you should get to bed, you have had a long day. Get some sleep." He said quietly. She stood up, she placed her cup on the kitchen sink and then walked into the bedroom and collapsed on the bed.

"Good night Red Flame." She called out as she rolled onto her side.

"Good night Ally." He took it that by her reaction he wasn't invited to share her bed. It was definitely for the best. He stretched out on the sofa and dozed off. He had a lot of thinking to do before the morning.

"Pssst. Red Flame," Ally's shoe hit him on the arm. It was Ally whispering to him.

He opened his eyes and looked towards the bedroom door without raising his head. Her shoe was on the floor. Ally was crouched on all fours behind the bedroom wall with just her head peeking around the corner.

"Red Flame, don't move." She said, whispering again.

"What's the matter?" He replied also in a whisper.

"The sheriff is at the front door, he's trying to see in. Don't move a muscle. I am going into the kitchen incase the deputy comes around back and looks in the kitchen window. He might see you. Do not move." Ally stood up and walked to the kitchen, brushing his legs as she passed the sofa and taking up her position at the window. Sixty seconds later she was waving to the deputy in the garden and purposely blocking his view as he peered in. He soon left.

"Thank you, God," she said quietly," he's gone. Don't move yet, I will check the front," she moved back through the parlor and looked through the curtains, "it's alright they have gone. You can get up now." She stood looking down at him as he still lay on the sofa with a huge grin on her face.

"What?" He asked embarrassingly.

"The great Red Flame cowering on the couch in front of a woman, a white woman too. That's what I'm laughing at." All the tears of the night before had gone.

"Oh, go away. Get some coffee on you evil woman." They both roared with laughter.

He went to the sink and washed while Ally got some food together for breakfast then they sat down at the kitchen table.

"Our plans are not going to work Red Flame, we need to face that."

He thought momentarily, he nodded.

"I know. The only way now we could spend our lives together would be if you came to the tribe with me, and we lived there. But you couldn't do that. That way of life," he shrugged, "it would be like stepping back in time for you. I don't think you could handle it."

"You are right, I couldn't. I thought I could but the constant threat of war...... I just couldn't do it. Not knowing if you were coming back alive. It would kill me."

"I know. I couldn't allow it. My life expectancy is like that," he snapped his fingers, "I wouldn't sleep at night knowing I would be leaving you in the tribe alone, it would be just a matter of time before the white men came and.........."

They sat, her fiddling with a loose thread on the table cloth, him pushing a small piece of bread with his fork around his plate. Finally, they both looked up and stared at each other, neither moving. Each recognizing the obvious.

"I wish this had worked out for us Ally, I was so looking forward to our lives together but...."

"I was too. Having you here meant......." She stood up and walked over to the window, gazing out over the trees. She was sobbing quietly to herself.

He moved over to stand behind her and wrapped his arms around her waist.

"I think I should leave. It's too dangerous for you if I get caught here, they would lock you up, and I couldn't stand that. I love you Ally, remember that, I always will." He said quietly releasing his hold on her. She was still staring out of the window.

"I love you Red Flame and I had wanted to spend my life with you, but with the way things are I feel we need to wait and see what the future holds. Who knows, they may pardon some of the tribes, this government doesn't have a clue what it's doing and I.........."
Just then she saw him crossing the trail into the woods, he had walked out very quietly and was heading to where he had left Laggon the night before. He hadn't said goodbye. She watched him disappear into the trees. She stopped crying, remembering his last words.

He soon found Laggon and untied him so he could get to fresher grass, he sat down on the ground next to him and ran through all the things he had learnt in the last twelve to fourteen hours. Loggan just looked and listened. Both his and Ally's plans had now changed completely, his ma would also be very disappointed, she had wanted grandchildren and this had been her best chance to date. He lay down on the grass with all their original plans swimming around in his mind, there was no alternative but to accept that he had to return to his old life and unfortunately his old ways. He dozed off.

Several hours later he was awoken by Laggon licking his face, maybe his good friend was getting worried about him, perhaps Loggan thought he was unwell. He sat upright and started chatting to him, Loggan just looked at him, no sign of interest what so ever, he just stared with his big bright brown eyes. Perhaps he did understand. He would wait until dark before leaving the woods and then he would head into town.

He couldn't remember where Billy lived but he knew of a way to find out. The problem was it meant waiting, just waiting and the hours dragged.

Just after sundown he led Laggon out of the woods on to the trail almost opposite Ally's house, he stopped and noticed the parlor light was on but all the drapes were closed. He wished he could see her again, just once before he left for good.

He mounted and slowly they made their way towards town alert to any traveler's that might be making their way from the opposite direction. It wasn't long before he saw the lights of Tallahassee, he paused at the end of Main Street. The only bright lights on were those of the saloon, he could hear chattering and laughter despite it being over thirty yards away in the distance. Perhaps the patrons inside were celebrating the demise of Donald. There were seven horses tied to the two rails outside the bar, he wondered if one of these was Billy's. He would wait and see. He hoped Billy was enjoying his last beer.

He moved Laggon around the back of the building opposite the saloon and tied him to a rail, he grabbed his bow and quiver and then he walked up a short flight of stairs and sat down on one. From here, sitting in the shadows he could see who and when the bar patrons left for the short ride or walk home for the night. He sat for over an hour on the same hardwood step, three men left the bar separately, each mounting their respective horses and riding off down the main street, one of the Ladies that worked upstairs of the bar stood chatting to a man for several minutes, he may have been her earlier customer, they were laughing and flirting a lot. Then he left and she went back upstairs, he watched her through the window, her long red gown sweeping the stairs as she went. Another man walked out and tried to mount his horse but the drinks he'd had were making it difficult for him, gradually he made it and trotted off down the street swaying slightly from side to side in the saddle.

Suddenly two men appeared through the swing doors, one was a small tubby man who he didn't recognize, the other was Billy. They both shouted 'good night' to each other and staggered off in opposite directions.

Red Flame watched until Billy disappeared into the shadows as he moved further away from the bright bar lights, then he stood up and followed. Staying on the darker side of the street he remained about forty feet behind. Billy was wearing a holster and hand gun.

Red Flame began to remember the town layout, Billy should, if he remembered correctly, take the next left and his house was the second house on the right. Billy did take the next left and then crossed over the street towards his house. He stopped at his gate before opening it and glanced back down the street. Had he heard him following? No. He couldn't have done.

Red Flame was now twenty feet away from him. He took off his bow and pulled out an arrow, he looked at it in the moonlight, it was one that he had taken from the Pawnee scout. How fortuitous. Nobody would know it was him that had killed the drunken slob. There would be no connection, no one would know he had even been in town. A smile spread across his face.

"Billy," he called out quietly, "is that you?"

"Yes," Billy spun around to face him. Squinting to see who it was in the darkness. Then he realized it was his old school adversary, "You. What do you want?" Perhaps it was the feathers that gave it away he thought to himself smiling.

"I hear you tied to rape Ally."

"What's it to you? Wait until I tell the sheriff you were here. He will hang you."

"No Billy. You're not telling anybody anything. You hurt Ally and you tried to rape her. Very manly of you, don't you think? Do you remember Ally?"

"Of course, I do."

"Well perhaps you should close your eyes and think of her now, as you die."

"Die?" Panic was in Billy's voice.

"Yes, die."

Red Flame positioned the Pawnee scout's arrow on his bow and fired. The arrow flew into Billy's chest, he slumped to the ground. Red Flame slowly walked over to where Billy lay, half inside his own garden and half on the sidewalk, his body was holding the gate open, he bent down and felt for his pulse, he hadn't got one. Good, he thought to himself. He turned and walked back across the street and on to main street turning right this time back towards where Laggon was still patiently waiting, making sure to stay in the shadows of the various buildings. He patted Laggon and mounted up and slowly they left town, the town he had grown up in, not knowing if he would ever see it again.

Despite one decision having been made for him, although he was struggling to admit it, he now knew he could never live as a Whiteman and so he had to throw himself into the protection of his tribe, and the never-ending war on the White soldiers.

CHAPTER 14

He travelled west throughout the night expecting the journey to rejoin his tribe to take about thirty hours, it was slow going as most of the journey would be done at night, sleeping through the day to avoid any bounty hunters or the like. It was dusk on the second day that he spotted in the distance a two-horse drawn wagon, it was stationary. There was no sign of the driver who, from the direction of the wagon had been heading east towards the Atlantic coast. He slowed Laggon to walking pace and withdrew his rifle from its sheath and placed it across his legs.

He moved slowly up to the wagon so he could see inside, it was empty except for a couple of old brown blankets. There was no sign of a driver or any weapons, was this a trap he wondered, he dismounted and still holding his rifle at the ready he moved around the wagon checking underneath as he went, nothing. Looking into the woods just to the north he slowly panned the trees, was there somebody hiding in there ready to take a shot at him? He couldn't see anybody.

Then in the long grass about twenty feet away, he noticed a man's boot, as he approached, he realized it was a white man's body laying spread eagled on the ground, there was a nasty gunshot wound to the man's upper arm with a lot of blood seeping through his white shirt. He knelt down next to the man and tore the shirt open to expose the wound. It appeared to be several hours old and because it hadn't been treated in any way, it had turned septic which obviously had got into the man's blood stream and looked very nasty, the smell had already attracted a brigade of ants. He felt the man for a pulse, he was still alive, but barely.

He dashed back to Laggon and grabbed his water pouch, kneeling down he raised the man's head and tried to get some of the water into his mouth, the man started to choke as the water gushed down his parched throat. Red Flame had to move him off this trail as quickly as possible incase other travelers should see them. He picked the man up and loaded him into the back of the wagon, with every move the man groaned in pain, but Red Flame took that as a positive. The man was tall and thin but looked as though he had been used to manual labor. The man's hair was light in color and tied back in a pony tail. He had a couple of strange looking blue drawings on his arms, what they meant he didn't know, he had never seen such things before.

He then picked up his rifle and jumped up onto the seat, calling to Laggon he drove the wagon along the trail until he reached a small break in the trees and then he turned off and into the woods, the rough ground was making the wagon heave one way and then another, the man moaned with each bump, for sixty yards he drove the wagon with Laggon following on into the tree's until they could not be seen by anybody passing by. He pulled the wagon up, jumped down and ran back to the trail, snapping off a sycamore branch as he did so, on reaching the trail he started 'brushing' away the tracks of the horses and the wagon wheels so no one would ever know that anybody had entered the woods. When he had made all the flattened grass 'stand up' again he gathered some kindling and some smaller twigs for a fire to boil water which he would need to quarterize the man's injury quickly as gangrene had already begun to set in.

In minutes the fire was alight and he had got the water on to boil, he ran to the back of the wagon and grabbed the two blankets, one he laid out on the wagon floor and moved the man on to it, the second blanket he cut two 12-inch strips off, one he placed into the pot of almost boiling water. The remainder of the blanket he folded up and used as a pillow for the patient.
Once the water was boiling, by using a couple of twigs he lifted the strip of blanket out of the bubbling water and strode to the wagon and knelt by the man, the man was drifting in and out of consciousness which was just as well as this procedure was going to hurt.
He placed the hot blanket on the man's arm and left it there for two minutes, then he peeled it off bringing layers of skin and poison with it. He dashed back to the fire and dropped the piece of blanket back into the water to re-boil. Two minutes later he repeated the same procedure, the man was still unconscious thankfully. Lots of poison,

lots. He scurried back to the fire and dunked the blanket piece in the water again and then placed his knife blade in the flames, he went back again with the blanket and placed it on the man's arm again, and then back to the fire holding the knife in place for a further two minutes until it was glowing and then back to the wagon, he slowly withdrew the blanket, the wound still looked bad even with the majority of the poison removed, he wiped any excess off that he could and then he laid the still red hot knife blade on the man's wound, the smell was awful, burning flesh and poison. The man flinched and then opened his eyes wide, he let out a spine-chilling scream. Was it because he saw Red Flame leaning over him with a huge knife or was it the pain of his injury. His eyes were wide open, Red Flame knew he should not be conscious, but how to put him out quickly? Red Flame stuck the knife into the floor of the wagon and punched the man on the side of the temple, he just wanted to knock him out not kill him, the punch wasn't hard enough to do either. The man was still staring at him in fright, he took a large breath and punched the man again, this time the man was out like a light. It would have been a lot easier if he'd had a bottle of whisky to administer as an anesthetic. He pulled the knife out of the floor boards and placed it on the area of the wound he had missed. The smell of burning flesh made him heave again, his stomach travelled up to his throat several times before he could look away and inhale fresh air.

At this moment he wished he had paid more attention to his father's medical lessons, it was certainly easier to kill somebody rather that to make them well again.

He studied the wound for a minute, it looked quite good, in fact he felt quite pleased with himself, no visible signs of poison, everything looked black or burnt but clear of poison. He hoped he had done enough, the thought of amputation frightened him.

He threw his knife out towards the fire and gathered the odd bits of blanket and threw them into the heart of the fire, while the smell dissipated he wandered into the trees picking up all the acorns he could find, he returned within several minutes and dropped them into a second pot of boiling water to make some acorn soup for when the man awoke. He then started to think about organizing a safer camp for the night, a bigger fire closer to the rear of the wagon to keep the nocturnal animals away was imperative, more water was required but not for tonight, he would find that tomorrow for both drinking and washing, and some food that would last a few days depending on the healing powers of the patient.

He immediately wandered around the periphery of the small camp noting all available clearings leading away from where they presently were, just in case they had to get away quick, although that would be difficult with a patient in the state he was in at the present time. He picked up twigs and branches as he walked that he would use for the new bigger fire and threw them towards the wagon. After looking towards the sun, he reasoned he had about an hour of usable light left, so if he needed food he had to go hunting fairly soon.

He quickly walked back to the wagon and after checking on the patient, who was still out cold, he snatched up his bow and quiver and jogged into the woods to his north so he wouldn't have to cross the trail or flatten the grass again, silently he moved through the trees and within minutes a large buck rabbit decided he wanted to challenge Red Flames hunting skills, not a wise move. He was back in the camp lighting the new fire and skinning the rabbit well before the sun set. He made a make shift spit and slowly roasted the rabbit, it would take several hours but he wasn't going anywhere so what did it matter. Also, it helped to take away the lingering smell of burnt flesh that had invaded his nostrils. He started to relax and pulled a log over to the new fire so he could sit while watching his meals progress and also hear if the patient awoke. He watched the stars again zipping through the heavens wondering if his father's relatives were watching the same stars overhead, he wondered if he would ever get to Scotland, see the croft his father was born in, see the Edinburgh University building where his father and Ewan had learnt medicine, would he get to see Loch Laggon, the name he had given his best friend, he hoped so, he really hoped so.

After daydreaming for a while, he heard movement from within the wagon, he jumped up and ran to the open rear of the wagon, he peered in and the man was obviously in a lot of pain, his eyes still closed and he was rubbing his arm, Red Flame grabbed the man's arm to prevent him from removing the make shift bandage, as he did so the man's eyes opened, again, in shock or fear they doubled in size.

"Don't, you will pull the bandage off."

The man looked at him, showing no emotion.

"Who the bloody hell are you?" The man replied in an English accent.

"My name is Red Flame." A long pause ensued.

"You bloody scalp people, don't you?"

Red Flame smiled. "No." He replied.

"Did you do this." He raised his arm.

"Yes."

"Bloody hell, I've been saved by a bloody red Indian." He burst into laughter and then suddenly stopped as the pain kicked in. He reached for the bandage again but then stopped.

"You have, but don't tell anybody."

The man roared with laughter again but, still in pain.

"You are alright mate. My names Eric, Eric Smif but my mates call me 'Smiffy''

"Thanks 'Smiffy' but we have to watch that wound. It's very nasty."

"Oh, ok, thanks. Your English is good Red Flame."

"My father was from the old country, how about you, you sound very English too."

"Yeah, well I'm from London, a cockney, I came over last year to Boston. I'm ex-British Navy and came over as a seaman."

"So, how did you end up here? With a bullet wound?"

"My mate and I, Harry, we took a job for a transport company in Boston delivering flour to Fort Dade, fifty barrels they said, no problems, deliver it and come back to Boston with the wagon, that was it. They didn't mention anything about Fur Hunters and Indians, no offence meant, no, it was just a short jaunt down the road they said, drop off the flour and back. Bastards"

"Flour?" Red Flame asked.

"Yes, that's what they told us, easy job."

"So, what happened?"

"Flour be buggered. It was bloody gunpowder. If it had gone off it would have blown us back to bloody London."

Red Flame just looked at him, staggered.

"Yeah, do you believe that? Bastards," there was then a short silence, "that was after a bloody Indian fired an arrow at us, it's still stuck in the wagon somewhere. Oh, sorry no offence meant mate."

"None taken. So, what happened to Harry?"

"We were attacked by two bloody grizzly bears on horseback."

"What?" Red Flame laughed at Smiffy's language.

"Yeah. Two blokes dressed from head to toe in bearskins on horses attacked us."

Red Flame thought for a few seconds.

"You mean they were fur hunters"

"Yeah, that's it. Bloody fur hunters. Bastards. They shot Harry in the head. Then shot me, but I managed to keep the horses going until I passed out. Bastards. Then I woke up and there you were." Red Flame expected him to say Bastards again, but he didn't.

"These fur hunters are not nice people." Red Flame said seriously.

"There are no nice people here, they are all Bastards. Present company excepted of course. They are all mad, always talking about wanting to kill people." Red Flame laughed again, but his sides were aching from laughing too much.

"Well......... I have some food if you want some, soup or meat? You decide."

"I'd like a bit of both if that's ok?"

"Of course. Do you want it here or by the fire?"

"By the fire Red Flame please," Smiffy paused, "I have heard of you, haven't I?"

"Have you, I don't know Smiffy."

"Yeah, you're a good man with a bounty on your head. Don't you worry about me though, once a mate, always a mate, that's my motto. I don't believe the shit they wrote about you anyway."

Red Flame laughed again. He liked Smiffy's sense of humor. Strange as it was.

"I won't ask what they wrote. So, what are your plans?" He asked.

"Get back to Boston and collect my pay check and then," Smiffy shrugged his shoulders, "I may head back to England, jump a boat,

I'm not sure yet. It all depends on whether I live long enough to get back to Boston." They both roared with laughter.

"That's a point, you never know in these parts. Well, you rest for a bit and I'll get the food ready. Ok?"

"Sounds good mate."

"By the way, what are those drawings on your arms?" Asked Red Flame.

"Tattoo's mate. Most British seaman have them. They are for luck."

"Oh, I thought you might be some sort of Witch doctor." They laughed again.

Red Flame left Smiffy to rest while he checked the food situation, everything was hot and so he served up for them both and placed their pots on the log ready for them to dig in. A short while later Smiffy joined him on the log and started stuffing the food down his throat as if he hadn't eaten for days. Finally, after clearing three loads of rabbit and two bowls of soup he sat back and while patting his stomach let out the loudest burp. Red Flame had never seen anybody devour so much food so quickly.

"Compliments to the chef. That was great mate, thank you. Bloody great."

"You are very welcome, I hope you enjoyed it."

"Best bloody meal I have had in years."

They sat quietly savoring the moment, the crackling of the fire, the orange glow and the black, black sky just full of white dancing stars.

"I envy you living like this, it's so bloody peaceful," Smiffy paused, "you've got it so right. Not worrying where the next pound or dollar is coming from. No bastards telling you to do this or do that, nothing to worry about."

"If only. It's not quite like that I'm afraid. People will kill you for twenty dollars out here. I think the folks in Boston are more cultured, but here women get raped, men, even white men are being scalped for the twenty-dollar bounty and once you get a bigger bounty on your head, men travel for miles to track you down. That's how they make a living."

"Bastards. You've got a bounty on you, haven't you?"

"Yes. A large one." He suddenly wondered if he should be telling Smiffy this, after all he didn't really know him and obviously the man needs money.

"How much are you talking about?"

"I'm not really sure now but it was five hundred." He thought it best to keep the amount down.

"What? Dollars?"

"Yes."

"Bloody hell. That's a fortune."

"Now you know why so many bounty hunters want to catch me."

"Well mate, I don't know what you did to deserve that sort of bounty and really I don't want to know. I just know that you're a good sort and I'm just glad you found me and not one of those fur wearing bastards. I'm quite partial to my hair." They both laughed again.

"Me too." Red Flame stood and got them both some water.

"Where did you learn your medical skills?" Smiffy asked.

"My father was a doctor from Scotland originally."

"Your dad was a 'Jock'?"

"A 'Jock'?"

"Yeah. That's what we call all Scotsmen. It's sort of English slang."

"Really? I have never heard that term before."

"Yeah, nothings meant by it. Them Scots call us 'Sassenachs'. But all credit to you, your dad taught you well."

"Good. Thank you. But what is a Sassenach?"

"I don't know. It's just something the Scot's call the English. Nobody takes offence on either side after all we have been fighting battles together for years, especially against the French, we call them frogs and the Spanish, we call them Diego's. They can't beat us, we have the best Navy in the world. A lot of the brits have come to America and now fight for them. That's what I did after my old women left me."

"Your old women?"

"Yeah, my wife. She ran off with a hairy arsed Matelot, the bastard."

"A Matelot? What's that."

"A Naval seaman, that's our nickname."

"You sure have a lot of nicknames you British."

"We do, don't we?" they both laughed again, "so your dad, did he marry an Indian?"

"Yes, she was from quite near here. He was murdered though and so she went back to be with her tribe."

"Murdered? The bastard that murdered him, did they catch him?"

"Yes, he got his just rewards."

"Good. I should say so, bloody good job."

Red Flame didn't always understand this slang that Smiffy used, he was pronouncing 'th' as 'f', but the man made him laugh.

"So, how are you feeling."

"Bit of a bloody pain in the arm, but ok, tired though."

"Well, when you need to go to bed just say so. I'm going to make some coffee. Want some?"

"Yes, please mate."

Red Flame stood and sorted through his bed roll, got some coffee beans and dropped them into a pot and added boiling water, gave them a stir and then left them to boil for a while.

"I first heard about you in Jacksonville," said Smiffy, "a sheriff it was, a bloody nice man, said that you were doing a lot for your people, somefing about defending them from the army and you'd killed a few of the bastards." Why hadn't he mentioned this before he wondered.

"Well, I suppose you could put it like that." He laughed to himself, not a bad way of putting it he thought, it sounds better than the real thing.

"These bloody soldiers are a waste of space, not a brain among them and lazy bastards too. Do you know they made Harry and me unload all those bloody barrels ourselves? Bloody heavy they were too. Not one offered to help. It was only after we'd unloaded them they told us it was gunpowder. Mind you there weren't many of them in the fort, it seems most of them have gone off to fight a bull or somebody, it seems they are all getting nervous about this Indian, he's got a great big bloody tribe and is going to drive the army back into the bloody Atlantic. Somefing like that anyway. Bloody good luck to him I say."

"You mean there are only a few soldiers left at the fort at the moment?"

"Yeah, they all pissed off up north somewhere."

Red Flame poured their coffees as he thought through what Smiffy was telling him. The army had left to meet Chief Sitting Bull and the united tribes that he had thought about joining? Perhaps he could do something to inspire the tribes a little, like blow the fort up. At least then they wouldn't have a permanent base for many, many miles. That would really upset the politicians up north. He laughed at the thought.

"What's funny." Asked Smiffy

"You know, your trip here might have been the work of the spirits."

"What bloody spirits?"

"The good Indian spirits, my Indian spirits. I might just blow the fort up."

"Bloody hell. You don't mess about do you?"

Red Flame thought what Smiffy had said.

"I try not to Smiffy."

"You do that and you'll be a bloody legend mate."

"That's not why I'm doing it Smiffy. If I told you what the Whiteman or particularly the Army had done to my people you wouldn't believe me, so I'm not going to bore you with the details. Only to say that if I did blow up Fort Dade, it would bring much joy to the Apalachee tribe of Indians and more."

"Much joy to me as well. Lazy bastards."

Red Flame roared with laughter again, his sides ached he'd laughed so much. He was crying with laughter.

"Is everybody from London like you." He asked.

"No. I'm better looking. I'm bloody good looking don't you think. Bullet hole or not."

Red Flame stood up holding his sides, he was in pain.

"I can't speak to you for a minute, I need a walk." He walked off around the camp.

Five minutes later he was back sitting on the log next to Smiffy. He raised his forefinger.

"Now, don't say a word." He said looking straight at Smiffy.

Smiffy just stared at him, not smiling, no hint of emotion. Then he burst out laughing.

They both sat there laughing together until they could laugh no more.

"Your making my bloody arm hurt again."

"Good, serves you right you bastard." Red Flame added, still laughing.

Smiffy laughed even more.

"I'm not a bastard. You can't be a bastard if you're from London." Smiffy said still laughing.

"Go to bed before I shoot you." Red Flame said jokingly.

"I think I need to," Smiffy stood up and slowly, but painfully walked to the back of the wagon, "goodnight Red Flame, and thanks for everything." He disappeared inside.

"Goodnight Smiffy, sleep well."

"Bastard." Smiffy yelled out from inside the wagon.

Red Flame laughed again. He slowly walked around the camp again throwing odd sticks and branches on to the fire. He poured another coffee for himself and sat back down on the log. All was quiet, no birds making any noise, always a good sign he thought to himself. He slowly took sips of his hot coffee and thought about the day, what he had learnt from Smiffy about the fort and the soldiers that had left to wage war against his people, what could he do to help? Could he possibly pull off the blowing up of the fort, of course he could. Just think of a decent plan.

He slid under the wagon with his bow and quiver and his rifle, laid out his bed roll right below where Smiffy was sleeping so he could hear if Smiffy got up. He could feel the heat from the fire. Laggon was about eight feet away watching. He felt safe as he closed his eyes and thought about obliterating a fort.

The next morning, he had refueled the fire, put the coffee pot on and was checking on Smiffy who was awake but just lying on his blanket.

"How did you sleep?" He asked.

"Bloody good. I slept like a log."

"How does the arm feel?"

"Sore, but ok."

"I have got some coffee on the boil; would you like some soup as well?"

"That would be great mate."

"Right." He turned back towards the fire when he heard somebody shouting.

"Hello. Is there anybody home?" The voice was coming from within the woods and approximately forty to fifty feet away.

"Hello. Anybody home?" Again, the same voice.

Red Flame moved quickly to the back of the wagon picking up his rifle, bow and quiver from the grass below the wagon. He stood next to where Smiffy was trying to raise himself on to his knees so that he could see through the front of the open wagon to where the voice came from.

Red Flame handed him the rifle.

"Just in case." He whispered. Smiffy nodded. Red Flame placed his quiver over his shoulder and took out one arrow and prepared to fire.

"Hello. Hello." The voice was now louder but no sign of any movement yet. He panned the trees and long grasses looking for whoever it was. Was there more than one?

"Anyone at home?" The voice was now very close.

Red Flame thought he had pinpointed the direction that the stranger or strangers would appear, he tapped Smiffy on the shoulder and pointed to the area.

"About there." He whispered. He then moved to the side of the wagon furthest from that point, he didn't want Smiffy to get hit if the stranger started shooting at him. The more distance between them the better.

Suddenly, a man dressed in furs pushed his way through the trees, he was carrying a long rifle. "Hello." He yelled again. Red Flame did not respond, but was ready.

Then crashing out of the trees a second fur hunter appeared just to the first ones left. Good, he thought they were close together, too close. An elementary mistake.

"It's the same bastards." He heard Smiffy say.

The man to the left had already seen him and was preparing to shoot, he raised his bow and arrow and fired hitting the hunter in the chest. The man dropped his long gun and sunk to the ground. He reached back to his quiver and grabbed another arrow, loading quickly he

215

glanced up to the original hunter who was running towards him aiming at him as he ran.

'Crack' The man fired and the bullet hit the wagon less than six inches from his stomach, he aimed at the charging man and fired. The fur hunters rifle flew in the air as the arrow hit him in the chest and he hit the ground. Red Flame paused, loading another arrow he was about to check on the two hunters when suddenly Smiffy ran past him clutching the rifle Red Flame had given him.

Smiffy stopped four feet from the first hunter and shot the man in the head, twice.

"Bastard. You bastard," he yelled. Then he moved to the second hunter and shot him twice in the head.

"Bastards. That's for Harry, you bastards." Smiffy was crying as he stood looking down at the men as they lay motionless, then he turned back towards Red Flame, he still had the rifle in his good hand. He was staring at Red Flame with a blank look on his face.

Red Flame suddenly felt uneasy, Smiffy was standing fifteen feet away from him with a loaded rifle and looking strangely agitated. Had he remembered the bounty money he wondered, after all he didn't know him properly, maybe the five hundred dollars meant more to him now he'd had time to think about it. If Smiffy was going to shoot him he couldn't miss from this range, injured arm or not, just be ready to move as soon as the rifle is raised, he thought to himself.

They stared at each other for what seemed to Red Flame to be an eternity. He was beginning to sweat.

"Bastards," shouted Smiffy suddenly, his face back to normal, he wiped the tears off his cheeks, "that was for Harry. I shot 'em Red Flame. Both of 'em. Bastards." He then strode past Red Flame still holding the rifle. He laid it down by the log, sat down on the log and looked straight ahead shaking as though he was in shock.

Red Flame followed him to the fire, nonchalantly picking up the rifle and placing it and his bow and quiver under the wagon again. Silence.

"You want some coffee?" He asked.

"Yes, please mate."

Red Flame poured two coffees and sat back down next to Smiffy who still seemed a little shocked.

216

"That's the first person I have ever killed," he paused, "well, first and second I suppose, but bastards like that deserve it don't they?" Said Smiffy.

"Yes, I find if you just remember that if you hadn't killed them, then they certainly would have killed you. It makes it a lot easier to bear if you look at it that way."

"Yeah, it does. Your right, it does. Thanks mate."

Nothing was said for a while as they both slowly drank their coffees.

"So, what are your plans?" Red Flame finally asked.

"Well I gotta get this bloody wagon back to Boston otherwise I don't get paid. After that though, I don't know."

"You can't drive this wagon with your arm the way it is. It will kill you."

"I know, but what else can I bloody well do?"

"I do have a suggestion, but I'm not sure how you will take it."

"I'm listening Mate." Said Smiffy moving forward so he could hear better.

"Suppose I could you get you some dollars, I mean lots of dollars, so if you didn't want to go back to Boston you didn't have to."

"That'd be bloody great mate, the dog's bollocks."

"What does that mean."

"Oh yeah, sorry mate, that means great, or the best".

"Right, hear me out. Firstly, you need to draw me a plan of the fort and where the gunpowder is stored. I will then go to the fort overnight and then return for you the next morning. I will then drive you to Jacksonville where you will sell what I have for you to make lots of dollars. You could also sell this wagon, you would probably get more for it than what the company owes you in wages. What do you think?" Red Flame asked, studying Smiffy as he was thinking about his offer.

"Why do you need to know where the gunpowder is and why are you going to the fort?" Smiffy either wanted him to spell it out or he wasn't as smart as Red Flame had given him credit for.

"I want to blow the fort up." He said matter of factly.

"Bloody hell," said Smiffy sitting back, "blow the bloody fort up? Your mad, your even more bloody mad than I am," he paused just staring at Red Flame, "no wonder you have got such a large bounty on you, no wonder they bloody want to catch you, they must be

217

shitting themselves all the time you're alive," he paused again and then a huge grin appeared on his face, "lets blow the bastards to hell." Then he roared with laughter again. Red Flame couldn't help but join in.

"Good."

"Just a bloody minute, what have you got that's worth money to me, I don't want no scalps, they give me the screaming abdabs."

"The what?" Asked Red Flame.

"The screaming abdabs, means make me feel sick."

"The screaming abdabs," he repeated slowly, "are you sure you're not just making up some of these words?"

"Nah, they are London slang." They both laughed again.

"When I first saw your wound, it gave me the screaming abdabs."

"I bet it bloody did. But, you didn't answer my question........what have you got that is worth money to me and not you?"

Ah, he thought, despite his bravado, Smiffy is brighter then he lets on.

"Just wait here, I will be back in a few moments. Pour some more coffee."

"Ok, will do."

Red Flame walked past the dead hunters and disappeared into the trees, four minutes later he reappeared leading two horses with saddles and another pulling a travois laden with different furs. He led them as close to the fire as he safely could.

"Bloody hell," said Smiffy, "what am I supposed to do with those bastards?"

"Not the horses Smiffy, it's the furs that are worth the real money. Not the horses."

"No? Really?"

"Yes. Don't get me wrong, the horses are worth money and the rifles too, but it's the furs that these men make their fortunes from. On average I think they get about forty to sixty dollars for each, more for the buffalo skins." Smiffy stood up and started counting through the furs, he turned and smiled.

"There has to be forty bloody furs here, gor blimey. That's over two hundred dollars. Bloody hell," Smiffy sat back down on the log looking into space, "you will give me all these just for a map of the fort?"

"Yes. But, it better be right, as accurate as you can get it, otherwise........."

"I know, you will bloody scalp me." They roared again.

"Well........," how could you be mad with this man, he just made you laugh all the time, a real comedian, "let's have some breakfast and then I will check your arm again, and don't give me any more of your slang or I will cut your 'bloody' arm off." He tried to say 'bloody' the way that Smiffy did but it didn't sound right. Neither of them laughed.

After eating and checking Smiffy's wound, which had improved immensely, he decided to hunt for some more food and water so that Smiffy would be alright if he did decide to go to the fort. Within an hour he was back in the camp with a fresh supply of water and a young buck Roe that he would prepare for several meals.

"More coffee?" He asked Smiffy.

"Yeah mate, lovely."

As Red Flame organized the two mugs of coffee, Smiffy picked up a small stick from the stock that Red Flame had piled up near the fire and started drawing a plan of Fort Dade on a baron piece of earth in front of where they were both sitting. He started with a three feet wide square and then he added smaller squares or rectangles within the larger square. Then Smiffy sat back and waited for Red Flame to join him on the log.

"This looks interesting," he said handing Smiffy his coffee. "is that the fort?"

"Yeah, these are the outside walls," said Smiffy pointing to the large square he had marked in the dirt," this one is the main office where the C.O is," he pointed to one of the smaller squares, "this one is the troops quarters where the most activity takes place, this one is the parade ground and this one is the stable block. These are the four staircases from the ground up to the upper walkway."

"What's the C.O?"

"The bloody commanding officer."

"Of course. Hmm.......... where are the main gates?" He asked.

"Oh, bloody hell, I forgot them. You need to know where they are don't you?" Smiffy started to laugh as he picked up the stick again, he marked the gates location, "in the center of this wall. Facing east. Ok?"

"Right," said Red Flame studying the plan for a minute or two," how many troops should there be in the fort at any one time do you think?"

"Christ knows, not a bloody clue I'm afraid."

"Well, how many bays in the stable area would you say?"

"I never thought of that.........about two hundred I would think."

Red Flame knew that was the approximate number of troops stationed at the fort most of the time, but it was good to have it confirmed by someone who had been there recently.

"About two hundred eh, and how many horses did you see when you were there?"

"Only about twenty I'd say." Said Smiffy looking to the sky while he visualized the area.

Twenty, Red Flame thought to himself, which meant that probably only ten were on duty at any one time. This plan was sounding better all the time.

"Where did you stack the barrels?"

"Right there," Smiffy made a large cross in the dirt, "furthest point from the troops quarters in case one of them lit a fag."

"A fag?"

"A bloody cigarette. Stupid really, they made Harry and me laugh, because if those barrels did blow, all that would be left would be a bloody great hole in the ground. Stupid bastards."

Red Flame picked up another stick that was lying nearby.

"The sentries, were they positioned in the turrets, here," he marked a small cross in the dirt, "and here, here and here," marking the four known lookout turrets.

"They should have been but no, they were only in the front two. No guards in the back two. And, you know what, there were no lights on at the back. We had to unload and stack those bastard barrels in complete darkness. And...... you know they didn't even offer us a drink. Bastards." Smiffy was getting annoyed, but then he laughed as did Red Flame.

It went silent as Red Flame thought through various plans to enter the fort.

"Your bloody quiet. Makes me nervous when your quiet." Said Smiffy.

"Why?"

"I keep remembering you leaning over me with your bloody great knife." They both laughed together again.

"You won't forget that in a hurry will you?"

"Bloody right I won't." Said Smiffy still laughing.

"I was just trying to work out from your plan the best way to get into the Fort."

"The guards where all on that front wall, at and above the gates, if that helps?"

"So, the back wall would be the place to enter?"

"Bloody right," said Smiffy, "the front is where they think any trouble will come from."

"Good, I just need to make a rope."

"A rope? I've got one under the seat in the wagon, it's there in case we needed to haul up the barrels anytime. Have a look, I'm sure it's still there."

Red Flames eyes lit up and went to the front of the wagon and looked under the seat, and there was a nice new rope. Smiling he went back to where Smiffy was still sitting.

"That's great, thank you Smiffy."

"That's three hundred dollars to you. No, as your one of those evil bastard Red Indians its four hundred dollars." Again, they both laughed.

Red Flame went back to the front of the wagon and pulled out the rope and laid it on the grass so he could see the full length of it. He estimated it to be about thirty feet long, the fort wall was about twenty feet high so he had spare if he needed it. He thought he would be best to make it a lasso so he could throw it over one of the forts spikes and haul himself over. Suddenly his train of thought was interrupted.

"How are going to blow it." Asked Smiffy.

"Blow it?"

"Blow it up. How are you going to bloody ignite it?"

"I haven't worked that out yet."

221

"You haven't worked that out yet? Probably the most important part of the whole plan and you haven't worked it out yet? Jesus Christ... I thought you were a smart bloody Indian."

Red Flame didn't know whether Smiffy was being serious or still joking. He wasn't laughing, so he was obviously being serious.

"Yeah, that is a vital part of the plan isn't it?" He admitted.

They both sat silently for many minutes thinking how to get some sort of fuse, or fire, that he could light when he got to the gunpowder.

"I suppose I could light just a small fire behind the back wall and take it over the wall with me."

"Don't be stupid mate, somebody would see the flames."

"Not if I..........., no your right. Stupid idea," said Red Flame apologetically, "forget that."

"What if you fired bullets into the barrels, would they ignite the bloody powder?"

"I don't think so. I have seen fire set off ammunition and powder," he answered slowly, "but not bullets. Where on your plan is the armory, is it near the barrels."

"Umm..... yeah, it's right there," he marked a cross on his plan with his finger, "just a few feet away. Stupid eh." There was along silent pause again as both men thought to solve the problem.

"It has to be done by fire. Only problem I can see is that I will need to get as close to that gunpowder as possible, light several fires on the barrels and then run."

"Run? I should coco, run like a bastard, I would." Added Smiffy laughing.

"How many troops were in the fort would you say? And how many horses?" He asked again. He needed confirmation.

Smiffy started slowly counting his fingers, then he started again.

"Six on duty, four were on the upper walkway and two at the gates, one either side.

Also, there would be the same number or more off duty, probably in their quarters. The C.O would be in his office or his quarters. So, I think if you said fifteen you'd be safe."

"Fifteen? That's better than I had hoped. What about horses, how many do you think?" Again, Smiffy went quiet as he visualized the fort he had seen two nights earlier.

"I still think it's no more than twenty."

"Normally there would be two hundred, you think the others had all gone to find Sitting Bull?" He needed Smiffy to confirm again what he thought he had seen.

"Yes, and I think one troop had gone to St. Augustine to escort some Indians they had caught to a big prison there. Something like that."

"That makes sense, there is a prison there, a big one where they now keep Indian troublemakers. They must have heard that all the tribes were travelling north west to join the fight with Sitting Bull and his mix of tribes."

"Yeah, the trooper that escorted us in the fort that night, lazy bastard he was, thought the troops were going to massacre the tribes once and for all. That's why I shit myself when I woke up with you and your bloody knife about to scalp me." Smiffy laughed out loud.

"I wasn't going to scalp you. I was going to stick it in your chest." They both laughed.

"So……….how are you going to blow it up?"

For the next hour Red Flame ran through his ideas, Smiffy listened but said nothing until he had finished.

"That sounds like a plan, one bloody thing though, when it does go bang, are you going to be far enough away?"

"I hope so." He said standing and getting everything together for the short ride to Fort Dade. He checked his arrows were true and in good condition, he then tied four-inch strips of blanket around six of his arrows, then he checked his rifle and knife were clean, and finally the rope was rolled in a tight loop. He would wait until sunset before leaving the camp for the five-hour ride to the fort, so the guards would be getting weary and not quite so alert. He hoped.

CHAPTER 15

It was just after sunset that they finished their meal and he mounted Laggon ready to get on his way, his plan running through his mind, over and over, trying to cover all eventualities and just get it done.

"I'll see you in the morning Smiffy, don't forget to keep the fire going, I don't want to get back here to find a bear or a cougar has eaten you. I will have wasted all that energy and food to keep you alive." He said as he turned Laggon westward.

"I'll be here you bastard," Smiffy yelled out, "good luck and take bloody care."

Red Flame thought he sensed some affection in Smiffys voice, no, surely not. He rode on.

After riding in the darkness for about four hours the fort finally came into view. Smiffy was right, there were several lights illuminating the front gate entrance area and the inner roofs of the two front turrets, silly really because he could plainly see the trooper standing in each. He could have shot them both easily. The C. O's office light was on but the trooper's quarters were in darkness. He hoped they were all asleep at this ungodly hour.

He wondered as he slowly edged closer to the fort which was the lazy bastard that had not helped Smiffy or Harry unload the barrels. Moving around the fort slowly at a safe distance counting the number of sentries, four on the upper walkway as Smiffy had said, he eventually reached the back wall which was in total darkness, huge tree trunks bound together with carved points on the top, he slowly dismounted. He needed to run through the plan again in his mind. Don't forget anything he thought to himself.

He took his bow and quiver off his back and placed them on the ground. Then he grabbed his saddlebags and placed them by the bow. Slowly he uncoiled the rope and positioned the loop of the lasso in his right hand, and the end of the rope in his left. He looked up at the 'point' some twenty feet above him, by Smiffys plan he should be at the back of the C. O's quarters, there should not be any sentries within one hundred yards. 'I will kill him if he's got this wrong' he said to himself quietly chuckling. He threw the rope up only to see it come hurtling back down and land on him, he repositioned his hands and feet and threw the rope back up towards the 'point', again it came crashing down, he bowed his head so it didn't hit him in the face.

He sighed loudly, this time he thought, he repositioned the rope and threw it higher. It landed on the 'point', he shook the rope and it slid down about two feet. It was now secure. He waited several minutes to see if it had been spotted by any of the guards. No, nothing. Replacing his bow and quiver on his back and the saddle bags over his shoulder, he climbed the rope, he was only half way when he realized this was hard work, he should have tied knots in the rope before he started the climb, something to remember the next time he wanted to blow up a fort. He giggled quietly to himself.

His arms were aching by the time he made it to the top and peered over the wall. He threw his arms around the pole to take his weight as he surveyed the upper walkway that the troops were using to guard the fort. There were four standing looking over the front wall, just as Smiffy had said, all looking eastward expecting any trouble to come from there. He looked down to ground level towards the gates, two more guards, again just as Smiffy had predicted. One either side of the gates.
He pulled himself up and over the top and yanked the rope up behind him so that it dropped down into the fort, he slid down as quickly as he could. He paused and waited. Silence. None of them had seen him. He dropped his saddle bags to the ground. He would need them later, hopefully.

He was standing next to the C. O's quarters if Smiffy was correct, the light was on. He snatched a look inside, there was an officer working at a desk with his back to the window, the window was ajar. He lifted the window latch and slowly opened the window, then loaded an arrow on to his bow and fired. It hit the officer in the back, who's head fell forward on to the desk with a bang. Red Flame climbed in through the open window and turned off the office light immediately. He waited again. Silence.

He looked through the office window towards the main gates, two guards on the upper walkway, two in the turrets and two down at ground level, still just one either side of the gates. So far, so good. The only lights now on were in the roofs of the two front turrets. He slowly opened the office door and staying in the shadows he moved around the building to confirm the gunpowder barrels were stacked where he thought. They were, lots of barrels, lots of gunpowder. Good.

He silently retraced his steps and proceeded to make his way along the south facing wall in the shadow of the upper walkway, passed the staircase to the upper walkway, he was getting closer to the guards at the gate who were talking to each other even though they were about twelve feet apart. One was smoking so he was easier to see, the other was just a shadow on the wall but his movements gave his position away. Red Flame was now only fifteen feet from being in the south east corner of the fort, directly below one of the lit turrets, that sentry was looking out towards the east and thinking of other things.

He watched as the smoking gate sentry walked towards him, it was pitch black in the shadows, only the man's glowing cigarette gave his position away, was the man going to walk the entire perimeter of the fort or only to the nearest corner where he would soon reach. He stretched behind him and took off his bow and one arrow without a blanket on, and waited.

The guard kept coming, the cigarette end was still glowing bright red. Now they were only thirty feet apart. He prepared to fire his arrow, now twenty feet apart, the guard was still walking, now ten feet away. Red Flame could suddenly see the man's features as he took one last drag on his cigarette, perhaps it was because of that glow so close to his eyes that the man hadn't seen him standing against the wall. Red Flame fired, the man slumped down backwards dropping his rifle which made a clatter as it hit the ground. He held his breath. Silence again.

"Jim…… you ok?" It must be the other gate guard he though. He quickly prepared another arrow to fire. He better answer he thought to himself.

"Yup." He replied bruskly. He waited for several seconds before starting to walk towards the next guard still staying close to the outer wall and under the walkway. When he got to a distance of thirty feet from the second guard he could clearly see him. Suddenly the guard turned away from him and proceeded towards the other corner, this had to be their routine, march from the gate to the corner of the fort and back to the gate. Red Flame quickly placed his bow and arrow on the ground and ran silently to catch up with the guard drawing his knife as he ran. He covered the man's mouth with his left hand and plunged the knife into his back, he grabbed the man's rifle and body before they hit the ground. He paused, still holding the guard and rifle from hitting the ground. Nothing, no noise what so ever. Slowly he lowered them to the ground. Turning back, he ran to where he had placed his weapons, quietly picking them up he moved back along the south wall until he could clearly see the other four guards silhouetted against the sky. Now this was the part of his plan that concerned him, he knew he couldn't just fire up from ground level to get each one because as an arrow hit one he would fall off the walkway and hit the ground some sixteen feet below, certainly making noise and he would be exposed in the middle of the open area by the moonlight. He couldn't use his rifle as that would alert the remaining troops who should be asleep at this hour of the night. No, he would have to improvise.

Silently he walked back to the rear staircase leading up to the upper walkway, up he climbed slowly, peering over the top he could see all four guards, still looking east. Good he thought as he crouched down below the wall and scampered along the walkway. He stopped twenty feet short of the turret. He now had to decide which guard to kill first, the one in the turret under the light or the one fifty feet away in the darkness. The guard furthest away was a harder shot to make but no one would see him drop to the ground, they might hear him but wouldn't see him. He momentarily paused, yes, he was favorite. He sneaked up to the turret, six feet behind that guard, he was now thirty feet away from the second guard, he fired his arrow, it hit the man, he couldn't see where but the man fell backwards the sixteen feet to the ground. He didn't hear any sound so he surmised that none of the guards did either. He placed his bow and arrow on the walkway and jumped the low wall into the turret and grabbing his knife stabbed the guard in the back and dragged him down on to the floor as quickly as he could, so neither of the two remaining guards would see him. He waited for several minutes listening for any raised voices. Nothing.

Suddenly he jumped up and over the low turret wall, he lay motionless on the walkway looking for the next guard who was about fifty feet ahead of him, still looking eastwards.

Keeping low he moved to within twenty feet of the third guard, he stopped, reloaded his bow and fired. The guard dropped to the ground with a thud. He quickly reloaded his bow. Guard number four didn't flinch, he just kept looking eastwards and occasionally south. Had he really not heard anything?

He's got to be deaf he thought, good. Then he realized being that twenty feet higher the wind noise was louder, no wonder none of the guards had heard anything. He moved forward again concentrating hard on the fourth and last guard, he got to within ten feet of the man before he released his arrow, the guard slumped to the floor. Red Flame immediately turned back to see if there was any sign of movement in the soldier's quarters. Nothing, no movement or lights being turned on. Stooping below the height of the wall again, he ran back around the walkway to the staircase down to ground level, taking two stairs at a time he ran to the gates, opening both wide he then continued to the stables, opening the doors he released all the horses, slapping the odd rump so they headed to the open fort gates and out into the darkness. He ran back to where he had dropped his saddlebags, grabbing the twigs and kindling he formed a small frame work and using two flints set it alight. He blew into it to get the flames to catch and then laid his six arrows with the attached blanket strips so they would catch fire. He sprinted to the pile of barrels, picking one up he then ran to the armory and placed the barrel at the door. He ran back to pick up another barrel, then to the troop's quarters, again he dropped it at the door. Back to the barrels, picking another up he ran to the stables, he dropped the barrel outside the structure and then back to the fire. The barrels were heavy, he was exhausted, he was light headed, get control he said to himself. Laggon, where was Laggon? He suddenly realized Laggon was still behind the back wall. He whistled and called out quietly hoping

Laggon would walk around the wall until he found an opening, this would be the open gates.

The arrows with the blanket strips were now burning fast, he picked up all six and ran towards the center of the forts parade ground, he stopped and loaded one arrow which was still burning, he fired, it hit the barrel at the armory door, he quickly reloaded and fired another at the barrel outside the troop's quarters, that one hit the barrel too. Then the stables, that burning arrow hit the thatched roof. He took a deep breath and then fired the fourth arrow at the pile of barrels, then another and then the sixth and last. He then ran faster than he'd ever ran before towards the open gates, he could see the soldier's horses disappearing into the night as he ran through them and out to see Laggon standing there, waiting. He pulled out an arrow and loaded it onto his bow and fired it into the ground about forty feet from the fort. He wanted them to find at least one of his arrows. He then jumped on to Laggon's back and they galloped eastward, for barely three minutes only before 'Ka-boom'. The sky lit up as though the sun had plunged to earth. The wind whistled past him as if pushing him forward. He pulled up and turned around to view the fire, flames a hundred feet high, it was no longer recognizable as a fort, just a shallow hole, a huge shallow hole.

He watched as ammunition in the remains of the armory continued to explode, and barrels that had been catapulted into the air bursting into flame. The main fort walls had almost disappeared. There was no sign that a fort had ever been built there. Just a few odd walls of different buildings smoldering away. Now, for the first time, he felt he had truly revenged the massacre of his tribe. He rode on excitedly to tell Smiffy the news.

Early the next morning he rode into their camp, Smiffy was still snoring away, but alive.

Red Flame put the coffee pot on and sat waiting for him to wake. It was a lovely morning and although he would be number one on the countries 'wanted' list now, he didn't care. It would take the army at least a year to rebuild the fort, if they ever did. It would be so much harder now for the Army to police this area, no more running back to the fort for protection, now they would have to travel several hundred miles to the next nearest fort.

He would take Smiffy back to Jacksonville to sell his furs and wagon and then he would head north west to join his ma and Sitting Bull in the ongoing war to re-establish their promised lands, the lands the President and the army now wanted to take back, whatever the cost to human life.

Lightning Source UK Ltd.
Milton Keynes UK
UKHW021258020419

340352UK00005B/680/P